The Reunion

by

Suzanne Rossi

The Reunion

Cover Art by *Kim Mendoza*

The Wild Rose Press, Inc.
PO Box 708
Adams Basin, NY 14410-0708
Visit us at www.thewildrosepress.com

Publishing History
First Crimson Rose Edition, 2013
Print ISBN 978-1-61217-801-1
Digital ISBN 978-1-61217-802-8

Published in the United States of America

She came into his arms and he pressed her close to his chest. His heartbeat accelerated. Damn, she felt so good, so right in his arms. She locked both of her arms around his neck and he nestled his into the curve of her back. Technically, they didn't dance, but swayed to the music never separating, even when the band changed tunes and tempos.

He steered her deeper into the shadows. The music stopped. They didn't. Zach, always analytical and ruled by logic, threw both out the window. For the first time in his life, he let emotion reign. Without thinking, he lowered his head and covered her mouth with his.

Like the flash of a meteor, it dawned on him that this was why he'd come to the reunion. He'd hoped she would be here. All these years she'd hovered on the fringes of his mind like a ghost. No wonder other women didn't appeal to him. He had wanted Meghan, and only Meghan.

His hand tangled in her hair pulling her head back to expose the delicate line of her throat. His lips trailed from Meghan's mouth to the pulse point by her collarbone. She moaned.

At the same time, a scream echoed from somewhere in the garden.

Praise for Suzanne Rossi

"I found [*ALONG CAME QUINN*] entertaining and a quick read. It's a fun road romance with a twist on the treasure that I think is different yet believable. And it just goes to show that sometimes you can't see what's right under your nose." ~ *Dear Author*

"I couldn't wait to turn each page to see what would happen next. Suzanne Rossi has definitely been added to my must-read list. The terrific twist on the run of the mill mob story makes [*ALL IN THE FAMILY*] a definite keeper."

~*Theresa Joseph, The Romance Studio*

"[*A TANGLED WEB*] has to be THE BEST romantic/suspenseful/mystery novel that I have read to date. The love scenes were perfectly timed with the plot, the suspense kept me turning the pages, and the mystery was superbly developed. Once I started reading it, I could not stop."

~*Happily Ever After Reviews*

"[*NEARLY DEPARTED*] is the BEST ghost story I have read in a long time. The wacky cast of characters is so colorful and fun that they bring the story to life."

~*Night Owl Reviews*

"I really got a good laugh out of [*HEAR NO EVIL*] and enjoyed the plot immensely which draws you in from the beginning... This author has done an incredible job penning this amazing tale."

~*The Romance Studio*

Dedication

This book can have only one dedication and that's to the
Carmel (Indiana) High School class of 1965.
(Yeah, I'm that old!) Our fiftieth reunion is looming
and I want to give them all something to think about—
BWAHAHAHA.

~

Seriously though, high school for me was mostly not
being part of the "in" crowd, but standing on the
sidelines. None of the characters in *The Reunion* are
taken from real life but are drawn from people I have
known over the years, including myself. Strange—in
1965 I graduated without a backward glance. Now I am
busy trying to reconnect with my classmates.

~

So to Cindy Hinshaw Weir, Carolyn Roth Richardson,
Avie Szabo Stamm, Pam Wisler Mills,
Judy Michael Roeder, Harold Lowry, Steve Perrine,
and so many more,
thanks for letting me back into your lives.
I hope you enjoy reading the story
as much as I liked writing it.

Prologue

May 10th

Obituary page of the *Grandview News-Journal,* Grandview, Indiana:

Tami Robinson McGovern

Tami McGovern, nee Robinson, age 38, died May 2nd at her home in Malibu, California. The former resident was a cheerleader at Grandview High School and had the distinction of being voted both Homecoming and Prom Queens two consecutive years. Ms. McGovern moved to the west coast shortly after graduation...

I stopped reading. The obit didn't say Tami had been stabbed in the back—by me. She answered the door of the opulent beach home totally unsuspecting.

"Holy crap! Who the hell sent this?" She snatched the huge bouquet of flowers from my arms without giving me a look.

I counted on that. Who really looks at a delivery person? As usual, Tami came first. Rage fueled my determination. It welled in my chest, threatening to crush my hammering heart. My doubts vanished. I had to kill her. She deserved it.

When she turned her back to close the door, I struck, plunging the nine-inch chef's knife between her shoulder blades. The arrogant bitch cried out, staggered forward, and fell face first into the thorny roses. I stepped into the house enjoying the gurgling noises coming from her throat and her feeble efforts to rise.

The blood flowing across her back and dribbling onto the cold marble tiles of the foyer gave me enormous satisfaction.

Leaning down, I whispered, "One down and lots to go. Roast in hell, bitch."

I waited until the choking noises stopped and she lay still, then turned, crossed the threshold, and closed the door behind me with a soft click. No one paid any attention as I walked down the sidewalk. After all, I was only a delivery person.

It was so easy. Much easier than anticipated.

I jumped up, ran into the den, grabbed the scissors from the desk, and carefully cut out the obituary, then slipped it between the pages of a book.

****

Page 3, Sports Section of the *Grandview News-Journal,* dated June 12th:

Former Grandview High School Football Star Dies

> *Edward Mancuso, age 39, died Wednesday, June 6th in Harrison, Texas, the victim of an apparent hit and run. Mr. Mancuso was the former quarterback of the Grandview Wildcats. His pin-point throwing accuracy carried the team to its only state championship in...*

I sipped my soft drink. *Yeah, Mr. Big-Football-Hero.* The paper didn't say Eddie was a total loser. With all of his so-called athletic prowess, he ended up driving an old semi across the country. Mechanical problems landed him in Harrison, a grubby little town not far from Ft. Worth. Lacking funds to make repairs, he lived hand-to-mouth at a seedy motel next to a truck stop.

I killed him, too. Just like his bitch of a girlfriend, Tami Robinson. Without transportation, old Eddie had been forced to walk the mile from the cheesy bar where he ate dinner every night to his room. The road was dark and narrow. Perfect for my purpose.

Stealing the pickup was a piece of cake. Nobody locked their cars in Harrison, and some even left the keys inside. I hit pay dirt on my third try.

I gave Eddie a ten-minute head start, and then followed in the rapidly descending dusk.

It was so easy. With my headlights off, he didn't see me hurtling down on him, and by the time he did, it was too late. I nailed him. His body flew backwards over the truck, his scream echoing in the still night air. A thrill went through me. I jammed on the brakes and watched in the rearview mirror as he hit the pavement, tumbling like a rag doll. I fist-pumped like a jazzed-up linebacker, reversed gears, and backed over him just to make sure.

Finished, I stepped from the cab and walked toward his broken, bleeding body. His eyes glazed and questioned. He didn't recognize me, but why should he? Twenty years is a long time.

"Have a good evening, Eddie."

I waited until the last breath gasped from his lungs, and then left.

"Number two has been sent to the hell he deserves. Time for number three to pay."

This article joined the obituary I cut out last month.

****

Obituary in the *Grandview News-Journal* dated July 13th:

Clara Sylvester, Educator, Dies

Clara Sylvester, age 83, died unexpectedly last July 11th at the Better Life Assisted Care and Rehabilitation Facility in Muncie, Indiana, where she had been recovering from a broken hip. Ms. Sylvester taught government and civics classes at Grandview High School for over forty years before retiring, but continued to work in the school bookstore for another ten years. She was revered by her students and fellow teachers alike. Ms. Sylvester was also Youth Coordinator for the Methodist...

Of course, the old bat died unexpectedly. I killed her. She was number three. Revered by her students? Not by me. I hated the old bitch. Meddling in other people's lives was her stock in trade, and because of that, she needed to pay just like Tami and Eddie.

This was both the easiest and the hardest to pull off. It's tough to breeze into a nursing home without someone asking who you're there to see, but a pair of white slacks and a baggy white coat made me look like a nurse or an orderly. I sailed in the front door as if I knew where I was going—which I did. I'd scoped the place out earlier pretending to be a visitor. The busy receptionist gave me the room number without hesitation.

The next night, I strode with confidence toward her room. No one questioned me. I was just another employee. I snatched a pillow from a gurney in the hallway.

Clara was watching television from her bed. She looked up and frowned.

"What now? You've already shoved all those pills down my throat."

"I'm here to make sure you're comfortable."

"I don't need another pillow," Clara grumbled as I approached.

"Oh, but you do." I took the remote from Clara's fingers, tossing it onto the covers just out of reach. When she fumbled for it, I shoved her back. *For once I'm in control, you old bitch.* I was about to exact the ultimate revenge for her actions those many years ago.

"Hey! Stop it! You have a lousy bedside manner."

"So I've been told."

The cranky old crow reached for the nurse's call button beside her head. I pulled it away. Elation at her look of surprise gave me confidence.

"Too late for that, Clara."

She drew in a sharp breath and opened her mouth.

With a swift move, I pressed the pillow over her face. She struggled, but the punches had no weight behind them. I pressed harder. Gradually, all movement ceased. I waited several seconds before tossing the innocuous murder weapon onto the foot of the bed.

I left the room and gloated. She paid—just like they'd all pay. I felt no guilt, merely a sense of justice finally being done.

I cut out the obit and slid it into the book with the others. My mission was more than half over. Strange, but I never expected murder to be so easy. I shrugged. *Easy is better than hard. And time is running out.*

The reunion was six weeks away.

Chapter One

August 25th
Grandview, Indiana

Welcome to the Reunion!!

Meghan Donahue read the sign over the doors to the ballroom of the Grandview Inn, her heart pounding with both anticipation and fear.

"Come on, Meghan, open the damned door. Don't be a jerk," she muttered to herself. She'd stalled in her room for over twenty minutes, hiding like a frightened gopher, before finally screwing up enough courage to emerge. "It's been twenty years. You can do this."

She lifted her chin, sucked in a deep breath, and entered the banquet hall. Conversation and laughter greeted her along with the clink of glasses.

A sign above a table next to the wall on her right read: *Welcome Graduates! Sign in here*. It was manned by a thin woman Meghan immediately recognized as Eileen Raymond. The hair had grayed and her skin sagged a touch, but she still displayed the same smile she'd had in high school.

"Welcome," Eileen greeted in a burbling voice as Meghan approached. "And whose spouse are you?"

"Nobody's. I'm Meghan Donahue."

Meghan had the satisfaction of seeing Eileen's eyes widen, her jaw drop, and her shoulders straighten in surprise. Her reluctance to attend the reunion vanished.

"Oh, my God, you've dropped a ton of weight," she said with a gasp.

It might not have been the most diplomatic thing to say, but Meghan didn't take offense. "Over a hundred pounds. I learned the value of exercise and diet my freshman year in college. You look good."

"Oh, well, I try." Eileen patted her elegant French twist and fumbled through the name badges in front of her until she found Meghan's. "Here you go. Please sign the register. We have cash bars located at opposite ends of the room. The buffet will begin at eight and dancing at nine. I'm so glad you could make it, Meghan. I'll be by to talk later."

Meghan signed in, clipped the badge to the top of her strapless cocktail dress, and turned away as three other people strolled up to register.

She gazed around the room. Close to half of the twenty-five or so tables had occupants.

A large bulletin board on an easel bearing the title *In Memoriam* caught her attention. It hadn't occurred to her that some of her classmates might have died, but twenty years after the fact and with a graduating class of two hundred, the idea wasn't unreasonable. The boards remembered not only classmates, but teachers as well. Still, Meghan was surprised to see ten pictures, along with the dates of death, on display.

Their old principal, Fred Sheridan, was there along with teachers John Noble and Clara Sylvester. Two of the names stunned her—Tami Robinson and Eddie Mancuso. The quarterback and the cheerleader—two of her tormentors. It didn't surprise her they were dead. Even in high school those two had lived life in the fast lane.

"Holy shit!" a female voice next to her exclaimed. "I didn't know Tami and Eddie died."

Meghan turned her head to see Tami and Eddie's best friends, Dave Coryell and Suzanne Wayland, standing nearby. They ignored her, but she expected that. The two of them hadn't paid much attention to her in high school either—at least not in a good way.

"This is the first I've heard about it, too," Dave replied.

"I wonder what happened." Suzanne had a dazed expression on her face.

"I have no idea. I need a drink," Dave muttered, cupping Suzanne's elbow in his hand. "How about you?"

"You got it."

The pair moved away and a woman approached Meghan. "Hi, I'm Glory Ecklund, Tom Ecklund's wife. I'm on the reunion committee."

Glory…Glory. The name sounded familiar. She remembered Tom Ecklund. He'd been average looking with average grades and a pleasant personality. Meghan's gaze drifted to the bulletin board and one of the pictures—Divine Prescott. Of course, Divine had a younger sister named Glory.

"I'm Meghan Donahue. I'm sorry about your sister."

"Yes, such a tragedy. I still miss her. She killed herself."

Meghan didn't know how to respond to such a blunt statement. She remembered her mother telling her Divine had died. Sometime following graduation wasn't it, after most of her classmates had left for college?

Glory smiled. "Well, it was nice meeting you, and if I can do anything to make the party more fun, feel free to ask." She nodded and walked toward the registration desk.

She resembled Divine—pale complexion, pale blue eyes, and light blonde hair. The Prescotts had been an odd family living on the outskirts of town. Meghan remembered they'd kept to themselves and been devoted to the Methodist Church.

"Kind of a morbid thing to have at a reunion," a male voice said.

She swung her head to the right and gazed into a man's face. It was a long journey. At five feet, seven inches, Meghan had to tilt her head. The man stood at least six-four. She fumbled for a name, wishing she'd taken time to study her old yearbook before coming to Grandview.

"Yes, but informative. I guess we should expect to lose some classmates. Tami and Eddie are a bit of a shock though."

"I think 'live fast, die young' was their motto back then," the man commented.

Feeling at a disadvantage, she decided to come clean. "Okay, I'll be honest. I should know you, but don't."

The man grinned as if anticipating her words. "I know you. You're Meghan Donahue."

"You recognized me? Or did you cheat and ask Eileen?"

"I never forget emerald green eyes." He paused. "Still can't place me? Try Zachary Dunbar."

"Oh, good grief! Four years of your locker being

just down from mine."

"Only Janice Donovan and Todd Duffy separated us. You've changed."

"A tad. At graduation I was well on my way to employment as the fat lady at the circus, had bad posture, and not one ounce of fashion sense. If I'm not mistaken, you were incredibly thin and wore thick glasses."

"I discovered the benefits of lifting weights and indulged in Lasik surgery. And for the record, you weren't that overweight. Are you with someone?"

"No, I'm alone."

"Me, too. Can I buy you a drink?"

"You certainly can. I'll have a vodka martini."

His right eyebrow rose as did the corner of his mouth. A dimple danced briefly, and his eyes crinkled with humor when he smiled.

"Shaken, not stirred, I assume."

"But of course."

He grinned again. "Why don't you find us a table while I get the drinks?"

Meghan couldn't take her eyes off Zach winding his way through the increasing crowd. Damn, he looked good. His light brown hair and blue eyes were just as she remembered. And while she'd lost weight, he appeared to have put on at least an extra fifty pounds—all of it muscle.

She shook her head and glanced around the room. Most of the tables had occupants now, but Meghan finally spotted an empty one and threaded her way past knots of chatting people. She slipped her purse from her shoulder, set it on the snow white tablecloth, and pulled out a chair.

"Allow me."

She turned to find Dave Coryell smiling at her. Returning the smile, she sat. Dave read her nametag.

"Donahue...Donahue. I don't seem to remember the name."

"No, I don't suppose you would. My locker was five or six down from yours."

He still looked puzzled. "I remember Patty Courtney and Janice Donovan. There was also some fat girl..." He stared hard, and then groaned. "Good God, don't tell me..."

"Yes, I was the fat girl. Needless to say, I didn't run with your crowd."

He pulled out a chair and sat. "Well, I wouldn't mind getting reacquainted right now." He took a long swallow of his drink and looked into her eyes, a smile on his face.

Meghan couldn't believe it. Dave Coryell, football hero, was hitting on her. Twenty years ago, she'd have been flattered into a stammering imbecile. No, twenty years ago it would never have happened. Now, she wanted to laugh.

Dave hadn't changed much from high school, still possessing a trim body and a head full of black hair untouched by gray. A closer look showed lines around the brown eyes and a slightly dissipated expression.

"So, are you here alone, Meghan?"

"Actually..."

"Nope, she's with me," Zach said from behind Dave's chair.

Dave rose and smiled. "Sorry. Didn't mean to step on your toes."

"You didn't." Zach set the martini in front of

Meghan, placed his drink in front of the seat Dave had just vacated, and extended his hand. "Nice to see you again, Dave."

Dave shook it while reading Zach's nametag. "Zach, you're looking good."

From the look in his eyes, Meghan suspected he was trying to place Zach in the proper niche. The fake smile told her he certainly didn't recognize him.

"Same for you. I hear you're in the commodities business in Chicago."

"Head of my own brokerage firm. How about you?"

"Head of my own software company in Phoenix. Maybe you've heard of it—Dunbar Electronics and Data Systems."

Dave's eyes bugged out. "Holy shit! That's you? You've had a good couple of years."

"Who's had a good couple of years?" Suzanne Wayland asked walking up and linking her arm through Dave's.

"This is Zach Dunbar and Meghan Donahue."

"I'm sorry, I don't remember. Did you graduate with us?"

The dismissive tone irritated Meghan, but then that had always been Suzanne's way. No interest in anybody unless they could benefit her.

"Yes, I was the fat girl. Zach was the computer genius," she answered in a crisp voice.

Zach stared at her and raised an eyebrow. "What Meghan is too polite to say is I was the skinny nerd."

The comments apparently didn't cause Suzanne any concern. She turned to Dave. "I could use another cosmo."

"Sure. Mind if we join you?" Not waiting for a reply, he placed his drink next to Zach's. "I'd like to hear more about your company." He winked.

Meghan hated people who winked like they knew a secret.

"Be my guest."

Zach's dry tone suggested he would have liked to avoid his former classmate.

Suzanne plunked her fanny down next to Dave's seat, clearly annoyed at spending the evening with people she didn't remember.

Meghan wasn't any happier, but tried to be civil. "What do you do, Suzanne?"

"Spend my late husband's money."

"Oh, I'm sorry. I didn't know you were a widow. Must be tough—being so young, I mean," Meghan stammered. She hated being put at an awkward position.

"It's not so bad. Charlie Crocker was twenty-five years older than me, drank like a fish, ate like a pig, smoked two packs a day, and never exercised a day in his life. He dropped dead from a heart attack five years ago."

As at the memorial display while talking to Glory, Meghan didn't know how to respond. Suzanne didn't sound particularly sorry her husband was dead. *As long as his estate pumps money into her wallet, I'm sure she's content. The sorry will come when the money runs out.* Guilt at the unkind thought tweaked her conscience.

"So, where do you spend his money?" Zach inquired.

Suzanne looked at Zach and smiled. "Wherever I

can. Charlie's one blazing talent was making money. Everything he touched turned to gold. At one time, he was Dave's boss. That's how I met him. Dave introduced us."

"Then you live in Chicago, too?" Meghan asked.

"Most of the time. I winter in Palm Beach."

Dave returned with their drinks and sat next to Suzanne, but before he could say anything Zach turned.

"What do you do, Meghan? Seems to me you always had good grades. Didn't you write short stories?"

"Poetry, too. Now, I write novels."

"No kidding?" Suzanne said. "What kind of novels? Are you published?"

"Mysteries and yes. I write under the name Meghan Bonaventure."

Zach sat back, eyebrows raised, and blew out a breath. "I'm impressed. I read *Cruise to Death*. You had me believing the doctor's wife was the killer right up until the end."

"Thank you. That was a fun book to write. Put a bunch of people on a boat in the middle of the ocean with a killer on board and no way off. *The Ghost Killers* was harder. I had so many suspects it was hard keeping them straight."

"So, you're rich and famous, now?" Dave's smile had a predatory gleam.

"My books have done well."

"That's an understatement," Zach told him. "I'd call the *New York Times* bestseller list better than well."

"Oh, shit!" Suzanne exclaimed, her forehead furrowing with a scowl.

"What?" Dave jerked his attention back to his date.

"Annabelle Peterson."

"Who?"

"Eric Peterson's wife. Three tables over. She graduated a year behind us."

All three of them looked. Meghan saw what had provoked Suzanne's expletive immediately and wanted to laugh, but managed to keep a straight face.

"What about her?" Dave said with a puzzled expression.

"Her dress, you asshole. It's the same as mine."

"You look better in it," Zach commented, and then turned amused eyes toward Meghan.

She couldn't contain her mirth and let it bubble out. An angry Suzanne didn't notice.

"Of course I do. That's not the point. Mine is a Gregoire original. I paid fifteen hundred bucks for it. Hers is a cheap knockoff. I heard Eric is a schoolteacher in Cincinnati. No way could she afford to pay what I did. Son of a bitch!"

Suzanne downed her cocktail and glared at the other woman.

Meghan had to admit, Suzanne did look better in the ice blue, halter topped, chiffon creation. Annabelle's legs were a bit too heavy to show off the swirling knee length skirt. But from a distance, the two women could have passed as sisters. Even their hairstyles were similar, although Suzanne's flowing red locks beat out mouse brown any day of the week.

"Dave, get me another drink."

Dave shot her a glance, but rose and walked away.

"Hi! Mind if we join you?"

Meghan looked up to see Jill Hardesty standing next to her. Jill hadn't changed in twenty years. Petite

15

with short-cropped blonde hair, her bubbly personality had made her a class favorite. Meghan couldn't think of anyone who hadn't liked her. A good-looking man stood behind her.

"Jill, how nice to see you. Of course, have a seat," Meghan said.

"Thanks. This is my husband, Ted Kramer." Ted waved and sat next to his wife. She peered at nametags. "Meghan and Zach? Holy cow! You two look fabulous."

Zach smiled. "Thanks, Jill. Nothing like extreme makeovers."

"Can we join the party?" Tom and Glory Ecklund, their fingers intertwined, stood behind the last two chairs.

"Don't see why not," Zach replied.

Meghan remembered Tom as a slender redhead with freckles. The years had not been kind. His hair had thinned, his stomach bulged, and a pair of glasses perched on his freckled nose. He set a glass of what looked like soda pop on the table and turned to his wife.

"Why don't you take a break, honey? You've been busy as a bee ever since we got here. Have a seat. I'll get you something to drink. Diet soda?"

"Oh, Tommy, that sounds wonderful."

Glory plopped down on the chair and hung her oversized purse over the back. She pushed some straggling strands of hair into the messy bun at the back of her head, and wiped a trickle of sweat from her temple with a tissue.

The temperature in the room had risen with the crowd, and the black, high-necked, long-sleeved dress didn't help matters. Even the material had a heavy polyester look. Meghan wondered why on earth she wore something like that in August.

Dave returned with Suzanne's drink and set it in front of her before once again casting his gaze on Zach. He opened his mouth to speak when a squealing microphone interrupted him.

"Testing, testing. Can everybody hear me?" The present principal, Roger Clark, stood at the podium on a stage by the dance floor. "I want to welcome everybody to this class reunion. It's a pleasure to see so many attendees. Is everyone having fun?"

A chorus of yeses and a smattering of applause greeted his question. Meghan politely clapped, too. Dave raised his glass and smiled. Zach leaned back in his chair. Suzanne sipped her drink.

"That's great. Now, I do have a few announcements before we get started." He pulled a slip of paper from his inside jacket pocket and unfolded it. "First of all, I would like to remind all of you about the dangers of drinking and driving. The hotel has assured me there are ample rooms available if anyone feels the need to stay over."

Zach slid his chair closer to Meghan and whispered, "I wonder if he'll tuck us in, too."

He grinned, and Meghan chuckled. She remembered Roger Clark as the stodgy vice-principal. He hadn't changed. Zach turned his attention back to the stage.

Meghan didn't remember Zach as being so good looking, but then she'd been no prize twenty years ago either. Tonight, an impeccable navy suit contrasting with a light blue shirt brought out the blue of his eyes. A multi-hued, conservative, patterned tie showed not only good taste, but spelled success as well. *When did nerd become so sexy?*

"I also want to take this opportunity to ask that we all observe a moment of silence for those classmates who are no longer with us."

He stepped back from the mike and bowed his head. Dave and Suzanne exchanged a look and bolted their drinks. This time Dave didn't wait. He got up and headed for the bar. Principal Clark returned to the microphone.

"And now, I'd like to introduce your class president, Dan Masterson."

Dan Masterson—still tall and beefy, his dark brown hair just beginning to gray around the temples—bounded onstage with a broad smile and shook Clark's hand like a pump handle.

"Thank you, thank you, Principal Clark. I want to welcome all my classmates. Some of you have moved from our lovely town of Grandview, and I hope you find us still the friendly folk you left behind. We have a great economy and lots of opportunities."

"He sounds like a fucking politician," Suzanne said with a curled lip.

She didn't bother to lower her voice and Meghan knew Dan had heard when his jaw clenched ever so briefly. Jill rolled her eyes while her husband shifted in his seat. Zach didn't react to the profanity. Glory shot Suzanne a shocked look, but Tom smiled.

"He is. He's a city councilman running for mayor. I'm one of his campaign workers," he commented.

"Thank God I live in Chicago," she muttered.

"And Palm Beach," Meghan murmured under her breath as Zach chuckled.

Dan droned on for a few more minutes, and then finally put an end to his campaign pitch.

"I have it on good authority that the buffet is now open. So, everybody come on up, have a great meal, and enjoy the dancing afterward. The cash bars close at midnight, by the way, but the hotel lounge is open until two. And don't forget, there's an informal get together out at Samson's Lake tomorrow from noon until three. Hope to see you all there." He left the stage to moderate applause.

"Are you hungry?" Zach asked Meghan.

"Starving. I was too nervous to eat lunch."

"You, too?" He glanced at the line forming by the buffet table. "Shall we?"

He pulled her chair out and placed his hand in the small of her back, steering her toward the food. A little zing zipped along Meghan's nerves. She caught her breath.

Oh, my goodness. I know he's good-looking, but I didn't expect this.

Her mind leaped to fantasy land and she tripped over a chair leg in her way. Only Zach's quick hand around her waist saved her from a fall. He swung her to face him her breasts just inches from his chest.

"Hey, careful there. Can't have you getting trampled by the hungry hoards." He smiled, his eyes taking on a brilliant color.

Meghan's heart thumped, and Zach ceased smiling as they swayed toward each other. Oh my God, was he going to kiss her in the middle of the dining room? In front of everybody?

Lord, I hope so.

19

Chapter Two

Zach swallowed the lump in his throat and stepped back. He'd been an inch away from kissing her right in front of God and all their classmates. And what would Meghan's response have been? A quick slap in the face?

"Thank you," Meghan said, a blush tinting her cheeks. "I guess I'm still not the most graceful person in the class."

"Not your fault. It's crowded and the chair was in the way."

Meghan turned and Zach followed her through the crowd heading for the buffet wondering where he'd dug up the courage to speak to her in the first place. He'd even made her laugh earlier. Since when had he developed the priceless commodity of wit? Zach Dunbar and women didn't mix. For some reason, he couldn't find the words to utter much beyond 'hello, how are you' and 'nice weather'. But give him a computer and a problem, and he could talk forever.

Yet, Meghan was no computer and they'd had a normal conversation for the past hour. He'd learned the art of hiding his nervousness years ago. But then, Meghan had never been an ordinary girl. He remembered a sensitive, shy person—not unlike himself—who'd always answered his greetings with a smile. Those incredible deep emerald eyes set her apart from the crowd. He'd sometimes wound elaborate fantasies around the two of them as only a high school boy with hormones could do, and had nearly asked her to the senior prom, but chickened out at the last minute.

"Wow, they've put on quite a spread," Meghan commented, stopping in the serving line. "If I'm not careful, I'll bust right out of this dress."

Zach didn't think that was such a bad idea. She looked fabulous. Her black hair hung to her shoulders where the ends curled under. The black dress was strapless and she held it up nicely. The top, covered with shiny things, fit snugly down to her hips where it flared out in a soft, lightweight material. Silver sandals adorned her feet. The pink polished toes peeking out looked seductive and he hoped he hadn't developed a foot fetish.

"I'm wondering if it would make sense to get salad first and come back later for entrees," she continued.

"From the looks of this hungry mob, they may scarf it clean."

Meghan chuckled. "I just hope I can balance the plates all the way back to the table. It would be just my luck to drop everything and look like a fool."

"In that case, I will promptly drop mine, too."

She sent him an amused look over her shoulder. His heart skipped a beat—or maybe added one. He wasn't sure. *For the love of God, pull yourself together before you say or do something stupid.*

Meghan took a plate from the stack and helped herself to various salads and fruit. When they arrived at the entrees, she selected a baked chicken breast, a dab of au gratin potatoes, and ignored the desserts.

Zach requested two slabs of medium rare roast beef

from the carver, and then heaped mashed potatoes and gravy on the plate. His mother was in his head ordering him to eat his vegetables, so in compliance, he added a moderate helping of green beans, also ignoring the desserts.

He joined Meghan at the table. "I see you made it. Too bad. I've never been the center of attention before."

"I can always go back through the line if that'll make you happy."

Now, Zach laughed. The teasing banter sped up his heart rate. When was the last time he'd had this much fun? He couldn't remember.

The table was empty except for Suzanne who nursed her cocktail. The rest of their classmates had apparently gravitated to the buffet.

Tom Ecklund returned with two plates, both overflowing. Glory followed with more modest, but still full portions. She sat heavily with a sigh. To Zach, she looked exhausted, but then the woman had been scurrying around the ballroom as if the success of the event rested entirely on her shoulders. And she wasn't even a classmate.

Jill and Ted resumed their seats.

"Glory, I envy you being able to eat that much and not gain weight. I look at food and my hips expand," Jill said.

"I've always had a high metabolism. I guess I'm just one of those people who can eat anything and not suffer the consequences."

"I, on the other hand, will suffer," Tom replied while patting his stomach.

"What do you do, Tom?" Zach inquired working

his way through his meal.

"I'm the regional manager for Everett Life and Casualty Insurance."

"He worked his way up from salesman," Glory added, a proud smile on her face. "I'm glad he doesn't have to travel so much anymore. He's only gone a few days a month. What do you do, Ted?"

"I'm Vice President of First National Bank and Trust in St. Louis."

"How about you, Jill? Do you have a career?" Meghan asked the bubbly blonde.

"I was a nurse, but now I raise three kids, two boys and a girl."

"That's a full time job," Zach answered. "What about you, Glory?" He cut his roast beef and popped a morsel into his mouth. Not bad, he decided.

"Oh, I keep the house neat and work in the garden. I do a lot of canning in the fall. I guess that seems boring to the rest of you."

Meghan smiled at the frazzled woman. "Not at all. It sounds sensible. You probably save a bundle at the grocery during winter."

Glory beamed. "You're so right. I never have to buy tomato sauce for my spaghetti and it's so much healthier. No pesticides for us. I'm organic."

"Oh, for God's sake," Suzanne muttered, draining her glass.

Dave returned with his plate piled high. "They've got a good selection of food. This roast beef looks terrific."

"It is," Zach told him. "Better than I expected.

"Thank you," Glory said. "I helped select the menu."

"I need another drink." Suzanne thrust her glass at Dave.

He gestured over his shoulder with his thumb. "The bar's in that direction."

Suzanne glared for a second, then shoved her chair back and strode away, none too steadily, Zach noted, but that could have been the result of the four inch heels.

Why do women wear those things anyway?

He gazed at her swaying backside as she walked. *Oh, I guess that's why.* He decided Meghan's modest height heels were sexier.

"So, Zach, tell me about Dunbar Electronics and Data Systems. How's this quarter shaping up?" Dave probed between bites.

If Zach had learned anything over the years, it was to identify fishing expeditions. The company's initial public offering four years ago had been good and the stock continued to creep up the index in respectable increments.

"Dave, I never talk business over a meal. Food's too important. I might forget to eat." Zach tried to keep the tone light. Dave, however, didn't take the hint.

"Are the rumors true Houseman Digital Services are sniffing around your back door looking for a hostile takeover?"

Dave's overt questioning sent up a red flag. Zach never divulged information that could be construed in the future as insider trading.

"Dave, even if I could answer that, I wouldn't."

Dave frowned and Zach read irritation with a touch of desperation in his eyes. The thought that Dave's business was not as successful as he claimed flitted through his mind.

Mental note: avoid discussing business with Dave Coryell.

Suzanne returned with her cosmo, set it on the table, and then wobbled her way to the buffet. Zach still couldn't decide if it was the liquor or the high heels. She came back with a plate full of salad.

"That's all you're eating?" Glory asked.

"It's all I want. I don't eat dry chicken, overcooked roast beef, greasy fried fish, or tortellini in thick sauce." Suzanne plopped down into her chair.

For a moment, Glory looked as if she would love to smack Suzanne right in the mouth. In Zach's opinion, she deserved it.

"I think the chicken is delicious," Meghan said. "Perhaps if you'd gotten there earlier, it wouldn't have dried out."

Now, Suzanne looked like *she* wanted to smack Meghan. She sipped her drink instead. Apparently, Meghan had learned the art of answering back over the years.

Before Zach could think of something to say, Jill turned her head toward the insulted woman. "Glory, what's this I hear about Tami Robinson being murdered?"

"Murdered!" Suzanne exclaimed, almost choking on a piece of lettuce.

Dave stared with a stunned expression, his fork poised halfway to his mouth.

Meghan also ceased eating to stare with a shocked gaze.

"Oh, yes," Glory replied. "She was stabbed in the back with a butcher knife in the foyer of her own house.

Can you believe that?"

"Good Lord!" Zach exclaimed, aghast at the news. "When did this happen?"

"Three or four months ago. The police contacted Eileen because they found the reunion invitation. Apparently, someone had just delivered flowers, and they were scattered all over the floor like a pagan offering." She shuddered and sipped from her water glass.

Jill placed her hand on her throat. "How awful."

"Do they know who did it?" Meghan asked.

Glory shrugged. "I don't think so."

"Who'd want to kill Tami?" Zach wondered.

Suzanne took a huge gulp of her cosmo. "Anyone whoever met her, I imagine. Tami could piss off the Pope. Can we change the subject?"

"From what I heard, she'd just divorced her fourth husband. I'd think four divorces would produce a whole slew of candidates," Tom said.

"And then there's Eddie Mancuso," Glory added with a smile.

"What about Eddie Mancuso?" Zach asked.

"He was murdered, too."

Jill gasped. "What?"

Dave's fork clattered onto his plate. His eyes bugged out and his jaw dropped. Suzanne stared, her fingers pressed against her coral-tinted lips. Meghan sipped her water with surprise on her face.

Both were murdered? How bizarre is that?

"Uh-huh. About a month later in some little town in Texas. He was run over while walking down the highway. The cops found the invitation in his pocket. Eileen got that call, too. Really shook her up."

"How do they know it was murder? Murder is deliberate," Zach commented. "This sounds like a hit and run."

"They found evidence that the truck stopped, and then backed up over him as he lay on the asphalt."

"That's gross. What did he do for a living?" Jill wondered.

"A friend of his is a client. Said when he last talked to Eddie about five years ago he was driving a semi," Tom told them.

"Eddie was a truck jockey?" Dave had a thoughtful look on his face. "The last time I talked to him he claimed he was in the advertising game in Los Angeles."

"When was that?" Jill asked.

Dave chased a bite of food with a generous gulp of his drink before answering, "I don't know, twelve or fifteen years ago. He was in Chicago at some seminar or something."

"The advertising business can be brutal," Ted commented.

"Yeah, he spent most of the time telling me how he almost made the NFL, but an injury screwed up his knee."

"Bullshit," Suzanne commented. "He flunked out of college in his first semester. Tami told me."

"That doesn't surprise me. Eddie didn't have much in the line of brains. His only talents were drinking beer and sliding out of trouble," Dave confirmed. "He was damned good at both."

"From football hero to road kill. How the mighty have fallen," Glory murmured. She forked chocolate cake into her mouth.

Zach was shocked at such a statement coming from Glory until he remembered that Tom Ecklund had been on the receiving end of more than a few of Eddie's bullying comments and actions during high school. The fact Tom was alive and successful while Eddie was dead probably gave even mild-mannered Glory a sense of satisfaction.

"Didn't the four of you hangout a lot?" Meghan asked Dave.

"Yes, we did, and I find this entire conversation disgusting," Suzanne snapped. She shoved her half-eaten salad away. "Change the fucking subject."

Silence fell over the table. Waiters came around removing the dirty dishes and serving coffee.

"Would you like something from the bar?" Zach asked Meghan.

"A white wine would be nice."

He left with his mind on the information Glory had enjoyed delivering. After twenty years, it wasn't unreasonable to find some of his classmates had died, but for two of the most popular to be murdered within a month of each other was not only coincidental, but downright sinister.

"A glass of chardonnay, and an amaretto on the rocks," he told the bartender.

He remembered Suzanne and Tami had been inseparable. The same could be said for Eddie and Dave, best friends for most of their lives. Strange how the two of them had drifted apart. Well, maybe not so odd. Eddie had always struck Zach as lazy and living for the moment, whereas Dave had the sense to plan ahead.

Zach paid for the drinks, returned to the table, and

found Meghan alone. On the stage, a band tuned up. Glory once again flitted around the room like a bothersome mosquito. Tom talked to a friend a few tables away. Ditto for Jill and Ted. Dave stood on the far side of the room with a group of former football players. Suzanne had disappeared.

"All alone?" he asked.

"For the moment. Thanks. How are you enjoying the reunion so far?"

Meghan's fingers touched his as she took the glass. The action resulted in a clutching sensation in his gut. Desire, pure and simple.

He pulled himself together. "Other than being with you, not very. Murder would not be my first choice of dinner conversation."

"I rather enjoyed it. My mind is already spinning possible plots from the information."

"Good Lord." He sipped his amaretto. "Is some disgruntled cheerleader working her way through the squad settling old scores? Or is the ninety-seven pound weakling knocking off football players out of revenge?"

She laughed. "Why not? And let's not be sexist. The cheerleader could be male. Reunions can be very revealing."

"How?"

"Think about it. The first is usually the tenth. Everybody is five or six years out of college and still climbing the corporate ladder. They have focus and are upwardly mobile."

"No time for envy or jealousy to surface."

"Exactly." She sipped her wine. "The twentieth and twenty-fifth are a whole different story. Careers are set and goals may or may not have been achieved. Some men attend to show off how much money they have—or pretend to have—while women go to see if the homecoming queen has put on fifty pounds. Envy and jealousy are rampant. People show up at the fiftieth to see who's still alive."

"Why are you here?"

She grinned. "I'm a successful author and I dumped a ton of weight. A part of me wanted to show off, yet I still had to screw up my courage to walk through the doors. In my mind, I'm still the fat kid. What about you?"

Zach toyed with the amaretto glass. "I'm not really sure. I was all set to drop the invitation into the shredder when something stopped me. I changed my looks—"

"For the better," Meghan interrupted with a smile.

He chuckled. "Thanks. I'm successful beyond my wildest dreams. I guess maybe I wanted to crow a little, too. And to repeat, you weren't that heavy in high school."

He liked how Meghan blushed at his words. The corners of her emerald eyes crinkled as she smiled.

"Thank you, but that's how I saw myself—as a float in the Macy's Thanksgiving Day Parade. In those days self-esteem wasn't one of my strong points."

He reached over and squeezed her hand. "Mine neither."

The band finished tuning up and swung into a slow song popular the year they graduated. Several couples hit the dance floor.

"I'm not the most graceful guy in the world, but if I promise not to step on your toes, would you like to dance?"

"I've got a flash for you. I'm not so hot either. Remember the chair? But I'm game if you are."

Zach draped his suit coat over the back of his chair, and led Meghan onto the floor, then held out his arms. She walked into them with a smile. He pulled her close and moved to the music. A tantalizing scent of something exotic wafted to his nostrils as the top of her head brushed his chin.

A zing of God-knew-what zipped along his nerves. Those high school fantasies flooded his mind with adult images of naked bodies, rumpled sheets, and sounds of pleasure. He hardened slightly.

Focus on dancing. If I don't, I'll embarrass myself and scare the shit out of Meghan.

It didn't work. Her breasts brushed his chest and his hands felt scorched from wherever he touched her. Even through those shiny things in the small of her back, the woman radiated heat.

Somehow they had drawn closer, her fingers playing with the hair in his nape, her warm breath whispering against his neck. He had an absurd urge to bury his face in her fragrant hair. A light, floral perfume made him dizzy with desire.

Knock it off, Dunbar. This close and she'll know how you feel any second. Think about something other than her body. Say something, jackass.

"Uh, you know, I don't think I've complimented you on your dress. It's gorgeous."

Terrific. Could I get any more ordinary?

"Thank you. I bought it for a party at my publisher's last year."

"What are all these shiny things?"

"Sequins and beads. Are you interested in

31

fashion?" She leaned her head back and smiled, a teasing look in her eyes.

Swell. She thinks I'm gay.

"Uh, no. I just wondered. They're very sexy."

Way to go, idiot. Now, she probably thinks I'm a sex fiend.

"Well, thank you again. I thought the same when I bought it."

Zach finally managed to laugh. Close proximity to Meghan addled his brains. For his libido's sake, he should take her back to the table. Her breasts against his chest nixed that idea. He enjoyed this too much.

They covered the dance floor through six songs until the band took a break. A trickle of sweat dribbled down his temple. The crowd had thickened and the temperature in the ballroom rose. He preferred that rationalization. *Her body has nothing to do with it.*

"It's getting hot in here. Would you like to go outside for a few minutes?" he asked.

"Sounds wonderful."

"Can I get you another wine?"

"That sounds wonderful, too. I'll meet you on the terrace."

She walked toward the terrace doors, her hips swaying just enough to set the skirt of her dress swirling. It was sexy as hell.

Zach swallowed, headed for the bar, got the drinks, and found Meghan standing by the stone wall at the far end of the patio gazing out over the garden. The lush greenery waved in a light breeze. The muted lighting threw shadows of gray and black over the pathways that serpentined through the trees and shrubbery.

"Here you go," he said.

"Thanks." She accepted the glass and took a generous drink. "Tastes good. Cool and refreshing after that ballroom."

Meghan set the glass next to her purse, and then rested her elbows on the parapet. The foliage rustled pleasantly. Zach mimicked her actions fumbling for something to say.

"How come you write under the name Bonaventure?"

"It's my ex-husband's name."

At least she'd said *ex*. The thought she might be married had never occurred to him. He didn't know what to say. Fortunately, Meghan did.

"I met Philip Bonaventure while getting my master's in English. He was a history professor working his way up the tenure ladder."

"How long were you married?"

"Seven years."

"I'm sorry it didn't work out." He wasn't really, but wanted to ask why in the worst way. Meghan supplied the information on her own.

She shrugged. "I have no one to blame but myself. Philip wanted a meek, compliant woman who followed the rules for a faculty wife. I attended all the social functions, and hosted the same. I tried to do the right thing, but never could understand why it mattered who sat where at a dinner party. The whole thing was based on who had the most tenure. Really stupid."

"So, you didn't always play the game?"

"No, and that led to arguments. He'd accuse me of deliberately jeopardizing his career and making him look foolish. And then there was my writing."

"He didn't like you doing your own thing?" Zach

sipped his amaretto already disliking this jerk.

"Phillip referred to it as a nice little hobby. It sounded good when he told his friends I was an aspiring author. Gave his image a boost.

"Everything was fine until I sold my first book. To his horror, it wasn't some high-brow work filled with angst and symbolism. He damned near had a heart attack when he discovered it was a mystery chocked full of murder, mayhem, and sex." She sipped her wine.

"What happened?"

"He accused me of sabotaging his career again. He'd climbed up the tenure ladder, and the banner of assistant dean fluttered under his nose. He forbade me to tell anyone at the university."

"And you went along with this? I'd have told him to go shove it."

"I almost did, but my self-confidence about being able to make it on my own was shaky. The first book made a modest amount of money and won an award. Then I wrote *The Campus Murders*. I used a university setting. The damn thing hit the *New York Times* bestseller list topping out at number thirty-four. My secret was out. Philip was embarrassed and spent less and less time at home."

Meghan sighed and sipped her wine again.

"I don't understand. If you'd been my wife, I'd have shouted it from the rooftops. Did he feel threatened by your success?"

"I didn't threaten Philip. According to him, I didn't have the brains for that. His biggest threat came from other professors lower on the tenure ladder."

"What a moron." Zach swigged amaretto glad she'd dumped this guy. "How could he say that? You had a master's degree for crying out loud."

"The academic atmosphere of a major college campus is a world unto itself. Philip was also a snob. He thought only the lowest of the low read mysteries and romance novels. Truly refined people read Faulkner, Hemingway, and the classics."

She sighed again and leaned over the parapet, gazing into the bushes. Partial shadows bathed their little corner of the terrace. Several people strolled out and into the garden, but paid no attention to them. Zach wondered if he dared to put his arm around her, but Meghan didn't look as though she needed sympathy.

"I suppose I should have seen it coming. The late nights, the out of town seminars, the students he said he enjoyed mentoring were all excuses. He found a graduate student named Marie who suited him better than I did."

"The son of a bitch dumped you?"

She laughed. "Don't sound so outraged. I was surprised, but in the end glad he finally admitted he wanted a divorce. Unfortunately, I wrote the first two books and the third I'd just submitted under my married name. My publisher didn't want to change. I already had a following."

"And name recognition translates into sales," Zach guessed.

"So, I kept the name—much to Philip's anguish—and continue to churn out a book a year."

"I'll bet he cringes whenever a new one appears. How long have you been divorced? Do you ever see him?"

"Six years come November and no, I never see him. He re-married as soon as the divorce was final."

She picked up her glass and rolled the stem in her fingers. "What about you? Am I hanging out with a married man?"

Zach sighed. "I've never even come close. The old cliché about being married to my work is true. Besides, computer nerds aren't sexy."

"Oh, I don't know. There's something incredibly sexy about a man with a brain." She slapped her fingers over her mouth. "Oh, my God! Did I just say that? Maybe I should switch to water."

Zach chuckled and hugged her without thinking, then dropped a light kiss on her forehead. It felt as natural as breathing. She didn't pull away or smack him one. Inside, the band tuned up again.

"Where did you go to school?" he asked.

"Undergraduate studies at Ohio State, and graduate studies at the University of North Carolina. How about you? Harvard, no doubt."

"MIT. I took every computer course I could, but officially graduated with a double degree in Engineering and Math. I immediately got my masters in Math, then turned around and received my MBA."

"I stand humbled."

He finished his amaretto. "Feel like more dancing or have I trampled your feet into bloody stumps?"

"My feet are fine, thank you very much, and you're a wonderful dancer."

He glanced into the ballroom at the crowded dance floor suddenly loathe to return to its cramped confines.

"Still looks crowded and hot," Meghan said, echoing his thoughts.

"We can dance here. Okay?"

"Why not?"

She came into his arms and he pressed her close to his chest. His heartbeat accelerated. Damn, she felt so good, so right in his arms. She locked both of her arms around his neck and he nestled his into the curve of her back. Technically, they didn't dance, but swayed to the music never separating, even when the band changed tunes and tempos.

He steered her deeper into the shadows. The music stopped. They didn't. Zach, always analytical and ruled by logic, threw both out the window. For the first time in his life, he let emotion reign. Without thinking, he lowered his head and covered her mouth with his.

Like the flash of a meteor, it dawned on him that this was why he'd come to the reunion. He'd hoped she would be here. All these years she'd hovered on the fringes of his mind like a ghost. No wonder other women didn't appeal to him. He had wanted Meghan, and only Meghan.

His hand tangled in her hair pulling her head back to expose the delicate line of her throat. His lips trailed from Meghan's mouth to the pulse point by her collarbone. She moaned.

At the same time, a scream echoed from somewhere in the garden.

Chapter Three

Suzanne sat alone at the table, sipping another cosmo and glaring across the room at Dave Coryell. He was drinking and laughing with a bunch of jocks.

Dammit, he invited me to this reunion. The least he can do is dance with me. As soon as I go to the ladies room, he's off hustling new clients. Fucking worm.

His phone call three months ago had surprised her. She hadn't heard from nor seen him since he, and his now ex-wife, had attended Charlie's funeral five years ago. Trying to revive old times, they'd had a few dates, but Dave's not-so-subtle probing into her financial affairs raised her suspicions.

If nothing else, Charlie had taught her to be wary of people's motives, especially concerning money, so she hired a private investigator. Charlie had done the same thing before popping the question. He knew she was a gold-digger and told her so, but married her anyway. All he demanded of Suzanne had been faithfulness and to look gorgeous. She'd lived up to the bargain. In return, he had given her anything she wanted. In her own mercenary way, she'd come to love him.

Her diligence in heeding Charlie's advice had paid off. Dave's divorce had cost a bundle and he was in deep financial trouble. Suzanne had no intention of replenishing his coffers. She suspected he juggled the funds of his client's portfolios. The report also revealed a cocaine habit.

Suzanne sipped her drink and wondered why the hell she'd agreed to attend this shindig. It wasn't like she gave a damn about any of these people.

He needs lots of money, uses drugs, and has sex on his mind. Someone tell me why I'm here. Good thing I insisted on separate rooms. No way will I sleep with the jerk.

Her gaze swept the room. Dave still schmoozed with the jocks and anyone else who'd listen. So far, this silly reunion had been a bust. Dammit, the diamonds on her ears and encircling her wrist were the real thing, as was the six-carat pendant around her neck. Nobody had commented on how great she looked. And working the room by herself might make her look desperate. Of course, sitting alone made her look pathetic. And Suzanne Crocker was anything but pathetic.

Suzanne sucked in an angry breath and sipped her cosmo. How many was this? She'd lost count and slowed her pace.

Charlie had also taught her how to drink at social affairs. A gorgeous wife wasn't gorgeous when drunk. Luckily, she had a high tolerance for alcohol, but now was not the time to test how high. She pushed the glass away.

Her gaze slid over the crowded dance floor. Jill and Ted swayed to a moody ballad. Tom and Glory shuffled their feet in a stiff attempt. Tom Ecklund had a case of terminally boring, yet Glory fitted him like a glove. At least she wasn't a self-righteous robot like her sister, Divine.

Suzanne shivered. The icy touch of a chill swept

over her bare shoulders and down her spine.

Don't think about Divine. It was a long time ago.

She heaved a sigh and fanned herself with her hand. It was hotter than hell in here. She'd give that asshole Dave ten more minutes of reliving the winning touchdown, and then go over and demand he dance with her.

Probably trying to pry money out of his football buddies.

Zach Dunbar had effectively slammed the corporate door in Dave's face earlier. She glanced at Zach's chair. He'd followed Dave's action by draping his suit coat over the back, but he and Meghan were nowhere in sight.

Zach had turned from geek to sleek and was probably worth a fortune. If Zach hadn't had eyes for the former fat girl, Suzanne would be all over him. Maybe she'd give it a shot later. Meghan might prove to be as boring as Tom Ecklund.

Now, *there* was a transformation. Once the names had settled into her mind, she'd placed the faces of twenty years ago.

Meghan Donahue, tall and built like a fireplug, Eddie had once commented she could play linebacker. Dave had countered that she was too soft. The opposing players would simply bounce off.

Suzanne tried, but couldn't stop her mind from swinging to Tami and Eddie. She could think of a lot of people who'd want Tami out of the way twenty years ago.

Her so-called best friend had been a vindictive, nasty piece of work. There had been times when her sharp tongue and caustic comments had taken aim at

Suzanne, especially when it came to being the center of attention. She wasn't unhappy they had drifted apart after high school and admitted part of the reason she'd agreed to this reunion had been to show off, especially in front of Tami.

On the other hand, Eddie had been a conceited blowhard, always bragging on how he'd make it in the NFL.

Suzanne shivered again. Now they were both dead; murdered in the prime of their lives. She was shocked, but not saddened.

The music ceased as the band took a break. Couples dispersed to the bars and tables. She caught a glimpse of Meghan and Zach near the terrace doors. Eric Peterson drifted toward the bar. Annabelle caught her eye and threaded her way between the throng. Without asking, she pulled out a chair.

"Hello, Suzanne. I guess we must shop the same stores," Annabelle said with a laugh.

The only reason she remembered the woman was because she'd been a member of the pom-pom squad. Tami had hated her. Everyone liked Annabelle and that had infuriated Tami. A couple of nasty rumors about the girl, instigated by the cheerleader, had swept the school near prom time.

Pissed at Dave, this whole reunion in general, at Annabelle because she wore the same dress, and just tipsy enough not to give a damn, Suzanne answered, "I sincerely doubt that. I don't shop at Target." She glanced at the fake diamonds hanging from Annabelle's ears and neck. "My, my, the cubic zirconia shines tonight."

The other woman's face reddened as she patted one

of her earrings. "Actually, I bought the dress at Macy's. Are you having a good time?"

"Not particularly. I find it all boring and pathetic, and could care less about people I didn't like or associate with twenty years ago."

Annabelle flushed and rose. "Nice talking with you, Suzanne. Have a good trip back to the rock you crawled out from under."

Suzanne gaped as Annabelle flounced away, and then sipped her abandoned drink.

I suppose I deserved that, but who cares? With any luck, I'll never see these people again.

Finally, Dave returned to the table and sat in Annabelle's abandoned chair.

"I've been talking to the guys. Would you believe not one of them has a decent portfolio?" He gazed around the room. "Where's Zach? I'd love to corner him about Dunbar Electronics. If there is a takeover bid floating around out there, I could make a butt load of money. What have you been doing?"

"Not a goddamned thing. I've been sitting here like a whore at a virgin sacrifice. The least you can do is halt trolling for dollars long enough to dance with me."

He frowned, and then smiled. "I'm sorry. The first dance when the band gets back. I promise. How's your drink holding out?"

She might have been half-loaded, but she recognized ooze when she heard it. "Fine."

"I need another. I'll only be a moment. Hello, Glory. I'm making a bar trip. Can I get you anything?"

Glory plopped down in her seat. "Oh, no, thank you. Tom's getting me another diet soda."

Dave left and Glory turned to Suzanne. "Isn't this

fun? I am so happy everything went off without a hitch. The food was good, the band is terrific, and tomorrow's going to be a blast. I just love picnics, don't you?"

"Oh, yeah, I adore insects crawling all over my food. The buffet sucked, the band is average, and needless to say, I won't be at Samson's Lake tomorrow."

For a moment, Suzanne saw loathing in Glory's eyes before the look vanished into hurt feelings. She bit her lip and gazed down at the tablecloth.

"I'm sorry you feel that way. Why did you bother to come?"

"I'm asking myself the same question."

"Of course, arriving only to find out your best buddies have been brutally murdered must have put a damper on your weekend. Divine said the four of you were a tightly knit group."

The mention of Divine's name brought back old memories for Suzanne, memories she could do without.

"Maybe the killer is someone you all knew, I mean like together. You know, during high school," Glory rambled on.

"If anyone wanted to kill Tami during high school, they'd have done it. Why wait twenty years? And if Eddie lived down to expectations, he was probably offed by an irate husband or boyfriend. I don't want to talk about this anymore."

"But don't you find it odd, and in a way fascinating, that the two most popular kids in our class were murdered within a month of each other?"

"I don't find it fascinating at all. And why should you care? They weren't your classmates, Glory."

"No, but Divine knew them. She didn't like them

much."

"Yeah, well, the feeling was mutual. Your sister was a sanctimonious, Bible-thumping, pain in the ass."

Glory licked her lips and shoved her chair back. "I think I'll go powder my nose." She hefted her large purse and left.

Suzanne shrugged. She shouldn't have insulted Glory, but the booze loosened her tongue. Her gaze settled on Zach's suit coat. She wondered if he and Meghan had sneaked off upstairs.

Swell, the former fat girl and the former geek are getting it on, while I'm stuck with Dave who will soon ask me for money. I should have stayed in Chicago.

The minutes passed, and still Dave didn't return. She finally spotted him talking with Dan Masterson.

You son of a bitch. Still on the make. Be careful, Dave, old buddy. Dan's a lawyer and a politician. He probably researches where and when to take a leak.

As though hearing her unspoken words, Dave looked up and waved, then nodded to Dan and came back.

"Sorry, I was just chatting with Dan."

"About what?"

He shrugged. "Oh, this and that."

"You mean you asked about his investments, and he gave you a campaign speech."

"Some, but we talked about old times."

"What good old times did you and Dan Masterson ever share? He was a target for you and Eddie."

"Not always." He gulped some of his drink and swiped his upper lip with his finger.

Dave talked and told what he thought must have been amusing stories. She knew how to play the game and laughed in all the right places when in fact, she was miserable, but damned if she'd show it to everybody in the room. To her classmates they probably appeared to be having a great time. Oddly enough, thoughts of her late husband popped into her mind. *I'd have had a good time with Charlie tonight. He was a great dancer and knew how to make a woman feel special.*

"Uh, Suzanne, I'd like to talk to you for a moment. How about another cosmopolitan?"

He looked jittery and wiped a fine sheen of sweat from his forehead with a cocktail napkin.

"No, thanks. What is it you want to talk about?"

Like I don't know. He's been oiling his way around the room all evening trying to get a fish on the line and been skunked. He was about to ask for money. Suzanne braced herself. *Oh, brother, do I have this guy pegged or what?*

"Honey, I know of a great stock for you—Royal Gemstones and Precious Metals. They're a small start-up group who buy only the best and at low prices. A simple hundred thousand this week will bring profits tenfold in a year's time. I can guarantee it. Gold is skyrocketing. Let me handle the entire transaction at a modest ten percent and you won't regret it."

"Why would I buy gold now when the price is up?"

"Because it's going to go higher." He shot her a surprised look.

As if he can't believe I understand the stock market. Asshole.

"And where does this company get its gems and precious metals?"

"Uh, all over the world."

"Including Africa?"

"A lot of diamonds are mined in South Africa."

"A lot of diamonds are mined in other African countries to finance war at the expense of the people."

"Suzanne, since when do you give a shit about other people?" Dave asked, his brow furrowing in a frown. His eyes held a hint of anger.

Not a good line to use during a sales pitch, jerk off. Charlie always said to trust my instincts. Good thing I listened. Dave Coryell is full of crap.

"Dave, I wouldn't buy Mississippi mud from you. The fact is, you are the only broker remaining at your firm. The last guy quit four months ago. Your ex-wife sucked your bank account dry in the divorce. Maybe she knew Tami and took lessons. With four divorces, I'm sure *she* did quite well.

"You're teetering on the edge of bankruptcy and none of my money is going down the drain with you. If I were a client, I'd demand an audit of my account."

His eyes opened wide and he shifted nervously in his seat. A drop of sweat dribbled down his forehead. He wiped it with his sleeve.

"Are you calling me a thief?" His voice didn't sound defensive, but scared.

"I wouldn't trust you with my last two nickels. And ten percent is highway robbery. I might not have been the brightest bulb in the pack twenty years ago, but Charlie Crocker taught me a lot."

She picked up her glass and downed the last of her cosmo.

"You had me investigated, didn't you?" Dave said in a stunned voice.

"Of course I did. Your first probe regarding my investments had me running to the nearest private detective. Oh, and while we're on the subject, you might want to do something about the cocaine habit you've acquired."

Dave sprang to his feet, grabbing the chair before it fell over.

"You bitch!" He gave the room a quick scan, and then hissed, "You can find your own way back to Chicago." He whirled, heading for the ballroom doors and the lobby.

"That should be no problem," she remarked to his retreating back. She'd stay the night and grab the first flight out of Indianapolis in the morning. Suzanne glanced at her diamond-embellished Tag Heuer. Geez, only ten-thirty? Early by her standards. The whole exchange had been refreshing. She decided to grab another drink—on Dave's tab—and blow this party from hell. She also wanted a cigarette.

It was the one bad habit she'd never completely kicked. The more she thought about it, the more she wanted one.

Suzanne snatched her evening bag from the center of the table and fished through it until finding the pack of Marlboro's and slim gold lighter. She shook one free, stuck it between her lips, and flicked the flame to life, then sucked the sharp acrid smoke into her lungs.

God, this tastes good. Why are all the vices in the world bad for you? Can't just one be beneficial? Guess if they were, they wouldn't be called vices.

She blew out a thin stream of smoke and sat back in her chair, closing her eyes. She'd finish this, get a drink, and make reservations.

"I'm sorry, but the hotel has a policy of no smoking in its public areas," a man's pompous voice broke into her thoughts.

Her eyes popped open to stare at Dan Masterson's disapproving face. "Excuse me?"

"There's no smoking in the ballroom."

Her gaze darted around the room. "I don't see any 'no smoking' signs."

"A law prohibiting smoking in public places was passed by the Indiana Legislature two years ago."

"Then the management should put up a sign for those of us who don't live in God's little acre."

"Nevertheless, it's the law. As even you must know, secondhand smoke is deadly on several levels. It can bring on asthma attacks and allergic reactions, not to mention it's just plain rude to pollute the air of those around you. If you must smoke, may I suggest you go onto the terrace or to your room, assuming you have one that permits the activity."

The former class president pissed her off. He sounded like an outraged spinster at the first sign of cleavage. He hadn't changed a bit over the years.

Suzanne squinted against the spiraling smoke. "Tell me, Dan, if I pull that stick out of your ass will your head fall off and roll across the floor?"

His nostrils flared, his lips thinned, and he glared at her from narrowed eyes. Dan leaned over until his face was a foot from hers.

"Twenty years is a long time, Suzanne, and I don't have to take any more of the arrogant bullshit you four handed out on a regular basis."

"You always were a self-righteous prick."

"I knew the difference between right and wrong."

"And you're in politics?"

"I'll be mayor of this town. You'll see."

"It still frosts your balls that we commanded more respect than you, doesn't it? Tami changed her hairstyle, and by the end of the week all the girls in Grandview High imitated it. Eddie hauls ass into school one day wearing a blazer over his t-shirt, and the next day guess what, so was every other jock or jock wannabe. We were the in-crowd, and the in-crowd always rules. You were the stuffy, self-important, class president who wore tasseled loafers and buttoned down shirts."

Dan straightened with a tight smile. "Tami and Eddie are dead and probably roasting in hell. If I were you, Susie Cute, I'd watch my back. Some people can hold grudges a long time."

He strode from the table and out onto the terrace.

"Well, shit," Suzanne muttered, absently dropping her cigarette into Dave's unfinished drink. "If I didn't know better I'd call that a threat."

Why stay? She'd get her drink and call it a night. She gathered her purse and made for the bar. No one spoke to her as she passed.

"Cosmopolitan," she told the bartender. "By the way, how much are they?"

"Eight dollars, ma'am."

"On second thought, make it two virgins— cranberry juice only." She fished in her purse and withdrew a twenty. "Charge me for the cosmos and consider this your tip."

She signed Dave's room number to the tab and hoped he choked on his bar bill. He deserved it.

Suzanne tucked her silver clutch evening bag under her arm, grabbed both drinks, and stepped around knots of chatting people on her way to the terrace doors.

****

I broke off my conversation with a group of classmates and wound my way through the crowd toward the terrace. Suzanne Wayland had just left the room—alone. Probably for a smoke, either on the patio or in the garden. While I was sure the foul-mouthed bitch wasn't a nature lover, her attitude tonight angered a lot of people. I doubted idle conversation was on the agenda and put my money on the garden.

I hurried through the doors just in time to see her blue dress disappear down the path toward the koi pond. Trying to look casual, I followed. A lot of people took advantage of the lull in dancing to gather and chat outside. I didn't think anyone would notice one more person in the throng.

The pathway was dimly lit and to avoid the sound of the gravel crunching under my feet, I tiptoed along the grassy edge. Rounding a curve, I paused and slipped my hand into my pocket. The cool metal of the stun gun met my fingers. The koi pond was just ahead and through the filtered glow of the tier lights, I saw Suzanne a few feet from the water puffing on a cigarette.

Time to die, you bitch.

I withdrew the stun gun, activated the switch and rushed forward. She didn't have a chance to even turn around. I jammed the weapon against the back of her neck and pressed the button, holding it down for a good five seconds. The cigarette dropped from her fingers as Suzanne lurched toward the pond. The smell of singed hair drifted to my nostrils. I released the button and pushed her to the edge of the rock rimmed pool. She fell just short, but still far enough for me to kneel on her back and hold her head underwater.

The stun gun effects didn't last as long as I thought. Within a minute, she came to life and struggled, but it was too late. I pushed harder until all movement ceased, then heaved her legs into the water.

Slowly, I backed away, my panting breaths the only sound other than the burbling from a waterfall in the pond. Suzanne's hair floated on the surface like seaweed. I stared, mesmerized by the sight. Distant laughter brought me out of my daze. I needed to get out of here. I moved and kicked something on the path—Suzanne's purse. No sense in leaving it here. I tossed it into the bushes. Casting one last satisfied glance at the pond, I hurried to the gate separating the garden from the parking lot, reentering the hotel through the main doors. A group of people sat in the lobby, but no one bothered to look up. I skirted along the perimeter and headed for the stairs.

Number four dispatched with almost no resistance. Soon numbers five and six will join the others.

The thought made me feel invincible—like a God.

****

Outside, Suzanne turned right and made her way to the far end of the long patio. The air had cooled, and a light breeze rustled the foliage in the garden below. She found a bench wedged between the waist-high stone balustrade and several potted plants. Sitting, she sipped one cranberry juice and set the other down, then lit another cigarette.

She exhaled and watched the smoke disappear on the wind. She sipped again. Several people climbed the steps from the garden. Their laughter irritated her. Suzanne was tired of people having a good time when she was miserable and pissed off.

She leaned back and puffed between sips. Someone exited the ballroom and crossed the terrace to gaze into the garden. Suzanne peeked around the edge of the potted plant.

Shit. It was Annabelle Peterson. The woman lifted the hair from her nape and raised her face to catch the breeze.

Not wanting to be seen by or talk to someone she'd insulted, she wiggled into the corner of the bench. Annabelle disappeared down the steps into the garden.

Suzanne breathed a sigh of relief and slid further along the bench until the steps were hidden from view. She crushed out her cigarette in one of the plants and finished her virgin cosmo. With her head laid back against the building, she closed her eyes. More footsteps crossed the terrace from the ballroom, hesitated for a moment, and then descended the steps.

Just a few moments of fresh air. That's all I need, and then I can go to bed. I'll call the airlines in the morning.

She willed herself to relax and forget about Dave, Glory, Annabelle, and that horse's ass, Dan Masterson. She especially wanted to forget about Tami and Eddie.

More people wandered onto the terrace, into the gardens, and back again. Small snatches of conversation drifted her way, but Suzanne shut them out. The booze made her groggy, and she slipped into that realm of twilight sleep—not awake, but not asleep either.

She had no idea how long she dozed. A loud bark of laughter brought her back to full consciousness. She sat upright and peered around the screen of greenery.

The band had resumed and music drifted out into the night. On the far side of the terrace, she noticed a couple dancing in the shadows. Five or six people stood near the doors.

"Laugh all you want, but I can feel my hips growing. The food was fantastic, but I need to walk it off." Eileen Raymond said. "Anyone care to join me in the garden?"

"Are you kidding? Those pathways are crushed stone. I'll break a heel," a woman responded.

"Not me. I'm afraid of the dark," a man replied with a chuckle.

Eileen waved at their jokes and sauntered down the steps, then turned left.

Suzanne sipped her second cranberry juice, and then dumped it into the plant.

She pulled another cigarette from her purse, and lit up. About to leave, the conversation stopped her cold.

"Did you see Suzanne Wayland? She was alone almost all night," one of the women said.

"Yeah, Dave Coryell practically ignored her," another female voice chimed in. "Wonder how she likes being on the outside looking in for a change. Serves her right."

"I feel kind of sorry for her," a man answered. "I heard her husband died."

"And left her pots of money," one of the women added in a scornful tone. "Must have taken her down a peg to see Annabelle Peterson in the same dress."

"How come women are so catty? So it was the same dress? So what?"

"Men just don't get it."

"Come on, let's go back inside. I'm ready to dance

again."

Suzanne gulped the anger burning at her throat.

"Jealous bunch of bitches. How many of them are wearing designer originals? How many of them are sporting fifty thousand dollars worth of diamonds tonight?" she muttered in distain.

She wanted to run over and kick all of them in the ass with her Jimmy Choos.

The laughter still echoed when a scream ripped the night air.

Chapter Four

Meghan jerked away from Zach as the scream was repeated, closer this time. Stumbling footsteps accompanied by ragged breathing emanated from the graveled pathway to her left.

"What the hell?" Zach said.

The high-pitched shriek turned into a wail as Eileen Raymond staggered up the terrace steps. The toe of her shoe caught the last one, and she fell to her hands and knees.

Zach and Meghan, along with several other people, ran to help her.

"Eileen, what's wrong?" Zach asked. He and another man lifted her.

"Honey, what's the matter?" the man questioned.

Meghan assumed he was Eileen's husband.

Eileen's teeth chattered. Hair straggled from the elegant French twist, hanging around her cheeks and bulging eyes, while she continued to sob. Her face was ashen beneath the tear-streaked make-up.

"Eileen, get a hold of yourself," her husband demanded.

Meghan doubted that would happen. The woman trembled from head to foot like a tree in a storm. Her eyes rolled back into her head.

"Keep her standing," Meghan ordered the men. She stepped in front of her hysterical classmate, and then slapped her hard across the cheek. "Eileen, calm down."

Eileen hiccupped, swallowed, but stopped the noise, even though she continued to gasp.

"What's wrong?" Zach asked again.

"Did someone attack you?" The husband's angry gaze swept the darkened foliage. "I knew you shouldn't have gone into the garden by yourself. Did you see who it was? Can you identify the man?"

The band still played, but a sizable crowd now pressed onto the flagstones.

Eileen pointed into the garden. She gasped a couple of times before finding her voice.

"Out—out there! In the pond! Oh, my God, it's awful!"

Meghan wanted to scream at the lack of information. "What's awful? Did someone attack you?"

"No, no!" Eileen sobbed and buried her face in her hands. "There's a body…in the fish pond."

"A body? Whose?" her husband demanded.

"I—I don't know. I was just walking and went to the edge of the pond, saw something floating, and ran."

"So, it might not be a body at all. You have had a couple of glasses of wine," her husband said.

"I am not drunk!"

He pulled Eileen into his arms. "Of course, you're not, but maybe you made a mistake in the dark and your imagination took over."

"I'm calling 9-1-1," a woman in the doorway declared.

"Wait a minute," Zach told her. "Let's make sure there is a body not just a tree branch or someone's sick idea of a practical joke. We need a flashlight."

"I have a small one attached to my key chain," a woman offered.

"I have a penlight in my purse," another replied.

"Go get them. What's your name?" Zach asked the husband as the women left.

"Carl Davis. I'm Eileen's husband. Do you think this is a joke?"

"I don't know, but we need to find out before calling in the police. If it is a body, a few more minutes can't hurt."

The women returned and handed Zach the items. He gave one to Carl and flicked his on.

"It's not much, but will have to do. Meghan, stay with Eileen. This won't take long."

Meghan nodded as the men trotted down the steps and disappeared into the night, the feeble glow from the flashlights bobbing down the path until they vanished.

"We should get her inside," a woman suggested.

Meghan shook her head. "Too hot. Someone bring a chair."

A man near the door complied, and Meghan eased a still shaky Eileen into it.

"Oh, God, I'm going to faint."

"No, you're not." Meghan pushed Eileen's head between her knees and rubbed her back. "Take slow, even breaths. You'll be fine."

A minute later the woman straightened pressing a hand to her chest. "Do you think it's a joke?"

"Well, if it is, it's not very funny."

Meghan thought back to the practical jokers in the class. This was just the kind of thing Suzanne and Dave would think up for entertainment—shove a mannequin in the pond and wait for someone to find it. She hadn't seen either of them since leaving the table.

Damn those two anyway.

She swore if that redheaded bitch was behind this, she'd punch Suzanne right in the nose. Dave, too. Money hadn't changed them. They still harbored a high school mentality.

Eileen cried softly.

"Someone get me a tissue or a napkin," Meghan requested.

A few seconds later, a man stuffed a wad of cocktail napkins in her hand. She gave them to Eileen.

"Here, there's no need to cry. You'll give yourself a headache."

Eileen wiped her face and blew her nose, then turned a watery gaze to Meghan. "I wish the guys would come back. What's taking so long?"

Meghan wondered the same. Zach and Carl had been gone almost ten minutes. Maybe they had trouble finding the pond or negotiating the pathways with those tiny flashlights.

The crowd milled around talking in low voices.

Dave Coryell bulled his way through the doors.

"What's going on out here? Has anyone seen Suzanne? I've been looking for her everywhere."

"Eileen thinks she found a body floating in the fish pond," Glory said. She and Tom stood just outside the doors.

"A body? You're kidding. Whose?"

Meghan wanted to smack him. As if he didn't know. His attitude confirmed her suspicions of a practical joke. Then from below, she heard the crunch of gravel.

Zach and a clearly shaken Carl mounted the steps.

"Well?" she questioned. Anxiety roughened her voice.

"Call the police, and notify the management they have a body on their hands," Zach told them.

"Who is it? Someone we know?" she asked.

"I think its Suzanne Wayland."

Meghan's head swung to Dave. He stared at Zach with a blank expression, and then downed his drink in a single gulp.

"Oh, my God, another one. I don't know why I'm so upset. I didn't even like her." Eileen moaned and sobbed harder.

"I'm not real fond of you, either," Suzanne stated, stepping into the light from the shadows on the opposite end of the terrace, her hands fisted on her hips.

Eileen yelped. Dave Coryell, his expression no longer empty but astonished, gaped at his former girlfriend. The glass slipped from his fingers, shattering at his feet.

Before anyone could say a word, Eric Peterson strolled out.

"Has anybody seen Annabelle? She wanted to get some air, but that was over thirty minutes ago." His gaze settled on the stunned crowd. "What's going on?"

The truth dawned on Meghan. She sucked in her breath and gazed at the people nearby.

Zach and Carl whirled to face Eric. Meghan's heart pounded and her ears buzzed.

Oh, my God.... Annabelle? Who'd want to hurt Annabelle?

Even as she thought the words, the facts stabbed her in the gut. Her attention turned back to Eileen who stifled another scream.

Glory Ecklund fainted dead away in her husband's arms. He lowered her to the stone floor, his face a mask of anger—and fear.

****

The police arrived and directed everyone from the terrace into the ballroom with orders not to leave until they'd been questioned. When the forensics team and the coroner arrived, they pulled the body from the water, and a distraught Eric made the gruesome identification of his wife.

Carl took over the care of Eileen, while Meghan helped Tom deal with a shaken Glory. They sat at the table while Glory mumbled biblical passages.

"Shall I get her a drink?" Meghan asked Tom.

"No, water will do for now, but I wouldn't mind a good stiff belt. Bourbon is fine."

She hurried toward the bar and glanced outside the terrace doors where Zach talked with the cops. By now everybody in the room knew what had happened. The band had ceased playing and the conversation had dwindled to a muted hum in the air.

Dave had grabbed Suzanne's hand and whisked her through the door. The two of them sat alone, heads close together, at a table in the far corner of the room. Meghan had never seen Suzanne so subdued, or Dave so tense. Several classmates shot covert glances at the couple.

Friends gathered around a stunned and sobbing Eric.

She ordered Tom's bourbon, a glass of wine for herself, and amaretto for Zach. She walked back slowly and deposited the drinks on the table.

Tom bolted the whisky in two gulps, and then

continued to comfort Glory.

"It's going to be all right, honey," he said, stroking the disheveled hair from her face.

Glory mumbled and stared straight ahead as if in a trance. It gave Meghan the creeps. She sipped the wine, waiting for Zach to return with news.

Glory clapped a hand over her mouth and rose. "Oh dear! I'm going to be sick!"

She turned and bolted toward the banquet hall doors, Tom running in her wake.

Meghan was tempted to follow, but Zach and the sheriff along with several deputies walked through the terrace doors. She recognized the sheriff as Ray Armstrong. Twenty years ago, he'd been a young deputy. He walked onstage to the microphone. Zach approached the table and sat next to her.

"Well?"

Zach shrugged. "Forensics is sifting through every piece of gravel in the path and under every lily pad in the pond. We'll know when they feel like telling us."

"May I have your attention, please?" the sheriff announced. The mike squealed and he backed away while one of the deputies adjusted the sound. "Ladies and gentlemen, your attention, please. I'd like you all to take the seats you occupied earlier this evening. We'll be around to get statements as quickly as we can. As soon as we finish, you can leave. I ask that you be patient. Thank you."

Several in the crowd groaned.

"I want to go home now," a woman whimpered.

"This is silly. None of us killed the poor woman," a man stated.

"That's right," another man added. "Some vagrant

came across her in the dark and tried to rob her."

"If I was Eric Peterson, I'd sue the hotel. They should have had security guards patrolling the garden," a woman declared.

A shaken Glory supported by Tom returned. He lowered her into a chair, seated himself next to her, and patted her hands.

Meghan leaned forward. "Glory, are you all right?"

She nodded and answered in a quavering voice. "I'm fine. I…I threw up."

"Well, of course you did. Perfectly natural," her husband said. "Can I get you something to drink? More diet soda?"

"No, thank you, honey. I'll just drink water. It was all such a shock."

Meghan silently agreed as she sipped more wine.

Sheriff Armstrong left the stage and pointed the three deputies to the first tables in front. He headed for theirs, wedging a chair between Tom Ecklund and Ted Kramer. Jill scooted closer to Meghan.

"This is horrible," Jill whispered as she wiped tears from her eyes with a napkin. "Eric is devastated. I was just talking to Annabelle a little while ago. They have four kids. The youngest is only two. She was so proud of them."

Dave guided a quiet Suzanne to her chair. Suzanne lit a cigarette. Dan Masterson walked up with a frown.

"We had this discussion before, Suzanne. No smoking."

The redhead looked up and snapped, "Fuck off, asshole."

"It is against the law…"

"Mr. Masterson, perhaps it would be better if you

returned to your table," the sheriff suggested.

"As a former senior class president and a city councilman, I feel it's my duty to remain visible. The people, many of them my constituents, need a calm, reassuring presence."

Suzanne glared. Dave curled his lip and sucked a sizable portion from his glass. Zach raised an eyebrow, giving Dan a cool look. Meghan wanted to follow Glory's lead and throw up. A woman was dead, and Dan Masterson sounded every inch the campaigning politician.

"My thoughts exactly, sir. Your leadership would best be served by setting a good example," Sheriff Armstrong answered in a soothing voice.

Dan straightened and adjusted his tie. "Yes, I see your point, Sheriff."

He shot Suzanne a nasty glance and walked away.

"You know, miss, there is a law against smoking in public places, and while I can understand your need for nicotine at a moment like this, I'd appreciate it if you'd put the cigarette out."

Suzanne sighed, but dropped it into a water glass where the glowing tip hissed and was extinguished.

"Satisfied?" she asked.

"Yes, thank you." He brought out a notebook and a pencil, and then turned his gaze on Ted Kramer. "Your name?"

"Ted Kramer. This is my wife, Jill."

"Which one of you is the graduate?"

"I am," Jill answered in a wavering voice.

"Where do you live?"

Ted gave an address in St. Louis.

Sheriff Armstrong jotted down the information in

his notebook, and then questioned, "What can you tell me about tonight?"

"To me, everything seemed perfectly normal," Ted told him. "We had a few drinks, chatted with some of Jill's classmates, and danced."

"Did you talk with Annabelle Peterson?"

"Jill introduced us, but that's about all. We talked to her husband for a couple of minutes, and then moved on to another table."

"When was this?"

"After dinner, but before the band started. I can't give you a specific time."

"How about you, Mrs. Kramer? Did you talk to either Mr. or Mrs. Peterson?"

Jill sipped some water and nodded. "Eric and I were classmates. Annabelle graduated the year after us. They dated all through high school. I wasn't surprised to find they'd married."

"So, you knew Mrs. Peterson prior to tonight," the sheriff stated.

"I knew her, but not well. She was on the pom-pom squad. Everybody loved her."

"What did the two of you talk about?"

Jill shrugged and raised her hands palms up. "The usual—kids, where we lived, the reunion—just ordinary things."

"Any idea who might want her dead?"

"None whatsoever. Annabelle got along with everybody. She chatted with a lot of people tonight. I saw her leave about half an hour or so before the screaming started."

"Which door did she use?"

"The one to the terrace."

"Did you see anybody follow her outside?"

"Are you kidding? It's hotter than hell in here. People were coming and going on a regular basis." Jill shuddered and swiped at her eyes again. "I just can't believe this has happened."

"Are you staying in the hotel?"

"Yes," Ted answered. "Room five-twenty."

"Thank you. You're free to leave."

Meghan watched Ted and Jill rise, then head for the lobby. Several people from other tables did the same as the deputies finished with them. At this rate, it would take hours to question everyone.

Sheriff Armstrong turned his attention to Tom and Glory. Meghan noted with relief that Glory appeared more in control.

"Tom, Glory, I'll be as quick about this as I can. Then the two of you can get home."

"Oh, we're staying at the hotel," Tom told him.

"Why? You live two miles away."

Glory smiled and sipped some water. "I'm on the reunion committee and thought it would make better sense to stay overnight in case someone from out of town needed something. I suggested it to Eileen a couple of weeks ago. She thought it was a good idea."

"What's your room number?"

"Four-nineteen," she replied.

"Tom, describe your view of the evening. Did you talk to Annabelle?" the sheriff asked.

"I spoke with her and Eric after we ate. It was just a quick 'hello, how are you' kind of thing. I don't even remember what we talked about."

"How was the party going?"

"Fine. I was having a lot of fun."

Ray Armstrong's eyes shifted to Glory. "How about you, Glory? Did you talk to Annabelle?"

"Some. I remember speaking to her just before the dancing started. I welcomed her and Eric back to Grandview. They live in Cincinnati, you know. We chatted for a few minutes about family and such, and then I moved on to another table."

"Was Tom with you the whole time?"

"What do you mean, was I with her?" Tom demanded with an indignant expression.

The sheriff raised his hand. "Relax, Tom. If the two of you were separated, then you may have seen different things."

"Well, you didn't ask that of Ted and Jill."

"Jill would have stayed close to her husband to introduce him to her classmates, whereas you and Glory already know most of the people present."

Glory laid her hand on Tom's arm. "Don't worry, dear. I'm sure Ray doesn't suspect us of anything. What else do you want to know?"

"Did you see Annabelle leave the room?"

"No, I'm afraid not."

"Did you leave the room at any time?"

"Yes, I went to the ladies' room a couple of times, and stepped onto the terrace for a moment to catch a breath of air." She frowned. "I'm afraid we didn't think about how hot the room might become with the dancing and all."

"Any idea who'd want to hurt Annabelle Peterson?"

Glory shot a nasty glance at Suzanne before smiling at the sheriff. "No. She was the sweetest person in the whole world. Are you sure she didn't stumble and fall, or have a stroke or something?"

"I can't say much right now, but we don't think it was an accident. Glory, I understand you fainted when you discovered the body was that of Annabelle Peterson."

"I'm afraid I did. It was all so shocking and I'd been so worried about everyone having a good time, I didn't eat much dinner. And it was so hot in the room. I guess it all just got to me. I feel silly about it."

"Are you all right?" the sheriff asked.

"Oh, I'm fine. Maybe when we go upstairs I can order a sandwich from room service."

"Can we go now?" Tom challenged in a rough tone.

"Yes, of course. I'll keep in touch."

Tom shoved his chair back and helped Glory from hers. With his arm around his wife's shoulders, he steered her out of the room.

Zach frowned. "Why don't you think it was just an accident? It's dark. The path is hard to walk on, especially for a woman in high heels. Why couldn't she have stumbled, fallen, hit her head, and tumbled into the pond?"

The sheriff's eyes bored into Zach. A chill raced up Meghan's spine. Zach had been as quiet as she during the interrogation. Was he also taking mental notes?

"I agree with Zach," Dave interjected. "This whole thing was a silly accident. And even if it wasn't, I say someone who shouldn't have been on the hotel grounds was lying in wait for a guest to stroll by, knock them on the head, and rob the poor sucker. I'm sorry Annabelle's dead, but you're just keeping us here to play policeman."

Dave had a surly look on his face along with a fine sheen of sweat along his hairline. His hands trembled. Meghan wondered if it was the booze or nerves.

Why would Dave Coryell be nervous?

She tried to recall the last time she'd seen him. Hadn't it been as the dancing started? He was across the room talking to some football buddies.

"Mr. Coryell, I assure you I'm not deliberately wasting either my time or anybody else's with foolish questions just to look official." Ray Armstrong's voice had a frosty tone. He looked at Zach who stared back. "We found bruising and cuts on her upper torso from the rocks around the lip of the pond. Her legs are also scraped. That's not consistent with a fall. A thief may have attacked, held her head underwater, and then heaved her in."

"Oh, my God," Meghan said with a gasp. This got worse by the minute.

She glanced at Suzanne who, pale as a ghost, stared at the sheriff with wide eyes. The woman's silence was out of character. She cast her eyes down and traced an invisible pattern on the tablecloth with a coral-tipped fingernail, then slid a sidelong glance toward Dave who sweated as though in a sauna, but not before Meghan caught the fear in her eyes.

Suzanne knows this was no accident.

Chapter Five

I killed Annabelle Peterson? How could I make such a stupid mistake? I was so focused on Suzanne, I hadn't given anyone else another thought. Never noticed that their dresses were similar, if not the same. And in the dark, I totally missed the hair color, especially once it was in the water.

You goofed. Get a grip. Act horrified. The last wouldn't be a stretch. And while I didn't really know Annabelle Peterson, I was sorry she died. *Collateral damage occurs. It can't be helped.*

I took a deep breath to steady my nerves. As usual, no one paid any particular attention to me. All eyes were on Suzanne and that obnoxious Dave Coryell. They sat talking in the corner, heads close together.

And Eileen Raymond was the perfect person to discover the body. Her hysterical reaction on the terrace helped fuel the fire. Then, Suzanne's appearance and Eric Peterson's emergence onto the patio spoiled the entire outcome. A totally wasted effort on my part. I was angry with myself.

I studied the guests when they took their original seats as per the sheriff's request.

Suzanne knows. She understands. So does Meghan. I can see it in her face. Zach's probably clued in, too. They all know it was a case of mistaken identity. Suzanne will be on guard now. I shook my head. *Never mind. Think about it later. You'll get her eventually. But for now, just answer whatever questions the sheriff asks.*

****

"Your turn," the sheriff said to Zach. "Name, address, and what you do for a living."

Trying to hide his disgust with Dave, Zach shot a quick glance at the man sitting next to him, seemingly impatient with the repetitive questions before answering.

"Zachary Dunbar. I live in Phoenix, and I'm the owner and CEO of Dunbar Electronics and Data Systems."

"Phoenix, that's a long way to come for a high school reunion."

Zach shrugged. "It was a last minute decision. I didn't e-mail my acceptance until a few weeks ago."

"You didn't answer my question."

"You didn't ask one," Zach replied.

The sheriff raised an eyebrow. "So, I didn't. Why did you suddenly decide to come back to Grandview?"

"Who knows? I've been working hard for ten years to build my company. When I came across the invitation in a stack of old mail, I thought why not."

"Nothing like success to motivate a person."

Zach gave the sheriff credit for being perceptive. Consciously, that was his reasoning, but Meghan had floated in his subconscious. *No need for the sheriff to know that.*

"I've heard about Dunbar Electronics. Is the home office in Phoenix?

"Yes, but I also have branches in Silicon Valley, Dallas, and just closed a deal to buy a small electronics outfit in Southern California."

The sheriff leaned forward and lowered his voice. "Do you know Paul Treadwell, the king of software?"

Zach nodded. "Yes. He's a nice guy and ten times smarter than me, which explains why he's worth billions and I'm not."

Sheriff Armstrong laughed, and then got back to business. "Let's see, according to my notes, you and Carl Davis found the body, is that right?"

"No. Carl's wife Eileen found the body. She was hysterical, so Carl and I went into the garden to see for ourselves. We thought she might be imagining things or that someone was playing a practical joke."

Sheriff Armstrong's eyes cut to Dave and Suzanne. He raised an eyebrow again and made a notation in his notebook.

Zach also spared the two a glance. Both squirmed and refused to meet anybody's eyes. If he remembered correctly, the two of them and Tami and Eddie accounted for a fair amount of mischief during their high school years.

"Obviously, it wasn't a joke. Tell me about it."

"Excuse me, Sheriff, but don't you already have this information?" Dave demanded.

"I spoke very briefly to Mr. Dunbar and Mr. Davis outside. Now, I want more details. Is that all right with you, Mr. Coryell?"

Dave bit his lip, rose, and left for the bar.

"I'll take another, too," Suzanne called after him.

"Get your own. And put it on your tab for a change," he snapped.

Suzanne mumbled something that sounded like 'jackass' under her breath and followed Dave.

"Give me the details, Mr. Dunbar."

"Carl and I decided to check out the pond before calling the police. If it was a joke, we saw no need to involve you."

"Did you know where the pond was located?"

"No, but Eileen had come running in from our left, so we followed the path until we saw a sign saying 'Koi Pond' with an arrow pointing down a smaller path."

"Pretty dark out there. How did you see?"

"A couple of ladies had tiny flashlights in their purses. We used them. The light wasn't strong, but combined with the tier lights in the garden and along the paths it was enough to see by."

"What happened then?"

"We saw something in the pond. Carl thought it might be a mannequin. He touched it and discovered the real thing. We both thought it was Suzanne Wayland. It was too dark to distinguish much else. I said not to move anything, and we returned to the terrace."

"Why did you think it was Miss Wayland?"

"The dress was blue, like the one she's wearing, and the hair was similar."

"I see. So, you returned to the terrace and called 9-1-1, correct?"

"I didn't, but someone else did. We also notified the hotel."

"Who else was on the terrace at that time?"

"A lot of people heard Eileen screaming and came out to investigate. I don't remember who all was there. I made the announcement we'd found a body and that it looked like Suzanne Wayland. Then, Suzanne stepped out from the shadows on the far side of the terrace."

"Can you tell me what you did this evening?" The sheriff wrote quickly, and then shot a piercing stare at Zach.

"The usual. I met Meghan at the sign-in desk. We renewed our acquaintance, had dinner, danced—that's about it."

Dave and Suzanne returned to the table with fresh drinks. Dave gulped. Suzanne sipped.

"If you want another drink you'd better get it now. This bar's closing in a few minutes," Suzanne informed them.

"I'll get them for you," Dave offered. "White wine for you, Meghan, right?"

Meghan nodded. "Yes, thank you, Dave."

"Zach?"

"Scotch, rocks." He pushed the remains of the amaretto away.

Dave left again while Suzanne watched him through narrowed eyes.

"Where were you when you heard Mrs. Davis screaming?"

"Out on the terrace."

"Alone?"

Zach shot a glance at Meghan, who sipped the last of her wine. He didn't want to tell the sheriff everything. It was none of his business. And Meghan might not appreciate him saying they'd been kissing like a couple of teenagers. But on the other hand, he couldn't lie. Too many people saw them come out of the shadows.

"No, Meghan was with me."

"Why were you on the terrace?"

"The ballroom was hot and Meghan wanted a

breath of air. I got us a couple of drinks and joined her."

"Did you talk to Mrs. Peterson tonight?"

"No."

The sheriff smiled. "Thanks for your cooperation, Mr. Dunbar. It sounds like you did an excellent job of keeping things under control. A mob of people trampling over the path by the fish pond would have destroyed evidence. The first instinct is to move the body, get it out of the water, and turn it over for identification. That would have made our job a lot harder. Obviously, nobody attempted CPR."

Zach bit his lip. God, he should have thought of that. "I don't think either Carl or I even considered it. I mean, to us she looked beyond any help CPR could provide. Unfortunately, I don't know the procedure. Could it have helped?"

The sheriff shrugged. "Hard to tell."

"I feel awful."

Meghan laid a hand on his arm. "Don't beat yourself up over it. Doesn't sound like it would have worked anyway."

"The lady's right. The paramedics performed brief CPR when they got here, but it was too late. Probably was when you found her. You did the best you could at the time."

"Glad I could be of help."

"What's your room number?"

"Five-oh-six."

The sheriff made the notation in the notepad and turned his attention toward Meghan.

Zach breathed a sigh of relief, glad the interrogation had ended, and not knowing why. It wasn't like him to feel so unsettled, but then he'd never seen a dead person before either.

****

Meghan swallowed a lump of nervousness when the sheriff's gaze landed on her. She had nothing to hide, but had never been involved in a real murder. Writing about one and experiencing one first hand wasn't quite the same.

"Your name, please?" he said with a smile.

"Meghan Donahue. And to save time, I live in Raleigh, North Carolina."

"What made you come to the reunion?"

"Why does anyone come to one of these affairs? I was the fat girl," she answered in a smooth voice.

"So, you wanted to show off a little?"

"Yes. I wondered if anyone would recognize me."

"Did they?"

Meghan shook her head. "Only Zach. He remembered my eyes."

She heard Zach suck in a breath and out of the corner of her eye saw him shift in his seat. *Hope I didn't embarrass him.*

The sheriff smiled. "I can see why. Are you married?"

"Not at the moment. I'm divorced."

"What do you do for a living?"

"I write mystery novels under the name Meghan Bonaventure."

The sheriff sat back. "You're kidding. I just finished *Death on the Gridiron*. It was damned good. You actually got most of the police and forensic procedures right. Plus, you know a thing or two about football."

"I went to Ohio State. It was hard not to learn

something about football in four years."

"So, you and Mr. Dunbar spent most of the evening together, is that right?"

"Yes."

"Never separated, even for a few minutes?"

"No—oh, well, yes, if you count going to the restrooms or the bar a time or two."

"Did you know Annabelle Peterson?"

"I knew who she was, but that's about all. She was one of the few kids in high school who didn't make fun of me."

"Talk to her tonight?"

"I said hello in the ladies room."

"When was that?"

"After dinner. I can't recall the time, but it was before the dancing started."

"Talk about anything special?"

"No. Just the usual 'hi, how are you, wow, you've really changed.'" Meghan sighed. "Annabelle was a nice woman. I felt so sorry for her husband, Eric, when he came out onto the terrace asking if we'd seen his wife."

"He did? When was that?"

Meghan caught the glance the sheriff pointed at Zach. He'd left out that piece of information. She assumed it was an oversight. Remembering every little detail in a time of shock was hard. Zach didn't make eye contact with her and shifted in his seat. She turned her attention back to the sheriff.

"It was right after Carl and Zach returned from the fish pond. Suzanne had let us all know the body wasn't hers, and before anyone could react, Eric popped out. I knew exactly who was in the pond then."

"Oh? How?"

"Well, Annabelle and Suzanne were wearing the same dress, an ice blue, chiffon, halter top, very chic."

"Thank you," Suzanne murmured, sipping her cosmo.

"What the hell has that got to do with anything?" Dave demanded, his words slightly slurred.

Only an idiot wouldn't see the significance. But then, Dave is an idiot.

The sheriff ignored both of them. "I'll be damned. Did you see Annabelle Peterson leave the terrace for the garden?"

"Uh, no. Zach and I were, ah, talking, and since the ballroom was so hot, lots of people came outside to cool off."

Sheriff Armstrong jotted her information in his notebook, then sat back and wiped a hand over his face, his eyes thoughtful. He shifted his stare to Suzanne who glared back at him.

"What happened after the body was found?"

Meghan gave him the details of trying to keep Eileen calm and of Glory's fainting. When she finished, he smiled.

"I take it you're staying at the hotel. What's your room number?"

"Two-fifteen."

"Thank you, Ms. Donahue," he said, and then turned his gaze onto Dave.

"All right, Mr. Coryell, it's finally your turn. Where do you live and what do you do?"

"I live on Lake Shore Drive in Chicago."

"What do you do," the sheriff repeated when Dave showed no signs of answering further.

"You didn't ask Tom and Glory what they did for a living."

Dave's petulant voice grated in Meghan's ears. He sounded half-plastered and well on his way toward total blotto.

Sheriff Armstrong sat back and massaged the skin between his eyebrows.

"Mr. Coryell, Tom and Glory live in Grandview. My car, house, and life are insured by his company. I know what he does for a living. Now, can we continue?"

His voice sounded tired. Meghan wondered how many times murder had reared its ugly head in her hometown.

And how far out of his league is he?

"What do you do for a living?"

"I'm a commodities broker. I own DC Commodities, Incorporated."

"And why did you decide to come to the reunion?"

Dave shrugged and took a drink. "I hadn't seen most of my classmates for a long time. It sounded like fun."

Meghan listened to Dave's words, but kept her eyes on Suzanne. The redhead rolled her eyes at the last statement and pushed her cosmo toward the center of the table.

She shifted her gaze back to Dave. He wiped a line of sweat from his forehead with a cocktail napkin, and focused his gaze on the tablecloth much the way Suzanne had earlier. His hands trembled.

"Did you talk to Mrs. Peterson tonight?"

"No. I chatted mostly with former teammates. I was the wide receiver on the championship team my senior year. Caught the winning toss from Eddie Mancuso. Maybe you remember?"

Sheriff Armstrong nodded. "Yes, Dave, I remember you—and Eddie."

Meghan squirmed in her chair. Dave hadn't caught the innuendo, but she understood the double meaning. The Fearsome Foursome as they'd sometimes been called back then had had more than a couple of visits from the law for their escapades.

Like the time they'd dumped laundry detergent into the fountain in the town square. Or rolled an ancient VW bug into the main hallway of the high school. She also remembered when they had stolen a dressmaker's dummy, clothed it, and tossed it on the railroad tracks. The entire town had awakened at midnight to the sound of air brakes hissing and iron wheels screeching on the rails. The four had been lucky. The engineer managed to keep the train on the tracks. It was that prank that made her think the body in the pool had been their doing.

They were nothing more than a bunch of vandals who always got away scot free.

Meghan glanced at Zach. He gazed at her with a half smile on his lips. So he remembered, too.

"Where were you when the screaming started?" the sheriff asked, back to business.

"I—I don't really remember." Dave's eyes shifted to the right.

He's lying.

"You came out onto the terrace asking if we'd seen Suzanne. Remember? Zach and Carl had gone down to the pond," Meghan reminded him, sipping her wine.

Whatever he was doing, it wasn't looking for his

former girlfriend.

He shot her a nasty look. "Oh, yeah, that's right. I was looking for Suzanne."

"Where?"

Dave raised one shoulder. "She wasn't in the ballroom or the lobby. I even dashed upstairs to check her room." He clenched his teeth and curled his lip.

"How long did you search for her?" The sheriff continued writing in his notebook.

The sweat trickled down Dave's cheek. He wiped it on his shirt sleeve.

"I—I don't know." Fear replaced his surly expression.

"Where else did you go looking for Miss Wayland?" Sheriff Armstrong pressed. The officer's tone sharpened.

"I—I went into the parking lot, and then stopped by my car for a few minutes. I needed my briefcase from the trunk. It—it contained some, ah, papers I had to have—business papers."

He stammered most of the answer and didn't sound convincing. Throughout it all, he stared into the depths of his whisky glass.

If he's not lying, he's being damned evasive. What the hell was he really doing? Meghan glanced quickly at Suzanne who curled her lips into a tight smile. *Like a cat lapping cream. She knows something.*

"You brought business papers to a high school reunion that would last two days?"

Apparently, the sheriff didn't buy his story either. Maybe he was a better cop than Meghan thought.

"The commodities market never sleeps, Sheriff."

"What did you do with the papers?"

"I, ah, took them up to my room. Are you about finished? I can't really add anything more."

Sheriff Armstrong stared at Dave who still refused to make eye contact. A deputy walked up and whispered in Ray's ear. He nodded and turned back to Dave.

"Stay put for a moment. I'll be right back." He left and followed the deputy to another table.

Dave swung angry eyes to Meghan. "Keep your goddamned mouth shut," he snapped with a snarl.

Zach reached over and grabbed a fistful of shirt yanking his drunken classmate forward to within a few inches of his face.

"Watch your mouth, Coryell." He released the man and shoved him back in the chair, then bolted the scotch in his glass.

A warm gush of emotion washed over Meghan. She'd never had a man defend her like that. It made her feel protected, wanted. It made her feel special. How strange that within the space of a few short hours, Zach Dunbar had become special to her, too. She could, however, defend herself. Time to let Dave know he's not that important.

"Funny, when you heard Zach say the body in the pond was Suzanne, you didn't have much of a reaction, yet when she stepped out of the shadows, you dropped your glass and looked as ready to faint as Glory did," Meghan said.

"Well, of course I did. It was shocking." He paused and licked his lips. "The sheriff thinks I'm lying."

"You probably are," Suzanne answered with a raised eyebrow. "I'll bet I know what you were doing in the car. Should I tell the sheriff my suspicions?"

"You bitch! I can't figure out what I ever saw in you."

"You dated me twenty years ago because I was a good lay. You started dating me three months ago because you need money. I got news for you. I'm still a good lay, but you're never going to find out."

"I could have done much better—and did. You never knew I was getting it from Tami, too."

Suzanne's eyes sparked like fire. "Sure I did. We used to get together and Tami would give me a blow by blow description. If nothing else you were good for a laugh." She snickered. "Your ego is a lot bigger than your johnson."

"Oh, for God's sake!" Meghan exclaimed, and then lowered her voice. "I don't need to hear this. You two were full of yourselves in high school and you still are. Some people just don't give a shit anymore. I'm one of them. Now, shut up."

Suzanne opened her mouth to reply, but Zach cut her off.

"Don't even think about answering back. Times have changed. Dave, I can probably buy and sell you a dozen times over. Suzanne, one of these days you'll wake up, fifty years old with sagging body parts, and no longer attractive to men—except for your money. So start acting civil to people." He waved a hand dismissively. "I don't know why I'm even talking to either of you. You're not worth the breath."

Meghan heaved an elated breath. She and Zach thought alike.

The sheriff returned as Zach spoke the last sentence. Meghan figured he had to have heard, but made no comment. He resumed his seat and addressed

Dave.

"Mr. Coryell, could I have your room number?"

He fished in his pocket and brought out the key. "Three-twenty-six."

"Thank you for your time. You may go."

Dave scrambled from his chair, grabbed his suit coat, and walked none too steadily toward the lobby. At the same time, Dan Masterson strode up with a frown.

"Sheriff Armstrong, I've been waiting for over an hour. What's taking so damned long? Let's get these people out of here. They're tired and not sure what's going on."

"Mr. Masterson, approximately two hundred people are attending this reunion. All are potential witnesses. I have five deputies. Three of them are conducting interviews. The other two are patrolling the town. We're working as fast as we can."

"Sheriff, I have a responsibility to the citizens of Grandview. They look to me for guidance. It's a job I take on willingly. I love this town and its people. That's why I'm running for mayor. A murder is very upsetting, and I'd also like to talk to you about what you've found so far."

"What I've found so far is not open to discussion." He shot Dan a hard glance. "You know, I think you're right. The sooner you're interviewed, the sooner you can leave. Have a seat." He gestured to the chair next to him.

A startled Dan did as told. Meghan stifled the urge to grin.

"I'll cut this short, Mr. Councilman. Did you speak with Annabelle Peterson tonight?"

"Of course, I did. I welcomed her and Eric back

home, chatted for a few minutes. She congratulated me on the fine job I was doing for the city and wished me luck in the upcoming election. I then continued to circulate among the crowd."

Meghan picked up her wine glass forgetting it was empty and set it back down again. *I can't believe what an ass this guy is. Please God, don't let me hit him.*

"Did you go out onto the terrace tonight?"

"No, not that I recall. I was busy meeting and greeting. It was my duty."

Zach kicked her under the table. Meghan glanced over, and he rolled his eyes.

"Thank you, Mr. Masterson. Are you staying at the hotel?"

"No."

"You're free to go."

Dan rose and placed his hands on the back of the chair.

"Perhaps, I should stay and help. As a representative of the city, I should have my fingers on the pulse of this case."

"That does it," Zach said. "Dan, go home. You were the class president, not President of the United States. You're not needed here."

Dan puffed up like a toad. "I beg your pardon?"

"What Zach's trying to say is, you're a pain in the ass," Meghan added. Funny how wine released the inhibitions, not to mention her tongue.

Suzanne threw back her head and laughed. The sheriff hid a smile behind his hand. Dan's jaw dropped, an outraged expression on his face.

"You've been strutting around like a peacock all night telling everyone how important you are," she continued. "A very nice woman is dead and all you can think of is how to turn the situation into a political advantage. Take a hike."

Dan whirled and stalked away.

"Way to go, Meghan." Zach leaned over and kissed her cheek.

Meghan's heart beat faster at the gesture as she remembered the heated kisses of earlier on the terrace.

"Congratulations," Suzanne murmured. "That was well done."

The sheriff looked at Suzanne. "I guess you're the last one."

"I can keep this simple," she said. "My name is Suzanne Crocker. I live in a lakefront penthouse also in Chicago. I came to the reunion because Dave Coryell asked me, and I'm in room four-twenty."

She spent the next few minutes telling the sheriff about Dave's business and his motives for attending the reunion.

"Did he hit you up for money?" the sheriff asked.

"Of course. I told him to drop dead."

"He hit on me, too," Zach added. "I refused to discuss it."

"Talk to his football buddies," Suzanne suggested. "He was jawing with them all night. Oh, and by the way, when I refused him, he left the room. I have no idea where he was until he showed up on the terrace."

"Tell me about your evening, Mrs. Crocker."

She gave the sheriff a description of her night, including the argument with Dan Masterson.

"And here's something to chew on. Mr. Mayor-to-be left me and went out onto the terrace."

The sheriff ceased writing and looked up, a frown

on his face. "Oh, really?"

"Yes. And I didn't see him return."

"I think I may have to have another conversation with our earnest mayoral candidate." He resumed writing, and then raised his head. "Did you talk to Annabelle Peterson this evening?"

"Yes. She came over to say hello and laugh about us wearing the same dress. I didn't find it particularly amusing. She left, and that was the last I saw of her until she came out onto the terrace."

"You saw her on the terrace? What time?"

"I have no idea. I was seated in an out of the way nook for a reason. I wanted to be alone." Suzanne sipped her drink.

"Did you see anyone follow Mrs. Peterson into the garden?" The sheriff wrote fast in the notebook.

"No, but I heard someone go down the steps a couple of minutes later. I didn't pay any attention because so many people came and went."

"You must have been stunned when Zach and Carl announced you were the body."

"I understood what happened immediately." She emptied her glass in one gulp.

"And that was?" Sheriff Armstrong inquired in a patient voice.

"Well, obviously, *I* was the target. *I* was supposed to be the body in the pond."

Chapter Six

"How do you figure that?" the sheriff asked with raised eyebrows.

Suzanne heaved a sigh, and sent him a "duh" look.

"I should think it would be obvious, even to you." She stroked the halter strap of her dress. "Annabelle and I wore the same dress. Mine is an original. Hers was a cheap knock-off." Suzanne's hand moved on to the jewels in her ears and around her throat. "These are real, too. And if you look close enough, you'll see that while my hair is red and cut by the best stylist in Chicago, hers was brown and not styled at all—merely the same length as mine."

Meghan wanted to shake the redhead until her teeth rattled. Annabelle was dead—murdered—and all Suzanne could do was criticize the poor woman's clothes and jewelry.

Why is she such a bitch?

She fingered her empty wine glass, watching the lights reflect off the rim. Maybe Suzanne had come to the reunion to gloat, expecting her high school cohort, Tami Robinson, to be impressed.

Only she found out Tami was dead, murdered. And she was always a bitch.

Zach rested his forearms on the table. "Suzanne, why would you wear jewelry worth more than some of these people make in a year to a high school reunion?

Why not wear fake? Nobody knows the difference."

Suzanne glared at Zach. "I would, and that's what counts. I gave up costume jewelry when Charlie gave me my engagement ring." She thrust her left hand under Zach's nose. "See? A five-and-a-half-carat, princess-cut solitaire, no flaws, surrounded by another two carats of baguettes. What's the use of having the real thing and not wearing it? Besides, it's insured."

Zach turned to Meghan with a puzzled expression.

"Would you wear the real thing to a reunion?"

Honestly, men. He'd look at me like I was crazy if I asked why men have to have the latest electronic gizmo.

"I agree with Suzanne on this one. Expensive jewelry should be worn whenever appropriate." She shrugged. "Okay, a high school reunion might be stretching it a little, but this is the twentieth. Remember what I said about reunions?"

"The need to impress." Zach shook his head. "I guess it makes sense to a woman."

"Sexist pig," Meghan murmured.

Zach's lips curved into a sexy smile. That sweet gushing warmth of earlier returned and her cheeks burned. *Damn, after all these years I can still blush. First time in a long time.*

"Could we get back to the subject?" Sheriff Armstrong interjected. "I still have a lot of people to interview. Now, Ms. Crocker, would you continue with what you were saying?"

Suzanne's lips lifted into a half smile for Zach before she turned her attention back to the sheriff.

"What was I saying?"

"About how this is a case of mistaken identity."

"Well, it is. I say the killer thought he saw me on

the terrace, followed, knocked Annabelle on the head, realized his mistake, and killed her to make sure she couldn't identify him."

"So, you think it was someone she knew?"

"Of course!"

"Suzanne, if that's the case, the killer must have come up behind her. How could she ID him? And if he met her in the garden, he'd know it wasn't you," Meghan said.

"How the hell should I know how he did it?" she snapped, her eyebrows drawing together.

"Besides, no jewelry was taken," Zach added.

"Just my point. He realized his mistake. No one steals fakes. Maybe Annabelle came to and recognized him."

"Any witnesses to your presence on the terrace?" the sheriff asked in a smooth voice.

Suzanne's jaw dropped. "You're fucking kidding, right? You think I killed her? Why?"

"I have no idea. Did you?"

"Of course not, you asshole!"

The sheriff stared her down. "Watch it, Ms. Crocker. That can be construed as verbal abuse of a law enforcement officer. Relax. It's just a routine question. Your assumptions could be correct."

"They are." Suzanne leaned back and pouted.

Interesting. Suppose Suzanne did leave the terrace for the garden. How many people might have assumed she was Annabelle?

Sheriff Armstrong snapped his notebook shut and pushed his chair back. "That's all for now. You're free to go." He strode to the next table.

Meghan gazed around the room. Close to two-thirds of the people still awaited their turns under the gun.

"Let's get out of here," Zach said. He rose and pulled out Meghan's chair, then draped his suit coat over his arm. "Would you like a nightcap in the bar?"

"I'd love one."

"Me, too," Suzanne replied.

Apparently, the redhead had decided Meghan and Zach worthy of her attention. They exchanged glances and shrugged. If Suzanne wanted to follow them to the bar, then she would.

Maybe she's afraid to be alone.

"I'd like to visit the ladies room first. You coming, Suzanne?"

"No. I'll see you in the bar." She curled her arm through Zach's and smiled up at him.

Meghan bit her lip. Heavy handed and obvious. Would it impress Zach? He looked surprised to find Suzanne clinging to him, but not beguiled.

She fought the urge to rip the pushy woman away from him, and was astonished at her reaction to Suzanne's flirting.

Good grief, I'm jealous.

She'd never experienced that particular emotion, but then tonight had been chock-full of surprises. Zach's kisses had sent her stomach quivering and her nerves humming.

She split off from the other two and opened the ladies room door. The restroom was jammed with her classmates. Most ignored her, but the comments centered on one subject.

"Poor Eric. What's he going to do with all those kids?"

"I resent being questioned like a common criminal."

"Why would any of us do it?"

"I heard they caught a guy in the parking lot trying to steal a car."

"My husband says it was just another act of random violence and people should arm themselves for their own protection."

Meghan listened, but did not participate in the conversations. Until the coroner had a cause of death, everything was speculation. She washed her hands, combed her hair, and left.

The bar was crowded. Too many people too upset to go home or to their rooms yet. She scanned the throng, spying Zach and Suzanne at a table along the wall. The woman snuggled close, a smile on her lips. Meghan scooted behind the seat of another patron and wedged herself into the remaining chair.

"I ordered another white wine for you. Is that okay?" Zach asked.

"Fine. From the looks of things, you were lucky to get this table."

Zach smiled. Meghan had no idea how to interpret it. A waitress arrived with a loaded tray.

"Scotch, a white wine, and a cosmopolitan." She set the glasses in front of the right people.

"Thank you. Run a tab, okay?" Zach told her. She nodded and moved on to the next table.

Suzanne sipped her drink, her eyes on Meghan. Meghan returned the look and wondered if some kind of war had been declared. It didn't take a genius to see Zach was Dave's replacement. She raised her glass to the redhead who cocked an eyebrow and returned the salute.

Let the games begin. Does Zach realize he's just become a prize?

"Look, there's Dave at the far end of the bar," Meghan said, firing the first round of cannon.

"Let him stay there," Suzanne countered. "The miserable bastard deserted me for most of the night."

"That's right. He was gone a long time. Did you get to dance at all?" She injected pity into her voice while keeping a straight face.

Suzanne shot her a filthy look.

Direct hit. One point for me.

"Of course I did. I don't guess you danced with anyone besides Zach, did you? Not that many guys recognized you."

Tie score.

"Just Zach. Right?" she answered, and let her fingers trail down his hand.

"I never forget beautiful eyes," he replied.

His gaze swiveled between the two women. Meghan figured he sensed something beyond casual conversation.

Suzanne frowned and took another sip of her cosmo.

Another point for me. No, make that two—with an assist from Zach.

Meghan had never indulged in this kind of feminine duel before. She enjoyed it.

"You know, Suzanne, maybe you should talk to Dave," Zach suggested interrupting the game.

"What? Why?"

"He was missing for a long time, or so you told the sheriff. You also insinuated you knew what he was doing during that time. What was it? Or were you just trying to rattle his cage?"

She sipped her drink again and cast her gaze at the table.

She's being evasive. She knows exactly what Dave was doing.

"I was just yanking his chain. Dave and I go back a long way. We'd fight, and then make up. No big deal."

Zach sipped his scotch. "Do me a favor. Go see what he has to say about where he was."

"Okay, but you come with me." She cast a snide look at Meghan. "I'm sure Meghan won't mind, will you?"

"He won't answer questions with me there. He looks hammered. I'll bet *you* can get him to open up. Buy him another drink. We'll wait here for you. I'd be grateful."

"How grateful?" the redhead purred.

"Very grateful," Zach answered, smiling down at her.

Suzanne curled her lips into a smug smile and shifted her gaze to Meghan.

I don't know how many points to award for that zinger.

"All right, but what do I ask?"

"Just get him to talk. Make up with him, like old times."

Suzanne rose and taking her drink ambled across the room, sliding onto a barstool next to her ex-boyfriend.

"Maybe she'll forget about hanging on to us," Zach said.

"I wouldn't count on that."

"What was going on with you two?"

"Never mind."

She paused and gazed around the room. Tom and Glory stood nearby, both with glasses in their hands, talking to another couple. He held a whiskey glass, while Glory's appeared to be a soft drink. They moved on to another table. Tom stumbled slightly.

Must have indulged in more than one.

She brought her eyes and her attention back to Zach. "Looks like Glory didn't get room service yet."

He stared also. "I guess a lot of people are still too keyed up to call it a night. I know I am."

"Same here. So, you wanted to get rid of Suzanne?"

"Can't discuss the case with her hanging on every word. You're the novelist. What's your take on the whole thing?"

She told him about the theories she'd heard in the ladies room.

"I'd be inclined to think it was a random act. Poor Annabelle was in the wrong place at the wrong time," he replied.

"I'd agree with that theory, too, if it wasn't for the dress and the uncanny resemblance to Suzanne."

"So, you think Suzanne was the target and her explanation to the sheriff the right one?"

"Could be." She sipped more of her wine. "And yet, it just doesn't feel right, if you get my drift."

"Sorry, but I don't."

Meghan shifted in her seat. "A thief—a stranger who didn't know either woman and just waited for an opportunity would have grabbed the jewelry and run. He wouldn't have known it was fake."

"So, it had to be someone who knew Suzanne."

"Dave's hit everyone up for bucks. He's also wasted. Mistaken identity isn't far off the radar scope with that. Maybe he attacked and actually said something that would give him away," she speculated.

"Not too smart, but then drunks don't think rationally."

"Maybe he thought Suzanne wouldn't turn him in—like for old time's sake—and let him go. She could always claim the loss on her insurance."

Zach drew his brows together. "Suzanne doesn't strike me as being that helpful. Unless..." he paused for a long moment.

"Unless what?" Meghan prompted.

"Unless, she was in on it. They could be closer than just casual friends. Maybe they concocted a plan in Chicago—old friends attending a reunion in a small town among a lot of people they haven't seen in twenty years. She claims robbery, he fences the items, and the insurance pays off."

She shook her head. "Not logical. Why go to such an elaborate charade? Just jimmy the door lock, and scream, 'I've been robbed'? Meanwhile, the jewels are hidden in the bottom of her suitcase. And if she's doing it on her own, why involved Dave? Besides, she's rich. Why do it at all?"

Zach sipped some scotch, a thoughtful expression on his face. "You're right. I'm logical about some things, but murder isn't one of them. Okay, maybe she wasn't in on it. Dave didn't mean to kill Annabelle and panicked. Remember his reaction on the terrace when Suzanne showed up alive and well? He might not have realized it wasn't Suzanne in the pond."

"To be honest, I don't see Dave Coryell having the guts to do it." She also sipped from her glass. "On the other hand, Dan Masterson looked like he'd have had no problem killing Suzanne."

Zach made a derisive face. "Dan? Now there's someone with no guts. He's all talk. How about another woman?"

His suggestion startled Meghan. "I never thought of that. But it doesn't read like a woman's crime."

"Now who's being sexist? Women kill, too."

"Let's assume the preliminaries are correct and someone held Annabelle's head under water. That takes a lot of strength. A dying person puts up quite a fight."

"Unless they're incapacitated," Zach reminded her.

"Like with a blow to the head. The sheriff didn't say anything about a head wound."

"Could be he's not telling us."

Meghan ran her hands up and down the condensation on her wine glass. An idea formed in her mind.

"Zach," she said slowly. "What if we offered to help with the investigation? You know, in an unofficial way."

"You mean play detective?"

"Why not? Ray Armstrong's been sheriff for quite a while, but I doubt he's seen that many murders, and the ones he has have probably been easy solves—drunks who live here in Grandview, domestic violence, people he's known most of his life. Something tells me this is more involved. He may be out of his league."

Zach leaned back and glanced at the doorway.

"Can't hurt to ask. He just came in."

Meghan turned. The sheriff stood at the door

scanning the room. She waved him over. The conversation level dropped. Patrons stared as he sat in Suzanne's vacated chair.

"How go the interrogations?" Zach asked.

"Less than half left. Most people didn't talk to Mrs. Peterson or Mrs. Crocker, and some never even heard the commotion. A few questions and they go home. My deputies can handle the rest. I'm going to grab a cup of joe, and then see if I can make sense out of what I've been told."

A waitress stopped by and the sheriff ordered coffee. Meghan played with her glass, and then lifted her gaze.

"Sheriff, how about Zach and I helping on this?"

"Helping how?"

"I was thinking we could ask people questions in a more casual setting, like this, and see if anyone might have remembered something."

Sheriff Armstrong sighed and shook his head. "Just because you write mystery books, doesn't make you an expert or a detective. This is not *Murder, She Wrote*. The crime isn't solved at the end of an hour with the murderer revealed in the last two minutes. It doesn't work that way."

"I know, but I do have some experience with police procedures. I research my books carefully. I talk to cops and have ridden with them on patrol. I understand how the system works. I like to think I understand human nature."

The sheriff rubbed his temples. "Miss Donahue, I appreciate the offer, but most criminals are stupid. Their crimes are often committed on impulse or without logic. They make mistakes. Sooner or later, we'll get this guy."

"You know, Sheriff, Meghan does have a point. She's got eight books to her credit. She knows how to conduct an interview, not..."

"Are you saying I don't?" Ray Armstrong cut in.

"Of course not. I was going to say she knows how to talk to the average person. A police officer asks questions and people have a natural tendency to clam up, whether from fear or not wanting to get involved in an official capacity. But Meghan and I making conversation is another ball game. We'd be one of them. They might give up information without knowing it."

His coffee arrived. The sheriff blew on the hot brew before taking a sip. "You could have a point. I take it you've been discussing the case. You both strike me as being intelligent and unemotional concerning the deceased. Have any theories?"

Meghan wasn't sure she liked the unemotional comment. It made them sound like robots or that they didn't care Annabelle was dead. Maybe what he meant was not emotionally involved. She sipped her wine while Zach told him about their conversation.

"I agree with Ms. Donahue. Mrs. Crocker wouldn't steal her own jewelry to help out Dave Coryell."

"Call me Meghan. This is Zach. Have you found out anything from your interrogation?"

He smiled. "I'm Ray. Not too much. I'm going with the stranger in the garden theory. The killer may have been one of the waiters or a delivery person who saw Mrs. Crocker leave the room and took a chance."

"And then didn't take the goodies? Why?" Meghan questioned.

"And why kill?" Zach added. "It's damned dark in that garden. Why assume either Annabelle or Suzanne could see well enough to identify him?"

"The sad truth is, a lot of people in this world just don't give a rat's ass. Taking a human life means nothing to them." Ray shook his head, and then paused to gulp half his coffee. "All right, you can talk to people, but any information you pry out of them is passed on directly to me. Is that understood? No chasing clues on your own."

Zach held his hands up. "Think of us as minions who do your bidding."

"Uh, there is one other thing, Ray," Meghan murmured.

"What?"

"Would it be possible for us to see the crime scene?"

"I've already seen it," Zach inserted.

"But I haven't."

"Forensics hasn't released the site yet. It's still taped off. They'll be back in the morning to search further. I can't let you in. You might inadvertently trample something important," Ray told her.

"I'll be careful. Like I said, I've been with police on cases as an observer before. I know not to touch or remove anything," Meghan begged.

Ray frowned and stared at the two of them.

"Aw, I guess it won't hurt for you to stand just outside the perimeter. Come on. It'll have to be quick. I have work to do." He drained his cup.

Zach waved down the waitress. She brought the bill and he charged it to his room, then the three of them left the bar for the koi pond.

****

"Dave, I want to apologize for the things I said earlier," Suzanne stated, sliding onto the stool next to him. "I was upset."

She batted her eyes and slid her fingers up and down his arm. She still had no idea what Zach wanted her to ask.

"Yeah, right. I suppose you told the sheriff everything about tonight," he replied with a sneer.

"Well, if I didn't, someone else would have. I mean, a lot of people saw me sitting alone. Where did you go?"

"Want me to tell you so you can go running to the cops?"

She shrugged and pretended to sip her drink. "I'm just curious. I know you didn't kill Annabelle, for Pete's sake. And I think you're right about it being some opportunist who realized the jewelry was fake."

Dave removed his suit coat and slung it over the back of his barstool. Sweat dribbled from his temple to his cheek.

If he took a break to snort, the high's wearing off. I need to get him drunker. Drunks and addicts love to talk when they're fully loaded.

"Bartender, another round for us, okay?" She turned to Dave. "I'm buying. So, did you go into the garden?"

"Why would you think that?"

"For starters, you looked totally shocked to see me alive. What *did* you see?"

Dave drained his glass as the bartender set a new drink in front of him.

"I was really pissed at you. I needed to take a walk

before I did something stupid."

"Like kill me."

"Maybe. At any rate, I went out to the car just like I told the sheriff."

Suzanne ignored her fresh drink. She knew damned good and well he hadn't retrieved any half-assed papers. She sneaked a glance toward Zach. He and that prissy Meghan had their heads close together.

Dammit, I'm over here pumping this jerk off for information, while she's beating my time.

"And?" she prompted, bringing her attention back onto Dave.

"All right, I took a walk in the garden to cool down. Then I saw a sign for the fish pond and followed the trail. I stopped at the edge of the pond and noticed something in the water. I saw the blue dress and long hair, and figured it was you."

"You found Annabelle? Why didn't you do something?" Suzanne demanded.

"I was going to pull you out, but decided too many people may have seen us argue and think I'd done it, so I just walked away. I hid out in my room for fifteen or twenty minutes, and then made my appearance on the terrace. It's the truth. I swear it."

She couldn't see Dave Coryell in the role of a cold-blooded killer. Accidental, perhaps, but not deliberate.

"Oddly enough, I believe you. You might feel like killing me, but you wouldn't. I don't suppose you saw anyone else." She wasn't convinced she believed her own words.

Dave shook his head and finished his drink in one gulp. Suzanne signaled the bartender for another.

"No, but for a moment, I thought I heard

footsteps."

"Like someone running away?"

"No, like someone walking. In a hurry."

Suzanne mentally chewed on that. The killer had no reason to think he might have been seen or heard, so why draw attention to himself by running? It made sense.

"You gonna tell the cops?"

"I don't know. You didn't see or hear anything that can be identified or even useful, so I don't see what purpose it serves."

She spared another glance toward Zach. Damn, now the sheriff was sitting with them. No way would she make it a foursome. The bartender arrived with Dave's drink.

"Good. Let's discuss you and your money again. I've come clean. Doesn't that deserve a reward?" Dave quaffed half the contents in his glass.

"I'll think about it."

"If you've had me investigated then you know my time is short. I need an answer now." His voice turned rough.

Suzanne's lips touched the rim of her glass, faking a sip. "I can't very well conjure up the money in Grandview, Indiana, on a weekend. Wait until I get home."

"Then how about we go to my room and you prove to me that you're still as good a lay like you bragged," he proposed, his words slurring.

"Dave, I think I made it perfectly clear before we left Chicago that I would not sleep with you."

She tried and almost succeeded in keeping the disgust from her voice. Luckily, Dave was too drunk to notice.

"Who said anything about sleep?" He bellowed with laughter, and then hiccupped.

Before she could answer, Glory Ecklund stumbled into Dave, jostling his arm and then dropping her purse. She bent to retrieve it, rising with a flush on her face. Tom leaned down at the same time and stumbled against Dave's barstool

"Sorry. Guess I've had a little too much to drink," he apologized.

"I'm so tired, my legs refuse to work. Did I spill your drink?" his wife asked.

"Just a little, but who cares? The party's over," Dave replied, wiping at the liquor stain on his shirt.

"Yes, I guess it is. I feel so bad. Everyone was having a good time, too. Eileen and Dan are canceling the picnic. I just can't imagine what poor Eric's going to do. I mean, how do you tell your children their mother's been murdered?" She shuddered.

Suzanne didn't want to listen to Glory's prattle, but it beat having to listen to drunken propositions from her former boyfriend.

Tom swayed and took a deep breath as though to stabilize his body.

"Oh, honey, you're practically out on your feet. Let's go up to the room." Glory sighed. "Poor man. You've been such a rock, so supportive during the last year while I worked on the reunion details. It took a long time to track down some of his classmates, although he helped with that. Said two heads were better than one—or rather two computers." She laughed lightly. "Did you know Mary Ellen Whitehall is a nun?"

"No kidding?" Suzanne replied. Who the hell was

Mary Ellen Whitehall?

"She's known as Sister Mary Benedict now. Eddie was hard to find, too. Luckily, Tom had a client who supplied information." She looked at her watch. "Gosh, I didn't realize it was so late. We'd better get to bed. Thanks for coming. Let us know if you move."

Glory took her husband's arm and steered him toward the door, bumping into another woman before sidling through and disappearing into the lobby.

What a combination—graceful as an elephant and dumber than a brick. What does Tom see in her?

"So, how about it, sweetie? You and me? In the sack?"

Dave's voice brought her back to the mission at hand, which in her view was over. She glanced again over at Meghan and Zach's table. It was empty.

Son of a bitch! Where the hell did they go?

If it was somewhere with the sheriff, she sure as shit didn't want to join them.

"Hey, you gone deaf?" Dave shouted.

She quickly looked around. The bar was noisy and only a couple of patrons showed curiosity at his words.

"No. Just thinking. Hey, bartender, my friend here needs another drink."

"About what? A simple yes or no will do."

Suzanne touched his nose with the tip of her coral painted fingernail, and forced a giggle.

"Before we get down to other matters, why don't you explain this mining company thing to me again in detail?"

Chapter Seven

Meghan stood behind the yellow crime scene tape gazing at the dimly lit koi pond.

"Can't see much," Zach commented from her left.

"Just a minute," Ray said. He skirted the barrier keeping close to the edge of the perimeter. He approached a sapling and a moment later strong light blazed to life illuminating the water and pathway. "That help?"

"Must be the world's longest extension cord," Meghan commented. In the darkness, she'd mistaken the ten foot tall pole lights for trees.

"Forensics brought them. The hotel has electrical boxes for the pump and maintenance work," the sheriff explained.

"Doesn't look any different from a few hours ago," Zach remarked. "Except for the body, of course."

Ray returned to their sides. "Not much in the line of physical evidence to find. Forensics will be back in the morning."

"Where was the body?" she inquired.

Ray pointed. "Here, floating in the front of the pool near the path."

Meghan decided the pond was nothing elaborate. The freeform structure reminded her of a pear. She estimated its length as roughly thirty feet and the width close to fifteen at the widest point—the area where

Annabelle had been discovered. Flat rocks stacked about a foot high surrounded the water like a necklace. She assumed they kept the pond from overflowing during a heavy rain.

"What's that in the middle?" she asked Ray.

"Artificial rocks with holes and tunnels for the fish to swim through. I was told the vegetation is simple aquatic plants. Something to do with nutrients and oxygen. The pump inflow is on the other end. The outflow is down here. At the moment, it's shut off. The staff transferred the fish to a tank somewhere else on the property. We're having it drained so Forensics can examine it."

That made sense to Meghan, especially if Annabelle had been cold-conked and the weapon tossed into the pond.

"Zach, exactly what did you see?" she questioned.

"A body floating next to the edge."

"Floating? That's unusual," she murmured.

"Why?"

"Because drowning victims usually sink to the bottom," Ray told him. "They float when the body gases expand with decomposition."

Meghan looked at Zach "How was she positioned?"

"Her arm may have been flung across the rim."

"It was," the sheriff confirmed. "Guess the killer didn't notice or care. That's part of why she was floating."

"Part?" Meghan said.

"Her other arm and legs hit the bottom and didn't let the torso sink."

"Why would you assume someone held her head

underwater?" Zach wondered.

"The victim's fingernails were ripped. The pond's only two and half to three feet deep, so she couldn't have fallen in and struggled to get out, even drunk."

"All she needed to do was stagger upright and stumble to the edge," Zach surmised. "How do you prove murder?"

"It's not easy," Ray stated "The coroner has to eliminate all other causes of death before labeling it a drowning. Then Forensics tries to piece the puzzle together."

"Any idea on time of death?" Meghan inquired.

Ray shook his head. "Everybody's vague on a time frame. Ms. Crocker saw the victim enter the garden, but has no idea of when. Mrs. Davis can't recall the time either. How about you two? Do you remember what time it was when you heard the screams?"

"Not a clue. Who thinks to look at their watch during a time of crisis? We heard the screams and reacted," Zach told him. "What about the 9-1-1 call?"

"We're checking it now. Actually, the coroner figures Mrs. Peterson was dead less than an hour."

Meghan turned toward the sheriff. "Any wounds like to the back of the head? A whack to the skull would incapacitate and make it easier to hold someone's head under water."

"Nothing we noticed. Of course, the coroner might come up with something."

"Any wounds other than the torn fingernails?" Zach asked.

"Some bruising on the upper torso, most likely from the rocks as she struggled. My guess is the perpetrator knelt on her back to keep her from thrashing around," Ray said. "She also had scrapes on her legs, probably from the killer pushing them over the edge to make it look like an accident."

Meghan shivered. Ray painted a vivid image of Annabelle's last minutes of life.

"And her jewelry was all in place? Nothing missing?" she pressed.

"All there—rings, watch, earrings, necklace."

She closed her eyes and tried to visualize what Zach had found and what Ray had told them. Meghan shivered again as she envisioned the murder, but wondered why Annabelle hadn't fought back until it was too late.

"She had to have been hit over the head. It's the only sensible answer. Sheriff, do you know where she was standing when the attack occurred?"

"When we first arrived, the gravel on the pathway was disturbed. I think Mrs. Peterson may have been attacked about four or five feet from the rim of the pond and perhaps pushed forward."

"Or someone carried her to the water," Zach suggested.

"And then later smoothed the gravel back in place as best they could," Meghan added.

"Factor in Eileen, Zach, Carl, and anyone else who wandered by and didn't look at the pond. The drag marks would have been obliterated," Ray finished.

"Sorry," Zach muttered.

"Not your fault. I imagine the killer did a fairly good job of covering his tracks."

"The killer must have gotten wet. Did anyone notice someone with sopping clothes?" Zach queried.

"No one said anything," Ray replied.

"A quick run upstairs and a change of clothing would be the best thing to do."

Meghan shook her head. "Too risky. Suppose someone noticed and asked questions? I'd go up and hit the wet spots with the hair dryer. There's one in every room for guests' convenience. It would only take ten or fifteen minutes. Even if the areas were still damp, I'd explain it as spilling a glass of water or a drink in the dining hall."

"And in that crowd ten or fifteen minutes wouldn't be so noticeable," Ray agreed with a frown. "I need to go back over my notes. Are you two finished?"

Something nagged at Meghan—something she was missing. She closed her eyes again and concentrated on Annabelle.

Zach touched her arm. "Meghan, what's wrong?"

She opened her eyes. "I don't know, but something's not right."

"What?" Ray asked.

"I don't know," she repeated, and then forced her mind to recall Annabelle as she'd last seen her.

Annabelle and Eric had bumped into them on the dance floor. The woman faced Meghan, one hand in her husband's and the other clutching her evening bag on his shoulder.

"That's it!" she exclaimed.

"What's it?" Zach and Ray spoke simultaneously.

"Her purse! Where's her purse?"

"What purse?"

"Yeah, why would a purse be important?" Zach said.

"Women take them everywhere, especially to the ladies room. I took mine when we left the ballroom for

109

the terrace. Annabelle's was a clutch—no straps. I remember she held it as she danced."

"Why would she do that?" Zach's face had a puzzled expression.

"Some women don't like to leave purses unattended. Others don't care when it's a crowded reception with people they know. I left mine at the table while we danced. Suzanne left hers whenever she went to the bar. It was still within sight and someone trying to swipe it could be noticed. However, if a woman leaves the room, the purse goes with her. Remember? I took mine onto the terrace. So, where's Annabelle's purse? If she was going for a breath of air or a walk in the garden, she'd have taken it with her. It's second nature."

"And if she was knocked on the head or overpowered five feet from the pond, then the bag should have been there," Zach concluded.

"We recovered no purse." Ray swung his head toward the water. It gleamed dark and menacing under the powerful lights. The breeze sent ripples lapping gently against the rocks. "Maybe the killer tossed it in."

"Couldn't leave it lying in the middle of the path for just anybody casually strolling by to find," she added.

"Would the killer chuck it into the water by the body or heave it further out toward the middle?" Zach said.

"I'd toss it next to the body. Or maybe Annabelle hung on and it fell in next to her. Either way, that evening bag is somewhere around here," Meghan declared.

Ray walked carefully across the pathway to the

rock rim. "The pond will be empty by tomorrow morning." He looked back across the path. "Maybe the killer didn't notice the victim had a purse until after the crime. I don't know how far into the bushes my people searched."

He returned to the vinyl tape and ducked under, then stepped into the foliage just off the path.

"You two stay put. The fewer people messing with this, the better. I hope I don't screw things up for Forensics. Let's see what I can find. How big was the purse?"

"About the size and shape of a large brick, but thinner. It was white satin and had a knob clasp in the middle."

The sheriff pulled his flashlight from his belt, flicked it on, and plunged into the bushes. Meghan held her breath listening to the rustling of the vegetation as he poked and prodded. Zach clasped her hand in his.

"Great logic, Meghan. I can see why you're a *New York Times* bestseller. I'd have never thought to look for a purse."

Her cheeks heated at his praise. "That's because you're a guy. Women just know this stuff."

Ray moved further into the garden the torch beam bobbing and weaving like a prizefighter in the ring. Then from the foot of a large tree about twenty feet away he called out, "I think I've got it." He returned and held up a white object. "This it?"

"That's it," Meghan confirmed.

"Open it," Zach said. "Or will that destroy evidence?"

"I doubt the killer bothered to open it," Ray said, but whipped a handkerchief from his rear pocket before twisting the clasp anyway.

They all peered inside the bag.

Ray removed a cell phone, a tiny compact, a tube of lipstick, a small comb, and an old-fashioned hotel room key, not a slide card.

"Room three-sixteen." He shook his head. "Annabelle Peterson was a nice woman. What a stupid goddamned waste."

"What's that?" Meghan asked pointing to a crumpled rectangular-shaped object.

"A pack of cigarettes." The sheriff removed it along with a slim lighter.

"Which means Suzanne *was* the intended victim," Zach murmured.

"It's dark. The killer thinks he's following Suzanne. There's just enough light to identify the blue dress, long hair, and maybe sees a cigarette being smoked," Meghan speculated. "Did the forensics team find any cigarette butts lying around?"

"Several. They bagged them all, but it'll take time to figure out who smoked what. A lot of people, including hotel staff, probably took a nicotine break here," Ray said. "I'd say there's one very surprised killer walking around."

"So, he kills her and gets the shock of his life later when Suzanne shows up alive and kicking," Zach mentioned slowly.

"Do you suppose he was on the terrace with us?" Meghan wondered.

Ray eyed them both. "How did everyone react to Zach's news and Mrs. Crocker's appearance?"

"Oh, God, I'm not sure. Everyone was upset. Eileen was hysterical and almost passed out. Glory did—fainted dead away. Dave was so shocked when Suzanne popped out from behind the bushes, he dropped his glass," Meghan told him.

Zach nodded. "For a moment I thought he would join Glory on the flagstones. And Tom Ecklund looked like he'd encountered Godzilla." He paused. "You know, I saw Dan Masterson, too. He turned and walked back inside."

"That's odd," Ray remarked with a thoughtful expression. "I'd expect him to run out and try to take charge."

The sheriff's ringing cell stopped further discussion. He walked several feet away to take the call.

"You really are good at this," Zach told her with a smile. "I can't believe you visit crime scenes for research. That takes guts."

Meghan cast a glance at Ray, and then lowered her voice when she turned back to Zach, "Don't tell Ray, but I lied. I've ridden with officers and talked to detectives, but never been allowed to view a crime scene."

Zach stared with raised eyebrows. "You'd make a good detective. You had me believing it. The fine art of prevarication might come in handy when we talk to other people."

Her gaze wandered to the pond and a chill chasing up and down her spine caused a shiver.

"Cold?" Zach placed his arms around her, drawing her close to his body.

Heat from his arms and from within raced through her body. "No, depressed. A part of me is thinking how I could use this as a book. I feel like a ghoul."

Zach hugged her closer. "Don't. How do you get your plots?"

"Mostly through newspaper stories or on the internet. I also watch crime dramas and those semi-reality shows like *This Case Is Closed*. The idea for *Higher Education Is Murder* came from an old episode of *Columbo*."

"Isn't that plagiarism?"

"No one has a copyright on a plot. The idea is to look at it from a fresh angle. I just never imagined I'd be freshening things with firsthand knowledge. Knowing my editor, she'll use it as a plug on my next book signing tour. I can see the promos now. 'The true life adventures of Meghan Bonaventure' emblazoned on posters in every bookstore in the country."

"Do you travel a lot? Where?"

"Frequently and all over. One of the reasons I'm here is because I needed a change of scenery. The reunion sounded like a good idea."

Ray snapped his phone shut and walked back, his face grim.

"What's wrong?" Zach asked.

Meghan was disappointed when he dropped his arms even though the warmth lingered.

"That was the coroner. He wanted to bring me up to date on the preliminaries."

"He's doing the autopsy now?" Zach inquired.

Ray nodded. "We have a lot of people who will haul ass out of Grandview tomorrow morning. He won't have tox screens for a few days, but he can give cause of death and any other pertinent information by morning." He paused. "I was right. The bruising we saw is from someone leaning a knee on Mrs. Peterson's back as she struggled. The marks on her torso are from the weight of that person pressing her into the rocks."

"And her legs?" Meghan probed with a shudder. She didn't want to think about how terrified and desperate poor Annabelle must have been in those last few seconds.

"Superficial scrapes from being thrown into the pond. He found bits and pieces of rock imbedded in the wounds. Same with her fingernails. Preliminary cause of death is drowning. He found foam in the mouth and nasal passages. Classic signs of drowning." He paused again and ran his hand through his hair.

Meghan glanced at Zach. "What else did he say?"

"He found a couple of burn marks about two and a half centimeters apart on the back of her neck. Her hair hid them."

"Burn marks? You mean from a burning cigarette?" Zach said.

"No. I mean from the electrodes of a stun gun."

"A stun gun!" Meghan exclaimed.

Zach nodded. "That would explain why she didn't fight back until the last. She couldn't."

"So it would seem," the sheriff added in a grim tone.

Ray switched off the lights and the three of them walked back down the darkened path. Meghan assimilated the information. A stun gun. Even the image sent a chill racing along her arms, causing the hair to rise.

Then a thought occurred to her. *I wonder what the killer will do now that he knows Suzanne is alive.*

****

Suzanne had just about had it with Dave Coryell.

He was hammered and rambling on about his company, the mining interests, and his ex-wife being a major league bitch. She could have told him that. All ex-wives were bitches.

The bartender wandered over. "He's not driving, is he?"

"No, we're staying in the hotel, but bring him a cup of coffee, will you?"

"You, too?"

"No, just keep the cranberry juice flowing in a martini glass."

She'd made that request several drinks ago. She wanted Dave loaded, not herself. He never noticed the switch. Her strategy had worked too well. Drunk, he was no use to her. Now, she had to sober him up.

"I'm—I'm still not sure where the headquarters are located. All I got is a website, but I think it's in Switzerland somewhere. Probably Zurich."

He slurred his words to the point of incomprehension. Not that it mattered to Suzanne—she wasn't about to invest. The bartender brought the coffee and her cranberry juice.

"What's this?" he asked.

"Coffee, Dave."

"Coffee? I don't need no damned coffee. You think I can't hold my liquor?" he demanded in a belligerent tone.

Not tonight at any rate.

"I was just thinking about later. I like doing it with an active participant. Remember the old days?"

He grinned and picked up the cup, blew on the contents, slopping some onto the bar, then took a cautious sip.

"Heh-heh! Remember that time when you showed up on the field after practice wearing a trench coat and a smile? Underneath you were naked as a jaybird. We made it on a table in the equipment room with the rest of the team only a room away." He laughed loudly. "Those were the days, hey, kiddo?"

"Yeah, yeah, we really rocked the joint."

"Yeah, you were great. So was Tami. You ever make it with Eddie?"

Asshole—double asshole. I should let you drink until you fall off the stool.

"No, I never did Eddie. He wasn't my type. On the other hand, everyone was Tami's type."

Dave threw back his head and hooted with laughter again. "That's for sure!"

Someone stopped next to Dave and draped his suit coat back over the bar stool.

"This was on the floor," Dan Masterson said, sending a hard glare toward Suzanne.

"Oh, yeah, thanks, buddy," Dave slurred.

Dan moved on to another table.

Officious clod. Wish it had been him in that fish pond.

The crowd had thinned in the last half an hour leaving most of the barstools empty and only half the tables occupied. Eileen Raymond—recovered from her earlier shock—held court over in the corner. The former class secretary waved her arms, and then clasped her fists to her chest. Suzanne shook her head.

Probably giving a blow by blow description of her role in the drama. No doubt disappointed it wasn't me.

"Enjoy it while you can, honey. Your fifteen minutes of fame will be gone in a few days," she

117

muttered.

"What?" Dave demanded in a booming voice.

"Nothing. I was just thinking out loud about how soon I could transfer the money you need."

Dave's face brightened. He finished the coffee and she signaled for a refill.

"Really? You'll let me have it?"

You have no idea how much I'd love to let you have it.

"I'll have to discuss it with my financial advisors, but I don't see a problem."

She was tired of this phony mining stock crap. It was a scam all the way. And for the life of her, she didn't know what else to ask him. And where the hell was Zach? He and the testament to controlled diet plans had been gone forever. Had they sneaked off upstairs?

The son of a bitch had better not be getting any while I'm down here stuck with Dave the Drunken Moron.

The second cup of coffee arrived along with a glass of ice. Suzanne spooned a couple of cubes into the brew. Dave smiled and patted her shoulder, then let his hand trail down to her breast.

"Pretty soon, baby."

"Good. I can hardly wait."

Dave swallowed half the cup. At this rate he'd be semi-sober in a few minutes and ready to rock and roll. He'd already told her what she—and the cops—needed to know. It was time to pull up stakes and get the hell out. She had no idea where Zach was, but if he and Meghan were still downstairs, she intended to find them.

Suzanne downed the fake cosmopolitan and

contemplated her next move. She had to make an exit but at the same time keep Dave in the bar sucking down coffee.

Where do I go? My room? No, first place he'd look, and I don't want a soused Dave Coryell pounding on my hotel room door demanding sex.

She didn't even have a car. Dave had driven.

He finished the second cup and called out, "Bartender, another one." He turned and gazed at her empty glass, a smug smile on his lips. "How about you? Another drink?"

"Yeah, that sounds good. I'll have more of the same." The bartender nodded. "Uh, Dave, would you excuse me for a moment?"

"Where you going?"

"The little girls' room, silly. I'll be back in a few minutes." She gave him a peck on the cheek, picked up her purse, and slid from the stool. "Now, you wait right here, okay?"

"Hurry it up. You women always take forever in the can," he muttered.

Suzanne threaded her way between tables and paused in the doorway to look back. Dave's eyes were trained on her, so she blew him a kiss and waved, then exited.

How long would he wait before he realized he'd been stiffed? Would he even remember she'd been with him?

Yeah, he'll remember. Men always remember promises of sex. And I'll bet his pillow talk would be all about mining investments, if he didn't fall asleep first.

Charlie Crocker, bless his heart, had never rolled over and snored.

Suzanne spent the next fifteen minutes hiding in a stall of the mezzanine level ladies room until she was sure even Dave had given up. He'd be pissed, but she didn't give a crap.

Opening the restroom door, she poked her head out and gazed up and down the hallway, then breathed a sigh of relief. Not a soul in sight. She trotted down the stairs and across the lobby, tossing a quick glance into the bar as she passed. He was gone.

Suzanne hurried toward the ballroom—and Zach had damned well better be there. But he wasn't. The deputies had released most of the tables. Less than half a dozen remained.

She whirled and retraced her steps to the lobby. The same people occupied the seating area. Zach and Meghan weren't with them. Then out of the corner of her eye, she saw Dave stagger out of the men's room and toward the elevators. He didn't look in her direction, but she dodged behind a potted plant anyway, remaining hidden until he entered the lift and the doors closed.

Suzanne stepped out and breathed a sigh of relief. If she didn't find Zach soon, she was going to bed. The hell with him.

He asks me to question Dave, and then doesn't stick around for me to tell him what I've learned. Unless, of course, the son of a bitch dumped me. Anger flickered along her nerves. *Why are all men assholes?*

Screw going to bed. She wanted to give Zach and that bitch Meghan a piece of her mind. No one, but no one, dumped Suzanne.

She strode across the lobby with long, angry strides.

****

"Do you think Suzanne is still in danger?" Zach asked.

"Absolutely," Meghan replied.

"But surely the killer knows there's no way he'll get the jewels now," Ray commented.

"He'll just wait for another opportunity. Let's face it, Suzanne may take precautions, but what if the killer is Dave. Would she fear him?"

"The safest place for Suzanne is locked in a hotel room, preferably not the same one as now," Zach added.

"Not a bad idea," Ray said. "I'll ask the hotel if they can do it without any fanfare."

They reached the terrace steps and ascended. In contrast to earlier, the area was deserted. Meghan wondered if people were too afraid to venture forth or just too damned tired.

She re-entered the ballroom with the two men. Several tables of people still awaited interrogation.

"Guess my deputies are a little slow. I'd better lend a hand. I'll talk to you later." The sheriff strode to table and took a seat, while Zach steered her toward the doors.

"I suppose we should rescue Suzanne from Dave," he commented.

A dart of jealousy stabbed in her gut. Was Zach attracted to the redhead? *Or maybe just bored with me? Could be he found all my theories ignorant. Zach's intelligent. Perhaps ignorance turns him off. But if that's the case, why mess with Suzanne?*

"Why bother with her?"

He shrugged. "I'd like to know if she managed to

pry any information out of him. What kind of game were the two of you playing earlier?"

"The kind of game men never understand."

Zach chuckled. She liked his laugh, deep yet sexy at the same time. It made for a potent combination. To her annoyance, her hormones elevated a notch or two.

"Don't tell me it had to do with me and one-upmanship. Are points awarded?"

She whirled to face him, aghast and more than a little appalled that he'd nailed it.

"Well, of all the conceited…"

"Where the hell have you two been?"

She turned back sharply to find Suzanne glaring at both of them from narrowed eyes with her fists balled on her hips.

"Busy," Meghan snapped. She decided the redhead's attitude was both irritating and satisfying at the same time. Meghan liked the idea that she, the former fat girl, aroused the green-eyed monster in a beautiful woman, but also found the outburst unbecoming and distasteful.

Jealousy—almost as corrosive as hate. Her mind flipped back twenty years to the taunts she'd endured at the hand of kids like Suzanne and Tami. She was shocked at how deep her resentment and hatred had run then. Meghan was even more shocked to realize she'd been the jealous one a few moments earlier. She bit her lip, embarrassed at allowing the emotion to creep into her psyche. She'd always considered herself above such thinking.

"Don't give me that, sister." Suzanne turned her attention to Zach and batted her big blue eyes, then curled her arm through his. "Zach, you left me all alone with Dave. He was drunk and boring." Her lips formed into a pout.

"Oh, for the love of God," Meghan began.

Zach held up his hand. "Hold it, ladies. Can we call a truce for the moment? We went with the sheriff to look at the scene of the crime."

The pouting lips and purring tone disappeared. "Why? What did you expect to find there? The cops have been all over it."

"True, but the sheriff thought I might remember more details if I went back."

"And did you?"

"A few. Let's sit down," he invited indicating a vacated table near the dance floor. "What did you find out from Dave? Where is he?"

Zach pulled out her chair and eased Suzanne down, then did the same for Meghan. She sat, relieved it didn't sound as though he wanted to tell the redhead anything that had passed in the garden.

"I have no idea where he is. I told him I was going to the ladies room and ditched him in the bar."

"Did he say anything useful?" Zach said.

Suzanne spent the next fifteen minutes telling them what Dave had told her.

"He found Annabelle and just left her there?" Meghan exclaimed. "Who the hell does something like that?" *Someone guilty of murder?*

"So he says. He was pissed as hell at me and afraid someone would think he'd done it. Dave's a lot of things, but he's not a killer."

"But what was he doing before he went into the garden?" Zach asked.

"He was in his car, and he says, in his room,"

Suzanne answered.

"Do you believe him?" Meghan wondered. *Would I? Probably not. I'd demand an explanation.*

"Sure. I think his stash is hidden in the car. Maybe in the trunk somewhere, like the spare tire well."

Zach raised his eyebrows. "His stash?"

"Coke. He probably grabbed a couple of packets, went to his room, and snorted a line or two."

"And he wasn't sharing, right?" Meghan inquired in a cool, but nasty tone.

Suzanne turned a frosty gaze her way. "Look, Miss Goody-Two-Shoes, I don't do drugs. A little pot in high school, but that's all. My husband made it real clear that if he ever caught me with anything stronger than a martini, I was history. Besides, drugs are for losers—like Dave Coryell."

Zach frowned. "So Dave's a cokehead. It sounds like he might have an alibi after all. The only problem is we don't have a timeline for any of it."

"He could have been in the garden, come across Annabelle, thought it was Suzanne, and killed her," Meghan said, thinking out loud. "Kind of taking advantage of an opportunity."

"Dave doesn't have the guts," Suzanne told them, contempt dripping from her voice. She glanced at her rival and pouted again, curling her fingers around Zach's wrist and hugging it to her bosom. "At least, I don't think he does. Oh, Zach, I'm not sure I'll be able to sleep tonight. Would you come back to my room with me? We can sit and talk. I'd just love to hear how the class computer geek ended up on the Fortune Five Hundred."

Meghan moved beyond awarding points. She

discovered jealousy, once entwined in the soul, was hard to ignore. Suzanne was in serious jeopardy of losing her eyes and most of her hair.

I'm jealous—so jealous I could kill her. She stifled a gasp at the sudden direction of her thoughts. *Oh, my God! Is that the answer? Is Annabelle dead because of jealousy?*

Her mind raced back through the evening. Suzanne had come with Dave, but Meghan hadn't paid that much attention to the two. Maybe Suzanne, bored when Dave ignored her, had batted those damned eyelashes at the wrong man. Could this be a woman's crime after all? Could a wife or girlfriend, angry at Suzanne for flirting, have been jealous and pissed enough to kill? And a stun gun was a woman's weapon. But who? *So many men, so much flirting, and way too much opportunity.*

She turned to voice her suggestion just in time to see Zach's reaction to Suzanne's flirting. He removed her fingers from his wrist and smiled.

"Suzanne, I'm not interested. I have a date. It's been twenty years. Grow up. Oh, by the way, the sheriff wanted to talk to you. I suggest you wait here." He turned to Meghan and smiled. "Would you like another drink?"

"I'd love one." She pushed back her chair and rose.

Suzanne's mouth hung open. Then she snapped it shut and glared, but said nothing.

Game, set, and match.

Chapter Eight

Meghan and Zach walked into the bar holding hands and found a table. Dave was gone. The lounge had also emptied. Instead of the crowd they'd left, she saw less than half the number of people including Eileen, who appeared well on the road to recovery from having found Annabelle. Her voice carried across the room.

"And I can't begin to tell you how horrified I was when I realized it was a body. I ran like the wind back to the terrace. I just knew the killer was right behind me. I swear I heard him breathing."

"Looks like Eileen is re-living the drama," Meghan whispered.

"I'm sure that by the end of the night, she'll have sold the movie rights," Zach replied.

The waitress stopped by their table looking as tired as Meghan felt. Zach looked at Meghan. "Don't know about you, but I'm having coffee."

"Iced tea sounds good to me."

The waitress nodded and left.

"Tell me more about stun guns," she asked. "Aren't those the things with the long threads attached that police use to subdue unruly suspects?"

"No, those are tasers and in some states are available only to law enforcement or people who are licensed to carry guns. Anyone can buy a stun gun," he informed her. "Our killer didn't use a taser. They're large and hard to conceal. Next to pepper spray, stun guns are the self-defense weapon of choice for women."

"How powerful are they?"

"They can zap an attacker with anything from twenty thousand volts to a real wallop of over a million."

"What! My God, the electric chair only sends twenty-five hundred volts. How come the streets aren't littered with dead bodies?"

Zach smiled. "It's not the voltage that kills, it's the amperes—amps."

"Amps?"

"Volts represent pressure and amps intensity. The higher the amps, the higher the chances of death. Even simple household items can kill, which is why those warning labels about unplugging the device before servicing are slapped all over."

"I've never seen a stun gun. What do they look like?" The weapon both fascinated and repelled her. She made a mental note to incorporate one into a future book.

"They vary. Some can be six to eight inches long and others much smaller. The business end has two protruding electrodes maybe an eighth of an inch long. Jam it against your opponent, press a button, and the gun sends a shot of volts right through clothing. The stronger the voltage, the bigger the zap. Some are disguised as cell phones and I saw one not too long ago that looked like a pen."

"How do you know all this?" Meghan wondered in amazement.

Zach shrugged. "I'm a technology junkie. A woman in my office bought one. I got curious and investigated on the Internet. I'd say that at two and a half centimeters, this one must resemble a large cigarette lighter. Just the right size to slip into a pocket."

"What happens when you're nailed with one? Do you go unconscious?"

"Not necessarily. It'll tingle and jolt, just like any shock, but the voltage disrupts the body's electrical impulses. Muscles go into spasm and while your mind might function, you won't be able to move."

"Incapacitated," she murmured. "How long do the effects last?"

"Depends on how long the contact is," he said. "A quick zap of less than a second wouldn't last long, but keep it buzzing for four or five and it would be several minutes until you regained full control."

"I wonder how long Annabelle had to endure it?" she murmured. "Would she have been able to move at all?"

"Maybe, but I doubt it. She was zapped just long enough for the killer to hold her head under water." Zach's lips thinned into a firm line.

"How do you keep from zapping yourself?"

"It has an on/off switch."

She pictured the killer creeping up behind Annabelle, thinking it was Suzanne, sending God only knew how many volts charging through her body, and then drowning her without having ever seen the face of his victim. And Annabelle would be conscious, aware of what was happening, but unable to defend herself until the effects wore off. By then it was too late.

The miserable, cold-blooded bastard. I want to find this guy in the worst way.

She shot a glance toward Eileen and her audience. "Are you ready to tackle our classmates with subtle questions?"

"How do we go about it? One on one or group sessions?"

"Ray's right. Most people wouldn't have seen or heard anything. But if we could corner those on the terrace during that time frame, we might be able to uncover new information."

"The only problem is finding out who was on the terrace. If I'm not mistaken, we were kind of busy."

Her breath caught remembering his lips and the heat they aroused within her. The other events of the night had almost wiped that from her mind—and Meghan wanted to remember. Oh, yeah. Remember and then some. Maybe repeat the experience later.

She cleared her throat. "Only for the last few minutes. We talked earlier. For instance, I remember Marcella Sanders and her husband walking down the steps into the garden. Elizabeth and Rudy Conrad did the same thing."

The waitress returned with their coffee and tea. Zach paid, adding a fifty percent tip for the young woman. Meghan's heart fluttered at the kind gesture. She liked generosity. *Another mark in the plus column for Zach Dunbar.*

Zach sipped his coffee before saying, "So Dave has a cocaine habit and needs money for a floundering business. What if he was checking the trunk of his car for a place to hide stolen goods—like jewelry?"

"He could have had a stun gun in the car, too.

Maybe he didn't realize his mistake until Annabelle was dead."

Zach frowned and rubbed a hand over his chin. "In which case, he put on a hell of a performance on the terrace later."

"Damn, I forgot. I don't think he's that good an actor." She lifted her glass of iced tea and drank. "Besides, if he was drunk and high like Suzanne says, then his reaction must have been real."

"Their exchange at the table when the sheriff left sounds like Suzanne threatened him, maybe more than once. Not a healthy thing given the circumstances. Should we warn her?" Zach asked.

"I imagine Suzanne can take care of herself under normal conditions, but there is a stun gun floating around out there. Maybe we should mention it to her."

"I don't think Ray wants that information released yet. I shouldn't have blown her off. I should have played along and kept tabs on her, at least until she was safely locked in a new room." He frowned, his eyes showing concern.

Another point in his favor. He's piling them up tonight. He doesn't particularly like Suzanne, but is concerned about her. Nice guys are hard to find. I need to hang on to this one.

The object of their discussion walked into the bar, scanned the occupants, and slid onto a stool. She spoke to the bartender who served her immediately.

"I wonder if Ray talked to her about changing rooms," Meghan said.

"If he hasn't, he will now," Zach replied, nodding toward the doorway.

Ray spotted them, strode over, and pulled out a

chair.

"How goes it?" Zach questioned.

"It won't be long now. I don't think there's anybody left who can give us anything."

The waitress paused beside the table. "Get you anything, sheriff?"

"A cup of coffee would be nice. I'm going to need all the caffeine I can get. It's gonna be a long night."

She looked at Meghan and Zach. "Anything for the rest of you?"

"I'm fine," Zach answered.

"Me, too."

The server nodded and walked away.

"I cornered Dan Masterson, and when I told him he'd been seen on the terrace he changed his story. He admitted going for a walk in the garden to cool off, both physically and emotionally. Suzanne really pissed him off."

"Enough to kill her?" Meghan wondered.

Ray shook his head. "Not Dan. He's too conscious of his image to risk anything like that, but I'll bet he thought about it." His coffee arrived, and he doctored it with a packet of sugar and two little containers of cream. "From what I've heard, Dan wasn't the only one Suzanne had words with tonight."

"Well, she never did have a problem speaking her mind," Meghan told him, sipping her tea.

"One woman walked past the table and heard Suzanne having words with Annabelle."

"About the dress?" she asked.

Ray nodded. "Suzanne was insulting."

"That doesn't surprise me," Zach said. "Dave was ignoring her, and for the first time in her life, she sat alone while others had fun." He finished his coffee. "If we'd found Dave in the pond, I'd have no problem suspecting Suzanne."

"She also gave Glory the rough side of her tongue," Ray told them. "Called Divine a pain in the ass and the reunion boring."

"So, she's an equal opportunity insulter," Meghan stated. "How is that new? She and Tami used to slice and dice everyone."

Ray eyed her. "Including you?"

"Occasionally. I once stepped on Tami's foot in gym class. She called me a fat cow. But for the most part, I stayed below her radar."

"How about you, Zach? Did you ever run afoul of Eddie and Dave?"

"Eddie tried to bribe me once. He wanted me to let him copy the answers during a math test. I refused, and later he gut punched me in the hall. As I recall, Dave just stood there and laughed."

Ray drank half his coffee in one gulp, rose, and glanced toward Suzanne. "I guess I'd better talk to Mrs. Crocker again. Get her side of the story."

"Don't forget to suggest changing rooms," Zach reminded him.

Ray nodded and sauntered over to the bar.

Meghan finished her tea. "I guess half the graduating class had run-ins with the four of them."

"Yeah, they thought they had the world by the tail. Hello, Ruth, Gary," he greeted two classmates who stopped next to him.

"Hello, Zach. Nasty business," the man said.

"Very nasty."

"Poor Annabelle," the woman replied, shaking her

head. "I was talking to her just before she left. Suzanne Wayland had made fun of her dress and jewelry earlier, and Annabelle was still upset. Claimed she needed a cigarette. Wish now I'd gone with her."

"Did you see anyone following her?" Meghan probed. Why not start interrogating classmates now?

"No. I stepped out about fifteen minutes later. Dan Masterson was coming up the steps so fast he nearly knocked me down. Didn't even apologize. He looked angry," Ruth answered.

"Masterson's an arrogant ass," her husband commented smoothing a hand over his dark hair.

Ruth's blue eyes filled with tears. "Honey, I'm tired. This reunion has turned out to be less than fun. Let's go home."

"I'm with you. Good luck. Hopefully, we'll meet again under better circumstances."

Zach waved a hand. "Good to see you, Gary. Goodnight, Ruth."

"Goodnight. By the way, the two of you look fabulous," Ruth remarked with a smile.

Meghan accepted the compliment with a nod. "Thanks, Ruth. Take care."

She watched the couple leave, and then turned to Zach. "So, Dan Masterson was in the garden at the same time as Annabelle."

"Interesting. I wonder if he told that to Ray. My guess is no."

Meghan shrugged inspecting her empty glass. "Maybe he didn't know she was out there. A lot of undercurrents flowed tonight—a lot of ulterior motives."

Ray rejoined them. "Well, I talked to Suzanne and

she admitted she'd been less than pleasant to both Annabelle and Glory."

"Did she agree to change rooms?" Meghan asked.

He shook his head. "Told me to eat shit, and go to hell."

"Is she drunk?" Zach quizzed.

"A little, but not enough to worry about. The bartender said she's been drinking cranberry juice, and just now switched back to the real thing."

"Sounds like Suzanne had a good plan. Get Dave loaded, and ask him questions all the while keeping her head above water," Meghan replied.

"What questions?" Ray wanted to know.

Zach explained what he'd requested of Suzanne and the information she'd uncovered.

"Dave found Mrs. Peterson?" Ray's eyebrows furrowed into a scowl. "I think I need to have another talk with Mr. Coryell."

"You might want to include Dan Masterson again," Meghan added, and then told him what Gary and Ruth had said.

"You two are just full of good news." Ray shook his head. "Why was Dave in the parking lot?"

"According to Suzanne, he has a stash of cocaine hidden in the car," Zach informed him.

"Well, I'll be damned. Now, I really have to talk to him and get a warrant to search his car. I guess there's something in this business of people talking to you instead of the law. Call me if you unearth any more information."

Ray rattled off his cell phone number. Meghan scrambled to find a pen in her purse and grabbed a cocktail napkin.

"Can you repeat that?"

To her surprise, Zach repeated it correctly. She gazed at him as did Ray.

"Sorry, I have numerical total recall."

"Remind me not to say anything incriminating around you," she murmured.

Zach grinned. "It only applies to numbers."

"Just be careful," Ray warned again, and then left.

As he passed the corner table, Eileen rose and walked toward them. "May I sit with you for a moment?"

Meghan nodded. "Of course. How are you feeling?"

"Much better. It was all so—so gruesome. I wanted to thank you for what you did for me out on the terrace. You handled it very well."

"I'm sure if the positions had been reversed, you'd have done the same." She glanced at Zach who nodded. Time to start questioning again. "Eileen, who was with you on the terrace—before you went into the garden, I mean?"

"Gosh, there were several people just standing around, but I talked to my husband, Carl, of course, and Jack and Mary Samuels. Carol Rutherford was there, too, along with her date. I can't remember his name— Allen? Adam?" Eileen paused and wrinkled her forehead.

"Anyone else?" she urged.

"Betty Coleman and her husband—don't know his last name. It seems to me Ruth Whisnett came out, and someone rushed up the steps and into the ballroom." She caught her breath with a gasp. "Oh, my God, could it have been the killer? Would he dare make such a public entrance?"

"I don't know." So, Eileen corroborated Ruth's information regarding someone rushing onto the terrace from the garden. Dan? "Who was it?"

"I don't know. My back was to the steps and the other side of the terrace. I never noticed. Do you think I should tell the sheriff?"

"I doubt that's necessary," Zach answered with a smile. "As you said, the killer wouldn't return with such a flourish."

Eileen rose. "Well, I guess I should be thinking about going home, although I'm sure I won't sleep a wink. Thanks again, Meghan."

Eileen returned to the table in the corner. Meghan mulled the information over in her mind. Robbery or something deeper? Mistaken identity or...

"Zach, what if Annabelle was the target after all?"

"What are you getting at?"

"Maybe *Eric* is the good actor. For all we know, the marriage might have been in trouble."

"And he used the dress angle as a cover-up? Men don't think that way." Zach shook his head. "Besides, how would he know about the dress beforehand?"

"It could have been a pleasant co-incidence for him."

"No, your theory is off base. Suzanne was the target."

"Never discard a theory."

Am I over-analyzing this?

Her mind slipped back twenty years. Tami, Eddie, Dave, and Suzanne had had things pretty much their way. Whenever questioned about their escapades, they all lied like rugs to get out of it—especially Tami.

She lied with the most angelic look on her face I've ever seen.

And God only knew the football coach would never do a damned thing to jeopardize his team, so Eddie and Dave got off without so much as detention.

Maybe this isn't about robbery at all. Maybe it's about revenge. Revenge for something that happened in high school. Then a more chilling thought sprang to mind. *No, it couldn't be.*

"Zach?" she said with a wavering voice.

He looked at her sharply. "What's the matter?"

"Zach, what if..." She paused and captured her lower lip between her teeth.

"What if what?"

"What if we were right?"

"About what?" he asked, a touch of impatience in this tone.

"What if Tami and Eddie's deaths are linked? What if Suzanne was meant to be number three?"

Chapter Nine

Her suggestion intrigued him. "What? You mean that nonsense about a killer working her way through the cheerleaders and the ninety-seven pound weakling stuff?"

Meghan shrugged, her eyes downcast into her empty glass. She rattled the remaining ice.

"Who holds a twenty year grudge? And for what purpose?" Mystery writer or not, he thought Meghan was reaching on this.

"I don't know, but think back to all the shit they pulled in high school, Tami especially. She got away with murder." She winced. "Sorry, bad choice of words, but maybe it took twenty years for the anger and resentment to surface. Think about it. Remember how it was? Eddie gut punched you for not doing what he wanted. How many other people did he victimize?"

Zach cast him mind back to those days. It had taken a long time to come to terms with the name calling during high school. He and Meghan had both been victims of bullying. He mentally added the names of other kids he knew to the list before answering.

"I think Tami and Eddie enjoyed making others miserable. She was sly, but intelligent enough when it suited her. In spite of his athletic prowess, Eddie Mancuso was a lightweight in the academic field. I remember Bob Ellis had to tutor him in history."

"Sharon Crawley did the same in English. Said he never did get the difference between a subject and a predicate," Meghan added rolling her eyes.

"And for all her self-centered ways, Suzanne was a follower. I suspect Tami and Dave were the instigators of the group."

She leaned her elbow on the table and cupped her chin in her hand. "Dave was more into practical jokes than physical abuse. Remember when he super-glued the combination dials on all the freshman lockers? And wasn't he the one who drilled a peephole into the girls shower in the gym?"

"A few people were embarrassed, but as I recall none of those incidents are a blueprint for revenge, especially murder," Zach replied.

"Someone could have snapped, discovered where Tami and Eddie lived, killed them, and then shown up here as a waiter or even a guest at the hotel, but not connected to the reunion. Someone no one would recognize—like us."

What she said could fly. How many other geeks and fat girls had the group victimized?

"So, he dons a waiter's outfit or a suit and tie, slips into the ballroom, follows who he thinks is Suzanne, and accidentally kills Annabelle? That's far-fetched."

"Humiliation can fester for years. If Eddie dealt out physical abuse, then Tami was queen of the verbal. She had the tongue of an adder. Her words hurt. I was often called 'lard-ass,' 'Beulah,' and 'Massive Meghan.' I tried not to let it bother me, but sometimes I'd close the stall door in the restroom and cry."

She swallowed what he suspected was a lump in her throat. Even now, those memories hurt.

Zach grasped her hand and brought it to his lips for a light kiss.

"I'm sorry. I was the 'geek,' 'nerd,' and 'beanpole.' I also took my fair share of pushing and shoving in the halls and locker room."

Meghan smiled and squeezed his hand before continuing. "The little bitch was sneaky, too. She once stole Helen Towne's book report, and presented it to the teacher as her work. When Helen pointed the finger and provided proof, the teacher gave Tami an 'F.' Tami got even by damn near running the poor girl down. Helen said Tami laughed and called her a name before driving off."

Zach drummed his fingers on the table and thought. Suppose Meghan was right. Had the four classmates pulled a prank or insulted someone enough to foster murder?

"I'm still not convinced, but it's an avenue we should investigate."

"It means Dave—and especially Suzanne—are still in danger."

"Yes, but why kill Tami in Los Angeles, Eddie in Texas, and wait for the reunion to take a shot at the other two? Why use the reunion at all? Knock them off one by one and no one suspects they're connected."

The whole thing had no logic and Zach's entire life and fortune were based in logic.

"I don't know. Maybe it was hard for the killer to get to everyone on an individual basis. It could be a money or a time issue. The killer probably has a family and a job. Taking a personal day or two off to commit murder might lead to questions by a spouse or a boss."

Zach's gaze traveled to Eileen and her friends at

the corner table. Eileen had been in charge of finding lost classmates and issuing the invitations. What had Glory said earlier? Something about the police in California and Texas notifying Eileen about the deaths?

"Meg, talk to Eileen again. Find out if Tami and Eddie had RSVP'd for the reunion. If they didn't plan on attending, then the killer may have *had* to travel."

"And if Dave and Suzanne had accepted the invitation they'd be here, then all the killer had to do was wait." She glanced at Eileen's table. "I count five women. Bob Harris and three other guys are over there along the wall. I'll do the women, you take the men."

"Good idea. Order everyone another drink."

"I think the nostalgia method will work best," she commented.

"The nostalgia method?"

"Yeah, ask about families first, and then bring up the 'do you remember' stuff? We might learn more about who had a serious grudge against the four of them. Do we warn Dave and Suzanne?"

"Let's see what we uncover first. Ray's already talked with Suzanne. Dave looks like he can take care of himself."

"But Dave is drunk on his ass, and according to Suzanne, lit up from cocaine. His judgment is impaired."

"Good point. Should I try to find and warn him?"

"If Dave was that wasted, he's no doubt passed out in bed by now," she replied. "Plus, you just brushed Suzanne off. I'm not sure she'd take any warning from you with style and grace."

"You're probably right."

Zach gazed at the redhead on the bar stool. She was

lovely, always had been, but the only emotion she stirred in him was amusement, although he doubted Suzanne would appreciate the knowledge. Her actions were so obvious—no subtlety at all.

He turned his head toward Meghan, who wiped the condensation from her glass, a frown on her face. Now, here was a woman of substance—successful, intelligent, and strong. That was a true turn on. Yet, he sensed vulnerability. He'd watched from across the lobby when she'd hesitated before entering the ballroom as if her confidence had suddenly vanished. He understood confronting past demons.

His hand stilled her fingers. "I guess we should take a crack at our former classmates."

Meghan nodded, pushing back her chair. "I guess. Meet you in the lobby."

She stood and walked over to Eileen's table. He waited a few seconds, rose, and sauntered toward the men.

****

Suzanne alternately sipped her cosmo and glared at Zach and Meghan. It had been a long time since she'd been rebuffed. And by Zachary Dunbar of all people— the class brainiac and dweeb! She could take that, but being told her charms were lost on Zachary Dunbar, millionaire, really rankled. *Am I losing my touch?* She drained her glass and ordered another.

At least Dave wasn't around. She wondered how long he'd waited. Not even Dave Coryell, drunk as a lord, could believe a woman would hang out in the john for almost a half an hour.

The bartender set a fresh drink in front of her. It was nearly one o'clock and the bar would soon close.

This whole evening had been a waste of time and energy. If she'd been smart, she'd have told Dave to go shove the whole reunion up his ass, but n-o-o-o-o, she had agreed to attend in the hope Tami would show. Now, she was involved up to her ears in a murder, and that damned sheriff had learned about her run-ins with Annabelle and Glory. She bet Zach and Meghan had also told him about her conversation with Dave. *Who cares? Let the bastard explain it to the law. I've done my civic duty for the night.*

She sipped her drink and ran a fingertip around the rim of the glass. The sheriff's attempts to warn her of further danger may have been ham-handed and less than subtle, but he got his message across. A determined thief could make a second grab for the jewels. Maybe she should consider changing rooms for the night. If nothing else, Dave wouldn't be able to find her.

She sipped again and suppressed a shiver. Second doubts pummeled her. What if Dave *was* the killer? Had he really been that pissed at her? Pissed enough to kill? Ordinarily, she'd have said no, but his circumstances were anything but ordinary. Between his ex-wife draining his bank account and lousy business decisions, he'd stretched the financial rubber band as far as it would go. When it finally snapped, the twang would reverberate throughout Chicago.

Maybe he only meant to scare me. Maybe the whole thing boomeranged when Annabelle died. It was an accident. Sometimes things get out of hand. She shivered and remembered events from long ago. *No, don't go there. Don't think about it.*

Suzanne bit her lip. So, she'd pissed off Dave. So

what? She'd pissed off several people tonight—Annabelle, Glory, Dan, and Lord only knew who else. She and Meghan had been dueling in an undertone she'd rather enjoyed. Suzanne didn't remember Meghan as having had the verbal ability to spar in the big leagues. And Zach hadn't seemed pissed—just bored and disinterested. *Damn him.*

She sipped and wished she could light up a cigarette. God knows she needed one. The last couple of hours had not been the best of her life.

Suzanne sighed. If someone wanted to kill her, they'd have done so in high school. The four of them had hacked off more than their fair share of people back then. She raised her glass and stopped with it halfway to her mouth when a sudden thought flashed through her mind.

No, that's not possible. Is it? Could someone be after all four of them—she, Tami, Eddie, and Dave?

"Oh, my God, who did we infuriate that bad?" she murmured to herself. Her heart raced and she had trouble drawing breath. The air stopped somewhere south of her throat.

Shit! Who? Eileen? Maybe the hysteria on the terrace was all an act. They'd made fun of the earnest young girl more than once. Her commitment to community service had been a source of amusement back then. Now, she admired the former class secretary for her efforts. Suzanne contributed both her time and money to various charities in Chicago. Charlie had always insisted on giving back. Of course, the payback had been mostly monetary, but what the hell, a contribution was a contribution.

She shook her head. *I don't see Eileen killing*

anything other than a spider.

Dan Masterson? As much as she hated the son of a bitch, she didn't think he had the *cajones* to actually follow through. *Too much riding on his political career for him to take the chance.* He might think about it, but that was all.

Glory Ecklund?

Skinny to the point of emaciation and dumb as an ox, Glory? Don't make me laugh. Besides, she wasn't even in our class. She graduated five or six years after us.

Tom Ecklund?

Mr. Excitement? She sipped her drink and mulled his name over in her mind. The quiet, almost introverted bookworm had been the butt of Eddie's so-called jokes on numerous occasions, but as far as she knew Tami hadn't singled him out for special treatment. Tami preferred dishing punishment to girls who may or may not have wronged her. *And I don't remember either Dave or I paying much attention to Tom in high school. No, someone who hated all of us did this if, indeed, the deaths are connected.*

Twenty years was a long time. Suzanne had trouble remembering *what* they had done let alone the names of the victims. They'd been so young, so caught up with a sense of their own importance. The feelings of others? Not a problem. Who cared? Their victims were the losers in the high school pecking order—social inferiors who didn't count.

Lord, how cheap and shallow it all seems now.

Tami had been the ringleader, but she'd been smart enough to let Eddie think he was *numero uno*. Dave had been more amused by their exploits. She remembered he'd pull off a prank, laugh, and then go on with whatever came next. *Usually sex with me—and sometimes Tami.*

Occasionally, Suzanne had hated her best friend. It galled her that Tami showed no conscience about balling Dave, then telling her and giggling about it.

Bitch. No wonder she's dead.

Maybe that was the answer. Tami had screwed the wrong husband or boyfriend and someone had made her pay. Eddie, too. The miserable sleaze had hit on her several times. Could jealousy be the answer for his death?

Suzanne downed her drink. In spite of having just ditched Dave, she now needed to find him. Ask him what he thought about all of this. Maybe he'd sobered up and coked out enough to remember the plots and plans of twenty years ago. He might recall something or someone she'd forgotten.

She glanced at Zach and Meghan. He now sat with a bunch of guys. Meghan was ensconced with Eileen and her bunch of eager listeners in the corner. Suzanne signed her bar tab, left a generous tip, and walked out of the lounge without a backward look.

The most logical place to find Dave was his room, but if he was there, he'd misconstrue her presence. Suzanne shrugged. She'd deal with that later.

The elevator crept up to Dave's room on the third floor. When she knocked, his door swung open.

"Dave? You in here?"

She walked into the room. The lights blazed in both the sleeping area and from the bath.

"Dave?" she called again.

Silence greeted her. He wasn't here—or was he? It

would be just his lame idea of a practical joke to hide, and then leap out trying to scare the crap out of her. Suzanne jerked open the closet door. Nothing. Just a couple of pairs of slacks and a few shirts.

Out of curiosity, she wandered into the bathroom, and noticed powdery residue on a hand mirror lying on the counter. Dave had been busy. But wherever he was, it wasn't here. She left, closing the door securely behind her.

Now where? Would he have gone back to the ballroom to search for her? She re-entered the elevator and stopped to think before pushing the button. If Zach and Meghan had relayed her information to the sheriff, then maybe Dave was having a discussion with the authorities. She punched the lobby button and hurried past a group of seated people.

But Dave was not in the ballroom. Suzanne estimated only about thirty people remained. Whirling, she headed to the bar again. Had he slipped in after she'd left?

She paused on the threshold and scanned the room. Zach and Meghan were still at the same tables as when she'd left, but Dave hadn't returned. She walked slowly back into the lobby. The seating area had several of her classmates grouped together, but no Dave.

She'd hung out in the ladies room. Did guys do the same? Casting a quick glance over her shoulder, she walked with determination to the men's room, pulled open the door, calling out, "Anybody in here?"

Silence greeted the warning. She entered, and checked under the stalls. The place was empty.

That left the car. Maybe he needed more coke or maybe he was so wasted, he'd fallen asleep in it.

Suzanne hurried out of the front doors and angled toward the parking lot. She had no idea where Dave had parked the car. He'd dropped her and the luggage off first. Suzanne scanned the spaces for a cream-colored Mercedes, before finally spotting it in the third row not far from the garden entrance. She hurried toward it and knocked on the tinted windows.

"Dave? Are you asleep? Come on, open up."

If he was in there, he was dead to the world. She shuddered at her choice of words and tugged at the door handles. Locked. Just to make sure, she pounded on the trunk lid.

"Dave?"

Okay, it was silly. Who the hell accidentally locked themselves in the trunk of their own car? Or even deliberately for that matter? Not even Dave could get *that* drunk or coked up.

She walked slowly back to the hotel entrance. Her heart pounded, and a growing sense of dread crept over her. She halted outside the doors, fished in her purse for a cigarette, lit it with trembling fingers, and paced. Could he have gone back into the garden? Suzanne shuddered. She wasn't about to investigate *there*.

Primed for sex, it would be just like the miserable son of a bitch to hook up with another woman and disappear to *her* room. That was the only explanation.

Goddamn him! I hope he gets some disease.

Yet something in the back of her mind rejected this. Dave Coryell might be a slug, but the chances of him scoring in the short time she'd been gone from the bar were slim. Most of the patrons had been classmates, and few of those single women.

Suzanne flipped her half-smoked cigarette into the

bushes and walked inside where her gaze once again searched the lobby.

Dammit, Dave. Where the hell are you?

****

Suzanne was proving elusive. At the moment, she was stuck like glue to Meghan and Zach. *Meghan doesn't look happy about it either. Good. That might work to my advantage later.*

With the redheaded bitch occupied, I turned my attention to Dave Coryell. He was disgustingly drunk and pitching his investment company to just about everybody, including me. Jerk. I didn't have that much against him really, but since he was best buddies with Eddie, Tami, and Suzanne, he had to die. Besides, he was in on all their antics years ago—the insults, the taunts, the whole poisonous atmosphere. I tensed remembering what I endured at their hands. I hated them all.

As I mingled with the guests, my mind focused on how to dispatch Dave to practical joke heaven. Suzanne's room seemed like the answer. I'd pilfered the key from her purse earlier intending to kill her there. Following who I thought was her into the garden had been an impulse.

You have a plan. Stick to it. You're logical and organized. Don't give in to sudden change, even if it does seem opportunistic.

But even the best laid plans go awry, so I pondered how to entice Dave to Suzanne's room. Then it hit me. Why not slip Suzanne's room key into his jacket pocket? He'd eventually find it. With the chaos of the evening, no one would remember who was where or for how long.

Placing the key in his pocket was simple. He, Suzanne, and half the attendees crowded into the hotel bar. Everyone bumped shoulders and spilled drinks. Dave was so drunk he didn't notice a thing.

My greatest fear was he'd discover the key while Suzanne was still with him. But my luck held. Suzanne hurried out of the bar and headed for the mezzanine. Fifteen minutes later, Dave staggered out—alone.

I requested a spare key from the desk clerk giving Suzanne's room number, and then ran up the stairs. The fourth floor corridor was empty. I hustled to the room and set the stage.

Her cosmetic bag was on the bathroom vanity. I rummaged through until finding a pair of manicure scissors, then returned to the bedroom, unplugged the lamp on the desk, and cut the cord fashioning it into a slip knot.

To further darken the room, I shut the bathroom door until only the tiniest sliver of light showed. The faint illumination revealed only shapes.

The wait was interminable. Where the hell was he? And what if Suzanne came back first? No matter. I'd take care of her instead. But what if they came back together?

No, Suzanne had been angry at being left alone and flirted with Zach half the night. I laughed softly in the darkness. The only person other than me who wanted to kill Suzanne was Meghan.

A bead of sweat trickled down my temple. What if someone came looking for me? What if my absence was a topic of conversation? What if…

Stop it! No one's going to come looking for you. Why should they? The sheriff doesn't have any suspects

*yet. Now is not the time to lose your nerve. You planned
this since the moment you heard about the reunion.*

Then someone inserted a key in the door lock. I
knelt on the bed, the stun gun clutched in my hand. My
heart pounded, but whether in fear or anticipation I
didn't know. All I knew was that whoever entered the
room would die.

The door crashed open. A man was briefly
silhouetted in the entryway before he slammed it shut
again. Dave Coryell had finally arrived.

"Suzanne, where are you, you little devil?"

He shed his coat and let it drop onto the floor.

I sighed, pitched my voice higher, and whispered,
"Here, Dave. Come and find me."

He moved forward, bumping against the desk. "Put
on the light, baby. I can't see shit."

"All in good time. I'm naked, Dave. Naked and
waiting. I have a surprise for you."

"Oh, yeah? What?"

"Come closer, and you'll find out."

He lunged for the bed.

I shoved the stun gun against his throat. The
sizzling zap echoed in the room. He fought back,
grabbing my arm. Surprise and fear rushed through me.
That wasn't supposed to happen! I pulled free, my
breath hissing in and out like an angry snake. Another
zap sounded and this time I held the button down.
Dave, jerking and twitching, lost all coordination. He
slid face down onto the floor. I laughed and bounded
off the bed.

This was more like it. I enjoyed all the flopping.
The great football player reminded me of a fish out of
water. For kicks, I zapped him again on the back of his

neck. Strange gurgling noises bubbled from his throat. Maybe he was strangling on all the booze he'd drank. The thought that the last thing he'd ever taste was the sour flavor of vomit gave me intense pleasure—almost as much as killing him. His life was about to end. I hoped he knew it.

I hit him again briefly with the stun gun, straddled his back, and twining my fingers in his hair, pulled his head up. Time to finish him off. I slipped the cord over his head and tightened. As with Annabelle, I placed a knee on his back, pulling harder.

He choked, but was unable to fight back. Something popped in his throat. He gagged. I envisioned his tongue forced out of his mouth. His arms, flopped up and down, but he was too weak to lift them in defense. I sniffed in disgust at the stench of feces and urine as he lost bodily functions.

"Did you think you could get away with it? You're all to blame." I used my own voice in hopes he'd recognize it. "Now you'll pay. Number four, rot in hell."

I put my last bit of strength into pulling one final time. Dave gasped, shuddered, and then lay still.

Panting from excited exertion, I slowly rose on shaking legs, staggered back against the wall for a moment, and waited until my breathing and heart rate slowed before crossing the floor. I paused at the door. The hallway was empty and the path to the stairwell clear. I left Suzanne's room and hurried to my escape route.

A good kill, but God, I'm tired. I never expected killing to be so exhausting. I took a chance, but it worked. Maybe I should wait for Suzanne to show.

Finding the two of them dead—together—would be a nice touch. No, leave now. Catch your breath, then go find the bitch. Find her and make her pay. Soon they'll all be dead, and I can rest.

I exited to the stairwell, the door closing with a dull thud.

Chapter Ten

Zach finished his classmate's interrogations first and strolled from the bar into the lobby. People still wandered about even though it was after one o'clock. A group of classmates sat on the sofas and chairs arranged in the center of the lobby. Someone in the bar had mentioned talking with Marcella and her husband on the terrace. One of the women spotted Zach and waved him over. He recognized a couple of other familiar faces and decided to join them.

"Good to see you," Rudy Conrad said as Zach sat next to a man he didn't know. "Do you know everybody?"

"I know Marcella, Carol, and you."

"This is my wife, Liz." Rudy gestured to a petite blonde next to him.

A man in a brown suit reached for Zach's hand. "I'm Stan Saunders, Marcie's husband."

The third man also shook hands. "I'm Adam Quincy, Carol's date."

"Nice to meet all of you. Sorry the reunion took such a terrible turn," Zach commented.

Everyone shifted in their seats and Zach wondered if he'd been too abrupt in bringing up the subject of murder. This group wasn't swilling booze in the bar where no one had questioned why he'd been so curious. These people would. The end tables were strewn with coffee cups.

Zach could handle business and binary codes, but this idle chit-chat disguised as info gathering was new to him.

"Mind if I join you, too?" Meghan requested from behind him.

He twisted in his seat and breathed a sigh of relief. Reinforcements had arrived.

"Meghan, good to see you. You look great," Marcie exclaimed. "How did you do it? I swear I gain weight on every diet I try."

Meghan laughed as Zach leapt to his feet. "Here take my seat."

She accepted the offer. "I looked in the mirror one day and decided it was time to either do something about my weight or have 'Goodyear' tattooed on my rear end. And since I have an aversion to needles, I chose the former."

Zach liked the self-deprecating humor. Showed Meghan was well-grounded emotionally and didn't take herself too seriously.

"Well, before you leave, please tell me the secret of your success. My ass could use it," Marcy added.

"And you, Zach, you've changed, too," Carol said. "I'll be honest; I didn't recognize either of you."

"I saw the two of you dancing and wondered if the reunion had been crashed by a couple of freeloaders," Rudy added with a chuckle.

Meghan eyed the coffee cups scattered on the tables. "Where can a girl get some coffee?"

"Complimentary over in the corner." Stan indicated the direction with his chin.

"I'll go. Cream and sugar?" Zach confirmed. At

her nod he left. Returning, he sat on the arm of the sofa next to Meghan.

"So, what have you all been up to these past twenty years?" she asked.

Zach eyed Meghan as she listened to the lives and times of her classmates, and then questioned them about the evening's more gruesome event. "I was having a good time until Eileen found poor Annabelle," she stated.

"I still can't believe it," Marcie said with a shudder. "I saw Annabelle leave for the garden and never thought for a moment something sinister lurked."

"That's right, you were on the terrace with us," Meghan commented. "Did anyone follow her?"

"Can't say. I saw Dan Masterson run up the steps, but we were joking with Carl and Eileen and didn't pay any attention to much else."

"I remember him," Stan added sipping coffee from his cup. "He ran onto the terrace, stopped to smooth his hair, and then walked into the ballroom."

"I heard they caught some guy trying to break into cars in the parking lot. Maybe *he* wandered into the garden and attacked her," Liz contributed. "Glad I didn't decide to commune with nature, too."

"Did you see her leave?" Meghan queried.

"I saw someone in a blue dress leave. A lot of people came and went, but I don't know who."

"I saw Dan on the terrace, and I remember Betty Coleman and her husband walking down the steps. And Tom Ecklund," Rudy told them.

"Tom? He was in the garden?" Zach asked in a surprised voice.

He glanced at Meghan who raised her eyebrows

and shrugged. This was the first he'd heard of Tom Ecklund anywhere near the terrace *before* the body was found.

"Yeah, but damned if I know when. Don't recall seeing him come back."

"I don't remember seeing much of anybody," Carol said. "I stepped out on the terrace for a smoke and talked with Alicia Raines for a while. Suzanne came out with a couple of drinks and headed for the shadows at the far end. She ignored us. I figured she had a guy stashed over behind the potted plants. I thought I saw her leaving the terrace, too. Guess now it must have been Annabelle."

"That's right," her date replied. "I came out about that time. I remember somebody else going into the garden a few minutes later."

"Who?" Meghan and Zach spoke as one.

"I have no idea. Just a figure. I caught movement out of the corner of my eye. By the time I turned my head, whoever it was had disappeared."

"Too bad none of us paid any attention," Meghan commented.

"Why would we? The place was crowded, and we all had our own conversations going," Zach answered in a bland tone. Conversation had been the last thing on their minds.

He wasn't sure where all this questioning was leading. So far, no one had seen much of anything that would help them find a killer.

"Hi, is there room for one more?"

Glory Ecklund stood at the edge of the group. She'd changed from the black dress into a pair of navy blue slacks and a matching long sleeved t-shirt. It wasn't much of an improvement. The garments hung on her thin frame.

"Of course not," Zach said, rising. He felt sorry for her. She'd worked her rear end off for her husband's reunion and Annabelle's murder had destroyed it all. Poor Glory.

Stan also stood. "Here take my seat. Can I get you a cup of coffee?"

She dumped her large purse on the floor and sank into the plump cushions. "Oh, no thanks."

"I thought you went up to bed," Meghan murmured.

"I did, but couldn't sleep. Tom's snoring like a buzz saw and the murder upset me, so I decided to come back down for a while. I sat on the terrace to think. Such a horrible end to what I hoped would be a memorable reunion."

"It was that all right," Carol replied.

"I meant memorable in a good way. I was on my way back upstairs when I saw you guys and came over."

"How are you feeling?" Meghan asked.

"I'm fine. It was silly of me to faint like that, but first you said the body was Suzanne's, and then when she popped out from behind the bushes, I just lost it. I guess it was the combination of the shock of another body, and the heat in the ballroom."

"Another body?" Meghan questioned.

"In addition to Tami and Eddie, I mean." She brushed a stray lock of hair from her forehead and rearranged a pin in the knot of hair in her nape.

"You should have cooled off on the terrace earlier," Marcie suggested.

"Actually, I did. Took a little walk in the garden, too."

"When was this?" Zach asked. Glory was in the garden, too? Seemed as if the entire class had taken a damned stroll. This interrogation wasn't going well. There were too many people and a huge time frame.

"Oh, I can't remember. I was looking for Tom." She shifted in her seat and flashed a smile before casting her eyes down. "I—I was kind of worried about him."

"Worried? Why?" Meghan wondered.

"He'd had quite a bit to drink tonight. His diet sodas had a little additive—bourbon, I think. At any rate, I couldn't find him for the longest time, so I went outside. I thought maybe he was sick or, well, passed out, somewhere. I noticed a few people on the terrace, but the garden attracted a lot of walkers."

"Do you remember who you saw?" Zach hoped his question didn't sound like he was playing junior sheriff. So far, no one had brought the subject up as to why he and Meghan were asking.

Glory shook her head and stared at him with wide eyes. "Gosh, not really. I only went a little way down the path on the right. It was dark and I didn't want to twist an ankle in that gravel. I was returning when I saw someone, Dan, I think, charge up the steps. I caught a glimpse of someone else near the pathway to the pond, but don't know who. I came back inside and worked my way around the ballroom again. I finally found Tom near the terrace doors." She smiled. "At least he wasn't drunk like I feared. It seems he was looking for me, and we just kept missing each other."

This was the most Glory had said all night, but for

such a short time outside, she sure packed in a lot of information.

"Did you see either Suzanne or Annabelle?" Meghan asked.

She shook her head. "No. Like I said, it was really dark. Tom and I were about to call it a night when Eileen screamed the house down."

Carol sighed. "We spoke with Mary and Jack Samuels for a minute, and then returned to the dance floor. I didn't even hear the scream."

"You sure ask a lot of questions," Adam commented to Meghan. "Are you a cop?"

Zach held his breath. Would everyone clam up now?

She drained her coffee cup and set it on the table. "Hardly. I'm a mystery novelist. I guess my mind works that way. I want to know why, and how, and who. Occupational hazard." Meghan crossed her legs. "You know who I didn't see tonight? Monica Evans. Is she here? I can't believe she'd miss the twentieth reunion."

"She's here," Marcie asserted. "I spoke with her just before dinner. Her husband wasn't feeling well and didn't come. I think she may have gone home before all the excitement."

"That's too bad," Carol replied. "If she thought for one moment she'd miss seeing Suzanne Wayland floating in the koi pond, she'd have stuck around."

Zach drank some of his now lukewarm coffee. *Seems a lot of people wouldn't have minded finding Suzanne in the koi pond.*

Glory sat up straight with an earnest look on her face. "Oh, don't be unkind, Carol. I know Suzanne's hard to get along with. She and I had words earlier this evening, but she was upset. Dave Coryell left her alone most of the night."

"If Monica wanted to see anyone in the pond, it would have been Tami Robinson," Rudy suggested. He winked at his wife. "Monica and I dated for a while in high school. She and Tami had one hell of a rivalry going for the head cheerleader spot. When Monica won, Tami did a lot of character assassination. Monica spent days afterward trying to think up ways to kill her."

Liz Conrad laughed. "I used to think up ways to kill the girl who stole my boyfriend in seventh grade. Monica—was she the tall brunette I met at the memorial wall?"

"Probably. Wearing a yellow chiffon dress?" Marcie quizzed.

"Yes."

"That's her."

"She seemed nice. She identified all the people who had died," Liz added.

"What was her reaction to Tami's death?" Zach asked.

"Nothing as I recall. She talked more about some teacher who'd died recently."

"Oh, that would be Clara Sylvester," Glory chimed in. "She broke her hip last spring and her son arranged for her to stay in a convalescent home near him in Muncie. I understand she died suddenly. She must have been over eighty."

"Eighty? Try a hundred and eighty. I think she was eighty when she taught government," Rudy joked.

Zach chuckled. "That's true. She used to head up the youth group at the Methodist Church. Stern and always wanting to know what we evil teenagers were doing. My mother made me go to the Wednesday night meetings, hoping I'd find a girlfriend. Boy, was she ever wrong."

"Oh, I don't know," Glory replied with a smile. "Divine talked about how smart you were. Said she wished she had your brains for math."

Silence settled over the group at the mention of her sister. Glory had spoken as though Divine was in the next room. Her voice had no inflection, but then, her sister's death had occurred a long time ago. Zach couldn't think of anything to say. *What do you say to someone whose sister killed herself?*

Zach remembered Meghan telling him Glory had informed her of Divine's death in very blunt, unemotional terms. *Maybe that's the way she deals with it. The whole family was a little odd. Used to quote Scriptures.*

Carol cleared her throat and broke the silence.

"Meghan, since you seem to have taken an interest in this case, let me ask you a question."

"Go ahead."

"What's this I hear about a stun gun being used to incapacitate Annabelle?"

"A stun gun!" Glory exclaimed. She turned a wide, shocked gaze onto Carol.

"No kidding? Did you know about this, Marcie?" her husband asked with a concerned expression.

"First I've heard."

Stan shifted in his chair. "I don't like it. Maybe we shouldn't stay here tonight. Go find another hotel."

"I—I don't think anything like that has been found," Meghan stammered.

"Why would you think that?" Zach demanded. Damn, had they been that careless?

"Because Jennifer Hutchins passed by your table in the bar and heard you talking about it."

"I heard about it, too," Liz added. "In the ladies' room. Two women were talking."

Carol raised her eyebrows. "How about it? Is there a stun gun?"

"I really don't know. Zach and I were just tossing out a theory, that's all."

"Hell of a theory," Rudy said with a frown.

Carol waved a hand. "I have a stun gun in the car. I suppose the cops are going to root through our luggage and strip search us now." She stood and straightened her skirt. "I think I'll go up to bed before Ray Armstrong can molest me. Goodnight, everybody."

Her date also rose, and the couple walked away.

Rudy looked at his watch. "I suppose we should be thinking along those same lines. It's late, and we have an hour's drive ahead of us."

"You're not staying in the hotel?" Zach had assumed everyone was at the hotel.

"No, we live outside Indianapolis on Geist Reservoir. You ready, Liz?"

Glory yawned as couple number two left. "Goodness, how rude of me." She rose, leaned over and picked up her purse, hugging it to her body. "I guess I should try to sleep. Maybe Tom's quit snoring. See you tomorrow."

She walked toward the elevators, her steps slow as if too tired to go much further.

"I'm about ready to leave, too," Marcie told her husband.

Stan rose, shook hands with Zach, and placing his arm around Marcie's waist, escorted her to the elevators, leaving him alone with Meghan.

"Boy, do you know how to clear a room or what?"

"We'd taken it about as far as we could anyway," she replied. "Still it was interesting. What did you find out from the guys in the bar?"

"Not much. They were all irritated with Dave for pushing investments. He even used my name as a potential client."

"You're kidding. What chutzpah."

"Another guy said his wife referred to Tami and Eddie as Satan and Beelzebub, and called Dave and Suzanne their evil minions."

Meghan laughed, uncrossing and then re-crossing her legs, giving Zach a tantalizing view of a smooth thigh. He shifted his gaze and took a deep breath.

"A couple of them saw Dan run up the terrace steps, but that's about it. Did you have any better luck?"

"Not really. Everyone was busy and didn't pay a lot of attention to who was where. Betty *thought* she saw someone walking down the path toward the parking lot." She paused, a thoughtful expression on her face. "Would someone who'd just killed a person walk or run from the scene of the crime?"

"You tell me. You're the mystery writer." His gaze strayed back to her legs where the dress had ridden up, once again revealing her thigh, making it hard for him to keep his mind on the conversation.

"True, but if I'd just killed someone, I'd run like a rabbit. And if I were a psychopath, I wouldn't care who saw me. I'd feel invincible."

"Walking would be the smart thing to do," he

suggested in a distracted tone unable to keep his eyes off her creamy skin.

"Not necessarily smart, just patient. I've got to quit playing amateur detective and get into this guy's mind."

"You can do that?"

She shrugged and smiled. "It's all part of writing convincing characters. Actors do it all the time."

"Anything else?"

"Betty also said she saw Dan near the koi pond with a cell phone in his hand."

"A cell phone or a stun gun?" Much to Zach's disappointment, Meghan uncrossed her legs and leaned forward, elbows on her knees and chin cupped in her hands.

"I wondered, too. Alicia was miffed at Suzanne for flirting with her date, but that's par for the course."

"It sounds as if we've got a great big bunch of nothing. Most people saw something, but can't remember what. And those that remember who have no idea of when."

"I did pick up some information. Eileen confirmed the police contacted her about both Tami and Eddie's deaths, but that neither of them had accepted the invitation yet. She seems to think Dave and Suzanne had accepted fairly soon after the invitations had been mailed. She dealt with much of the communications, but said Monica was in charge of compiling a data base for future reunions."

"Monica of the rival cheerleader fame?"

"The same. Eileen also told me Dan, Tom, Glory, and others tracked down addresses of lost classmates, and verified others."

"Which means a whole lot of people had access to

the information, including the person who stuck the labels on the envelopes." Zach ran a hand over his face, suddenly tired. "Are we getting anywhere with this?"

She sighed and sat back. "I have no idea. It's much easier in a novel."

"Are you hungry?"

She sighed and nodded. "Starving. Think the kitchen's still open?"

He grabbed her hand, hauling her to her feet. She used his shoulders to steady herself. Zach took advantage of the opportunity to drop a light kiss on her lips. "If it's not, there must be leftovers from the reunion banquet. Maybe we can raid the refrigerator."

Eating might not be sexy, but it was the best he could do.

****

Meghan wandered back into the lounge while Zach headed for the kitchen. The room had cleared out, so she chose a table near the bar. Eileen and her group were gone, as were the men Zach had questioned. She nodded to a few classmates enjoying a nightcap. A couple sat at the bar where Suzanne had been, and a man sipped a beer a few stools down. She didn't recognize any of them, and assumed they were not connected to the reunion.

"Hey, is it true someone was murdered in the garden tonight?" the lone man asked in a loud voice. The couple ceased their conversation and stared.

The bartender, wiping down the bar, answered, "I haven't heard anything about a murder, but some woman got drunk, fell into a fish pond, and drowned."

"Good Lord, how bizarre," the woman remarked.

"I've been a bartender for ten years and you

166

wouldn't believe the things I've seen. Why, once there was this guy…"

Meghan tuned out the story. So, that was the hotel's official stance on the events of the evening. She supposed it made sense.

Hotels do not like the word 'murder' bandied about in reference to their establishments. Bad for business.

Zach returned with two Styrofoam plates filled with sandwiches and potato salad.

"This looks delicious." she said as he set one in front of her. From his pockets, he produced two cans of cold soda. "And complete with good service, too."

Zach laughed. "My pleasure, ma'am. Please remember I work for tips. Hope roast beef is all right with you."

"It's fine. How did you manage this?"

"There were a couple of line cooks cleaning up. I slipped them each a twenty, and they spent five minutes dishing up the grub."

More generosity to a couple of tired people who put in a long night over a hot stove. And I thought nice guys were a myth.

Hungrier than she thought, Meghan took a bite of medium-rare roast beef sandwich. A sharp pain zipped along her jaw to her salivary glands. She chewed the tingle away, licking a dollop of horseradish sauce from her finger. She swallowed, and then told Zach about the conversation at the bar.

"That makes sense," he affirmed, echoing her thoughts. "Hotels and restaurants are real touchy about murder."

"I can't believe the news about the stun gun got

out. Do you think Ray will be mad at us?"

"Could be, but I can't see how he would have kept the news quiet much longer. Just like the hotel's story will be blown away by the news reports tomorrow." He took a bite of his sandwich, forked potato salad into his mouth, and ate before continuing. "*Did* we get anything of interest from the conversation in the lobby?"

"I had no idea Monica Evans hated Tami so much."

"Somehow, I think Monica's moved on. Besides, why would she want to kill Eddie Mancuso or Suzanne?" he asked.

"Good point, but maybe she held a grudge against the women. Where Tami went, Suzanne followed. Monica was like the invisible cheerleader tonight. Nobody recalls seeing her after dinner."

Zach popped the top on his soda can, took a long swallow, and then shrugged.

"If her husband was sick, she may have left. If I hadn't met you, I'd have left early." He wiped a morsel of sauce from the corner of her mouth, and popped it onto the tip of his tongue.

Her heart rate accelerated. *Wonder what else that tongue can do.*

"Thank you." Not to be outdone, Meghan set the sandwich on the plate, and licked, then sucked imagined condiments from her fingers, her gaze never leaving his. "I find it interesting Tom was running all over looking for Glory—and they were both in the garden."

Zach ceased staring at her fingers, heaved a deep sigh and took another bite of his sandwich. "But once again, we have no time frame. Do you remember seeing either of them while we were talking?"

"No, and we weren't talking much." She chuckled, opened her soda, and sipped. Under the table she crossed her legs, allowing her foot to slide a couple of inches up his leg. "At least not all the time. I don't remember seeing either Tom or Glory outside of the ballroom. Although I do remember Tom stumbling like he'd had one too many in the bar."

Zach made a noise deep in his throat before saying, "And Glory ran all over the place tonight. I suppose if her husband hadn't seen her in an hour, he'd have gone looking."

She inched her foot closer to his knee. "You know, if I had to name a suspect right now, it'd be Dan Masterson. He was pissed at Suzanne, took a walk in the garden to cool down, mistook Annabelle for her in the dark, and accidentally killed her."

"And the stun gun?" Zach leaned forward, his fingers stroking her hand.

The light caress made her stomach flutter. "I don't know. Maybe he habitually carries one, or just wanted to scare the crap out of her—zap, and then laugh—only got carried away."

"There could be something in what you say. I was the President of the Math Club my senior year and a representative to the student council. Dan didn't like anyone contradicting or disagreeing with him. As senior class president, he chaired most council meetings. He was a real stickler for following parliamentary procedure and Roberts' Rules of Order."

"We know he's a tight-ass, but did he ever get angry?" Meghan asked. Without removing her hand from Zach's touch, she finished her sandwich and pushed the empty plate away. Never had she eaten under such sexy circumstances.

"Not exactly angry, but he tended to lecture when the rules weren't followed. I remember one kid telling him this wasn't the halls of Congress and to lighten up. Dan didn't like it."

"Repressed anger," Meghan mused. "The worst kind."

"This is all speculation, of course." His fingertip drew little circles on the back of her hand.

She drew in a sharp breath as a vibration zipped up her arm. Meghan's foot rose higher on Zach's leg, and her reply sounded breathy. "Of course. There's...there's absolutely no proof to any of this."

Zach leaned forward with a wicked smile.

The sexual by-play ended when the sheriff walked through the door, slapped his hat on the table and called for a cup of coffee. Meghan and Zach removed hands and feet from sensitive areas of each other's bodies. The bartender poured one, brought it to him, and carted off their plates as he left.

Ray sighed heavily and sank into the chair. "Hell of a night." He doctored his coffee with cream and sugar, blew on the steaming liquid, cautiously took a sip, and then fastened his gaze on the two of them. "I hear the news is out about the stun gun."

Warmth flooded Meghan's face. Zach raised one shoulder and turned his hands palms up.

"Sorry, Ray, but someone must have overheard Meghan and me talking. The bar was crowded and noisy."

"I guess our voices rose to compensate. Did we screw things up for you?" she inquired.

"Well, I didn't want that information revealed to the public, but I should have told you not to discuss it. What did you find out from the people you talked to?"

Meghan and Zach told him of their discussions in the bar and in the lobby.

"Sheriff, I'm not sure you're ever going to find the killer," Zach added with a shake of his head.

Meghan took a sip from the soda can. "I find that Tami and Eddie being killed before accepting the invitation interesting but have no idea where to run with it. If I were writing this, they'd accept, and all the murders would occur here."

"But this isn't a mystery novel. It's real. I've already contacted the police in California and Texas. They'll fax or e-mail me the files overnight. The killer may have slipped up and left evidence. God knows, there's not much to go on here."

Meghan told him her theory about Dan Masterson as the killer.

Ray drank more coffee and raised an eyebrow. "It's an interesting theory, but that's all it is. I can't put him and Mrs. Peterson at the pond at the same time. I do, however, want to have another chat with Mr. Coryell, as soon as I find him."

Zach's eyebrows rose. "He's missing?"

"I wouldn't call him missing, just not around. I knocked on his door and got no answer. Of course, if he was as drunk as Mrs. Crocker says, he may have passed out. In which case, I could have used a battering ram and he wouldn't have heard me." Ray finished his coffee.

"Did you check Suzanne's room?" Zach said.

"He wouldn't be with her," Meghan declared.

"Suzanne was furious with him most of the night. I don't think she'd reward his actions with an invite to her room."

"She didn't have a whole lot nice to say about him when I talked with her earlier," Ray confirmed. "Besides, I think I saw her in the lobby not too long ago."

Ray's cell phone rang. He jerked it from its holder on his belt and answered with a crisp, "Armstrong."

Meghan fingered her soda can and tipped the remainder of the lukewarm contents down her throat.

The sheriff listened for several seconds before saying, "Is the forensics truck still here? Bag it and get Joey to print it asap. I doubt we'll find anything other than the waiter's prints, but it's worth a try. Let me know what you find out." He snapped the phone shut.

"More evidence?" Zach asked.

Ray nodded, and swiped a hand through his hair. "Yeah, a waiter bringing down a room service cart made too sharp a turn out of the service elevator and overturned a trash receptacle. Guess what fell out?"

"What?" Meghan held her breath in anticipation.

"A stun gun."

Chapter Eleven

Meghan rested her forehead on her hands and moaned. "Oh, God, this is our fault. The killer heard about the stun gun and ditched it."

"I'm sorry, Ray. We screwed up," Zach admitted.

The sheriff ran his hand through his hair. "Not all your fault. Like I said, I should have told you not to say anything. Puts a crimp in my plans. Even the waiter knew about its importance. Unfortunately, he handled it. The stun gun's being checked now, but my guess is his will be the only prints we find."

"Ah, nuts," Meghan said with another moan. "I write mysteries for crying out loud. I should have known better."

Zach clasped her hand, squeezing gently. "You're a writer. I'm a software exec, which means we're not professional criminologists. Nothing we can do about it now." He turned back to Ray. "It's getting late. Are you still interviewing?"

"The deputies are finishing up as we speak. Most people have been remarkably patient, considering the chance of actually finding someone who saw something is slim."

"Ray, do you mind if I have a look at the stun gun? I've never seen one before. It might be something I could use in one of my books."

"I have no objection, but you'll have to wait until

after it's been printed."

"No need to wait. I've got one in my room," Zach told her.

"You have a stun gun?" Ray asked with raised eyebrows.

He shrugged. "I prefer it to the .38 Smith and Wesson revolver in my suitcase. Only use deadly force as a last resort."

Meghan stared as a sudden breeze from the air conditioning vent sent a chill racing along her skin. She shivered, rubbing her arms.

"But you flew here. How did you get them past airport security?"

"I used the corporate jet." He rose. "Let me go get it. I'll be back in a couple of minutes."

Meghan bit her lip as he left the room. Zach had come to the reunion armed? Why?

"You must lead an interesting life," Ray said bringing her attention back. "I heard you've been on a book signing tour. What do you do? Besides, travel and sign books, of course."

Meghan laughed. "That's about it. People think it's so glamorous going to different cities and spending an hour or two inside a bookstore, then lounging by the pool the rest of the day. Doesn't happen. If I'm not signing my name over and over, I'm holed up in hotel rooms writing. I live and work out of North Carolina, but the last three or four months have been crazy. I've been all over the country. At least I got to see my folks this time."

"Where do they live?"

"Dallas. Dad retired three years ago. He plays golf every day and lies about his score, while Mom indulges her passion for bridge. I was there in early June, and swear both of them look younger than ever. Hope it's a family trait."

"Do you ever forget which city you're in?" Ray wondered.

"Believe it or not, that did happen. I was on a tight schedule, and whipped from Seattle to San Diego in less than two weeks in late April. I signed a book for a lady in Fresno and commented on how much I enjoyed being in Sacramento. Major embarrassment." She leaned forward. "Don't tell anybody, but sometimes I have to stop and think if it's Monday or Tuesday."

Ray grinned. "I can imagine."

Zach returned and handed her the stun gun. Small and compact, it fit easily in her hand. An on/off switch on the side was millimeters from her thumb. She slid it upwards and a tiny green light glowed.

"I take it this is the business end of things," she said indicating a red button above the switch. Without waiting for an answer, she pressed it. The resulting arc of electricity sizzled, startling her.

The few people remaining in the bar stared.

She dropped the device on the table. "Holy shit! I wasn't expecting that. Sounds like it can do major damage."

"It has a lot of voltage, but unless you hold the button down for a long time or zap someone repeatedly, it merely incapacitates."

"Why do you feel it necessary to bring a stun gun and a .38 to a high school reunion?" The sheriff echoed Meghan's thoughts of earlier.

Zach resumed his seat. "About three or four years ago, I had to fire a guy. He sent me threatening letters and e-mails. Also harassed me with voicemail. Then one night while driving home from the office, a car rear-ended me and drove off. The police eventually arrested the guy, but I decided personal protection was the route to go."

"I assume you have a license and know how to use the Smith and Wesson."

"Of course, I do."

Ray smiled. "Just checking. Meghan and I were talking about family and such. What about you, Zach? Do your parents still live in Grandview?"

He shook his head. "Mom and Dad moved to St. Louis shortly after I graduated from high school. Dad was an engineer with a large chemical company until retiring last year. They loved the area, but can't take the winters any more. Southern California is home now. That's one reason why I bought out a small software company in Los Angeles. It gives me an excuse to drop in and check on them every few months. Neither of them is in the best of health."

"I've talked to so many people tonight, I can't remember where you hang your hat," Ray commented.

"Phoenix."

"House or condo?" Meghan inquired.

"House. I don't like rules, or people with nothing better to do except sit on condo boards telling me what I can and can't do. On the other hand, for my parents, a condo was the only answer. I helped them set up housekeeping in Brentwood last spring."

Ray's phone rang. "Armstrong." He listened for a few seconds, and then said, "Okay, thanks, I'm on my way." He snapped the phone shut. "The last person just left the ballroom. I'd better go see if I can locate

Coryell." He slapped his hat on his head and left.

"It sounds as if you and I were in the same parts of the country at the same time," Meghan remarked.

"Too bad we didn't know. We could have met for dinner or something." He gazed toward the bar. "I'm thirsty. Would you like a bottle of water?"

"Thank you, yes."

Zach returned with two and unscrewed the top of one before handing it to her. "What do you think of all this? Is it fodder for a new book?"

"Maybe. What I'd really like to do is take some time off. No writing, no tours, no nothing. I'd love to go someplace warm for the winter and just vegetate."

"Why don't you?"

"It's called a contract. I owe my publisher two more books, and she's demanding the next one in six months. Until tonight, I didn't have any ideas regarding plots."

"Sounds like you might be suffering burnout."

"That's what I told my agent, Beth. She said to keep writing."

Actually, Beth had told her to find a man and have a little fun, but Meghan didn't think Zach needed to know that. Besides, Beth could be right. She pigeonholed the thought of a naked Zach into a corner of her mind.

"Not very sympathetic."

Meghan tilted the bottle to her lips and drank. "Which is why I'm seriously considering finding a new agent. What about you? Do you intend to own all of Silicon Valley?"

Zach grimaced. "Never crossed my mind. I like my company the size it is now. Nothing further east than

Dallas. I can travel to and from all of them in less than three days, and get back to Phoenix with a minimum of effort."

"What do you do for fun?"

"Play video and computer games."

"That's it? No sports?"

He grinned. "I never cared for sports, but have a pool and swim laps when time allows. I also have a home gym I use on a regular basis. I hate golf, tennis, and jogging, and while I play a mean game of bridge, I hate that, too."

"Any weaknesses I should know about?" Meghan tilted the bottle again.

Zach leaned forward, smiled a killer smile, and whispered, "Yes. Twice a year I go to Vegas and play Texas Hold 'em. How about you?"

She mimicked his actions, their faces inches apart. "I pretend to be Broadway star and do high kicks to soundtracks on my iPod. My favorite is *Chicago*."

"We lead such decadent lives." He closed the gap, giving her a brief, hard kiss, and then extended his hand palm up.

Meghan's lips tingled and heat suffused her body. She had the most incredible urge to say screw it, pull him down on the table and rip his clothes off. Instead, she slipped her hand into his. If they had left the terrace two minutes earlier, they'd have never had to deal with Eileen or any of this. They'd have been upstairs in her room tangled in the sheets.

He's fabulous. Why couldn't I have found him years ago?

Zach rubbed his thumb over the back of her hand sending a zing of electricity up her arm.

She inhaled a deep breath to clear her head of erotic fantasies. "Okay, so you don't want to own all of Silicon Valley. You're happy with your little slice of the American dream. What do you see yourself doing at, say our fortieth reunion?"

"Lord, I have no idea. I'll be fifty-eight years old and probably retired."

"Retired? At fifty-eight? What would you do to keep busy? Swap fishing stories with your buddies?"

He grinned. "I don't like drowning worms either. To be honest, I doubt if I'll ever retire. That's the beauty of technology. It's always advancing, changing. Something new comes along every day. What about you? Will you be writing on your deathbed?"

Meghan drank from her water bottle before answering. The heat within hadn't subsided. His kiss had fanned the embers, and she still tasted him on her lips. Her skin burned from the touch of his hands.

"God, I hope not, but if I am, I want it to be for my grandchildren."

"Don't you have to have children before you contemplate grandchildren?"

She leaned forward again and gazed into his eyes. "Yes. And I'd love to have oodles of them—uh, grandchildren, that is."

He squeezed her hand. "Maybe the right guy will come along and get you started."

"Maybe he will."

Maybe he already has.

Meghan looked up when a figure passed the table. The real world cut off her fantasies. "Suzanne's back."

Dammit. Just when things were getting interesting.

Zach frowned and released her hands. "She

shouldn't be wandering around alone. Someone's already taken a crack at killing her. What's she thinking anyway?"

Meghan sat back, a little jab of jealousy darting through her. Why was Zach so concerned about a woman who had no problem taking care of *numero uno*?

****

What's wrong with me? I should be holed up like a gopher, but instead I'm running around looking for Dave, and I have no idea why.

Suzanne entered the bar and noticed Zach and Meghan, holding hands, their heads bent close together and smiles on their faces.

Glad someone's having a good time. Bitch. What does he see in her? Or maybe tackling a real woman scares the shit out of him.

Being dumped by two men in one night was a first and left a bad taste in her mouth. She needed a drink.

She sailed past their table and headed for the bar. She spied a couple of familiar faces and nodded as she slipped onto a stool. The bartender didn't bother asking. He set a cosmopolitan in front of her. She sipped and sighed.

Damn all men to hell, she thought. Her irritation at being unable to locate her so-called date had transformed to worry. She'd trod every square inch of this stinking hotel and come up with zilch.

She eyed the man and woman at the table next to the bar. He was a big guy and she vaguely remembered he'd played football. Dave had pitched his investment scheme to every other teammate tonight. Why not this guy, too?

She hated to admit, and have others realize, she'd been dumped, but finding Dave had taken on an urgency she couldn't explain.

Swallowing her pride, Suzanne asked, "Excuse me, but didn't you play football with Dave Coryell?"

"Sure did. Linebacker. Name's Bill Rafferty. This is my wife Jane."

"Have you seen him tonight?"

The man rolled his eyes and made a face. "I'll say. He hung me up for close to twenty minutes jawing about some investment opportunity. The minute his back was turned, I disappeared."

"Yeah, I can understand that. He did the same to me. But I mean have you seen him lately?"

"I saw him getting into the elevator," the woman replied.

"When was that?"

"I don't know. We had just been interviewed by the police and decided to come in here for a drink. Maybe an hour or so. Isn't it awful what happened?"

"Yeah, awful," Suzanne muttered. "Was he alone?"

"I can't remember. There were a bunch of people in the lobby and others heading toward their rooms. I imagine someone got on the elevator with him." The woman shook her head. "I'm really upset about Annabelle. I graduated with her and she was the sweetest person I've ever met. Is it true she was killed with a stun gun?"

"A what?" She stared in consternation. A stun gun? She owned one. Charlie had bought it for her. She carried it whenever she went out at night.

"That's what I heard. Why would anyone want to do that?"

"Stun guns don't kill. They incapacitate." Suzanne brushed a lock of hair over her shoulder. She wished she'd brought the damned thing with her.

It might come in handy now.

Unfortunately, it was back in Chicago. She remembered how Dave had laughed when she carried it on one of their dates a few months ago.

"Well, I just know I won't sleep a wink tonight." Jane turned to Bill. "I could use another drink."

"I think we should go to bed." The couple got up to leave. "Nice to see you again, Suzanne. Have a safe trip home.

"Yeah, you, too," she said to their backs as they walked away.

She sat, sipping a cosmo she didn't really want and tapped her fingernails on the counter, then straightened when a thought occurred to her.

When was the last time she'd seen her stun gun? She bit her lip and tried to recall the image. She remembered carelessly tossing her purse onto the foyer table one night about two weeks ago. She and Dave had been out to dinner, and come up to her place for a nightcap. For the life of her, she couldn't recollect if she'd put it away or even seen it since.

A nasty thought ran through her mind.

Could Dave have taken it?

"But why?" she whispered. "Why would he steal my stun gun unless…"

A chill traced down her spine like the finger of death.

No, it's not possible…or is it?

She gulped the rest of her drink and gripped the edge of the bar when her head spun. Giddy, she pressed her fingers to her mouth and breathed deeply. The room stopped tilting.

"Get a grip, Suzanne," she muttered to herself. "If Dave wanted to bump you off, he'd have done it in Chicago, not Grandview, Indiana."

She wished she'd quit this silly vacillating between thinking one minute Dave was a killer, and then declaring him too much of a weenie to murder anyone.

A quick scan of the room showed Meghan and Zach still seated at their table. Another couple sat at the end of the bar. A lone man a few stools away shot her a glance and a smile. She looked away.

She needed to resume her search for Dave. Could he have gone into the garden? In view of the night's events, the thought of traversing those dark paths made her skin crawl.

Maybe we've just been missing each other.

She had no clue how long she'd looked earlier. Dave had been pretty hammered, not to mention high. She'd try his room again.

Signing her tab, she slid from the stool.

"Suzanne," Zach said. She paused next to the table. "What?"

"Have you changed rooms yet?"

"No." His earlier brush-off still rankled.

"You shouldn't be wandering around by yourself," Meghan added. "I have the feeling this nastiness isn't over. Please, don't take unnecessary chances."

"Are you telling me to go hide in my room?"
Prissy bitch.

"No, Meghan and I are just concerned about you. Whatever the motive, Annabelle's death was a case of mistaken identity," Zach answered with a frown. "You were the target."

Suzanne read the concern in their eyes and her irritation ebbed. She agreed. And while she didn't believe anyone was so angry they'd kill her, the robbery angle by a stranger—perhaps a persistent stranger—was still a possibility. She drew a deep breath.

"Thanks, but I'll be all right. At the moment, I'm looking for Dave. Have you seen him?"

"Not lately. The sheriff's looking for him, too," Meghan said.

"He's probably passed out in his room. By the way, what's this I hear about a stun gun?"

Meghan blushed and Zach shifted in his chair.

"Yeah, we heard a rumor to that effect," he muttered.

Rumor my ass. I'll bet it's true. They both look guilty as hell about something.

"Well, I'll see you in the morning." She turned to leave.

"Don't forget about the room," Zach reminded her.

She waved a hand, exited the bar, and headed for the elevators. The doors opened. She stepped inside, punching the button for the third floor and tapping her foot, until the car stopped. She hurried down the hallway to Dave's room.

Her knock went unanswered, and she risked calling, "Dave, are you in there? Open the damned door."

Suzanne shivered. She could swear she wasn't alone. A nervous glance up and down the corridor reassured her.

She knocked again, harder this time. "Dave, you asshole, open the goddamned door."

When the door remained steadfastly closed, she pressed her ear against the wood. The interior was quiet as a tomb.

The miserable slug. If he's ignoring me, I swear I'll kill the son of a bitch.

Remembering how it was unlocked earlier, she twisted the knob. It didn't turn. Suzanne gave up and walked back toward the elevators. She thought she heard a breathy sigh followed by a creaking sound. It made her stop and turn, her heart in her throat.

The corridor was empty, yet she had the impression someone watched. Her flesh rose in goose bumps. She whirled and ran. Reaching the elevators, she frantically jabbed the down indicator and cast a panicked eye toward the stairwell exit.

The elevator hadn't moved from its previous ascent. The doors opened and Suzanne stumbled inside, punching the button for the lobby. She held her fist over her pounding heart. Now, safe in the cocoon of the steel car, she felt like a fool.

Idiot. I'm letting my imagination run wild.

While her heartbeat returned to normal, she still pondered her problem of finding Dave. They had to talk.

Back in the lobby, Suzanne hesitated. *What do I do now? The garden? No, not alone. Ask Meghan and Zach to go along? And watch them hold hands like a couple of teenagers? I don't think so.*

Then an idea popped into her mind. She pivoted and walked toward the registration desk.

It would be risky, but she had to take the chance.

****

Suzanne is an idiot.

She wandered all over the hotel like she didn't have a care in the world. Spying on her was easy. She sensed someone in the shadows, but I was too clever to let myself be seen. I chuckled. I did, however, make just enough noise to scare the bitch into panic mode. It was fun watching that perfectly made up face disintegrate into a mask of fear. I almost laughed out loud as she scampered toward the elevator, her gaze darting from side to side. I came out of the stairwell when the doors closed. Not time yet to show myself.

Until I want to, that is.

Attacking her in the hallway or her room was off the agenda. She might make noise and rouse other guests. Then I'd be seen. And I no longer have the stun gun. Too bad. The stun gun was my secret ingredient. I laughed. Secret ingredient, like on one of those cooking shows. Only my main course was revenge with a side of murder.

The elevator indicator showed the car had reached the lobby. Maybe I should have taken the chance and nailed her right outside Coryell's room. It had been tempting. But it's good to resist temptation.

No, I'd keep following and wait for her to make a mistake. She wasn't that bright, plus she had a lot to drink—just like her late boyfriend.

I'll get you sooner or later. That's a promise, bitch.

Chapter Twelve

Suzanne rested her arms on the cool granite of the front desk counter. The area was empty, but a lighted doorway along the back wall and the distinct chattering of a printer told her the clerk was probably back there retrieving a computer printout.

"Hello, anybody here?" she called impatiently. Suzanne wanted to get this over and done with before her nerve failed.

A young man stepped out. "May I help you?"

"Yes. I can't find my key. Must have left it in the room. I wonder if I could have another."

"Of course," the clerk replied with a smile. "What's your name and room number?"

"Uh, Coryell, and the room is three-twenty-six."

The man disappeared, and then returned a moment later with the key.

"Here you go, ma'am." The clerk hadn't bothered to check that Dave had a single occupancy room or have her show ID.

"Thanks." She turned and blew out a breath.

Well, that was easy. Thank God for incompetency.

Suzanne clutched the key and scurried for the elevators.

She exited on the third floor and paused, remembering her fear of a while ago. Her gaze scanned the hallways, but her ears picked up no sound.

Convinced she was alone, she hustled to Dave's room. Three-twenty-six was almost at the end of the hall, two rooms away from the vending machines, and another stairwell. She inserted the key and opened the door.

Dammit!

The room was just as she'd left it earlier. The lights still blazed and the bed remained in pristine condition. Wherever Dave slept, it wasn't here. A quick check of the bathroom showed the mirror with its powdery residue had not been moved.

Maybe the son of a bitch found a willing partner, after all.

If that was the case, then he wouldn't return for hours. And she needed to talk to him now.

Suzanne walked to the closet door, opening it slowly. No one jumped out. Feeling foolish, but safe, she patted every piece of clothing hanging from the rod. No stun gun surfaced.

She turned her attention to the drawers. Empty, but his suitcase was on the old-fashioned suitcase rack. She unzipped it and searched among the clothing, holding up a pair of red silk boxers. Suzanne stifled a laugh.

You've got to be kidding. Red? Did he plan on impressing me with these?

She stuffed them back into the suitcase and rifled through all the side pockets, then slammed the lid down in irritation. No stun gun.

Suzanne sat on the edge of the bed. Maybe he didn't have it after all. *Maybe* all those damned cosmos and the warnings from Meghan, Zach, and Sheriff Andy had made her paranoid.

Then, the barest whisper of footsteps on carpet sent a chill slithering down her spine. Her scalp prickled.

Slowly, she turned her head toward the door. It stood ajar by less than an inch—the way she'd found it earlier in the evening.

I closed it when I came in, didn't I?

With her heart pounding, she rose and walked stiffly toward the door, grasped the doorknob with a shaky hand, and yanked. She faced...nothing. The corridor was empty. Suzanne poked her head out. No one lurked. In the vending space, the soda and ice machines hummed. She jumped when ice tumbled into the bin with a muted clatter.

Exhaling a pent up breath she hadn't realized she'd held, Suzanne inspected the latch, pushing it in and out. It sometimes stuck in. Sighing, she shut the door, and leaned against it until she heard the click.

She turned and spied Dave's briefcase on a small table next to a chair on the far side of the bed. A sense of urgency, perhaps a residual of her fright a moment before, sent her striding across the room. The briefcase was closed, but not locked. She opened it.

Suzanne riffled through the papers and the compartments. No stun gun appeared. Then, she stopped to read the contents in her hand.

I,_____, on this date,_____, do hereby authorize David Coryell to buy and sell on my behalf any and all investments in Global Mining and Precious Gems, LLC. I understand that this is a speculative enterprise, and absolve David Coryell from responsibility in case of severe financial loss.

Her jaw dropped. Did Dave really believe she or anybody with an ounce of sense would sign a document as silly as this? He had close to fifty of the blank affidavits. None had been signed.

He must be a cock-eyed optimist. How high was he when he printed this?

She shook her head. Dave was a bigger jerk than she thought. A key tucked into the back corner caught her attention. Suzanne picked it up and tossed the papers into the briefcase. An alarm fob dangled—a spare car key. She hesitated and fingered the embossed letters on the head.

If Dave had stolen her stun gun, she assumed he must have kept it in his room. But what if he hadn't? What if he'd hidden it in the car?

And if he's as drunk as I think, could he be sleeping it off in the Mercedes after all? Just because he wasn't there earlier, doesn't mean he isn't now.

She closed her fingers over the key. There was only one way to find out. She'd go look in the car again.

Slipping the room key into her purse, Suzanne emerged into the hallway, looked right and left, then walked swiftly to the elevators. The doors opened, and as they slid shut, she thought the stairwell door opened a crack.

Her breath stuck in her throat until the car descended. When the doors opened again, she faced an empty lobby.

Ignore your heebie-jeebie nerves. Concentrate on finding Dave and your stun gun.

Her high heels clacked on the terrazzo floor, the sound echoing. She pushed the front doors open and paused. Instinct told her to forget about searching the car. To steady her shaking hands, she lit a cigarette and surveyed the parking lot through the wispy smoke. Nothing moved. A light breeze stroked the leaves on the trees. She shivered. The rustling reminded Suzanne of taffeta skirts on a dance floor. She hated taffeta—a stiff, noisy fabric that had always seemed sinister. Like snakes wiggling through the underbrush.

Boy, am I ever jazzed with imagination tonight. Come on, get it over with.

She crushed the cigarette under her sandaled foot and paced for several minutes not wanting to walk down the steps toward the parking lot. Screwing up her courage, Suzanne swallowed and shivered again in spite of the line of sweat trickling down her back as the humid night air cloaked her skin. With a pounding heart, she hurried, winding through the parked cars until spotting the Mercedes.

Breathing a sigh of relief, she approached the car and knocked on the tinted windows again. When no one answered, she pushed a button on the alarm fob. The lights blinked twice. She grasped the handle and opened the driver's side door.

Dave's car was as empty as his room. Suzanne slid into the front seat and rooted in the console. The only gun she found was a Beretta. The temptation to take it was strong, but in the end left it alone. She leaned across and checked the glove compartment pulling out the owner's manual, the registration, a three-pack of golf balls, leather driving gloves, and a bottle of aspirin. Everything except a stun gun.

She slammed the lid and searched under the seats. It was squeaky clean. Detailing had its drawbacks. Suzanne leaned over the console and checked the back seat. The pockets in the seat backs were also empty.

That left the trunk.

She pressed the trunk release. It popped open and she strode to the rear of the car. The trunk was cleaner than a dog-licked plate at a family reunion. Curiosity got the better of her. She poked around the spare tire well, and then tugged at the corner of the carpet near the left taillight. Nestled under the covering lay Dave's stash—five small baggies containing a white substance.

Suzanne was tempted to dump it in the koi pond. Instead, she closed the trunk, turned, and leaned against the car.

Now what?

She gave up. She'd go to bed and tackle the asshole in the morning. Pushing away from the trunk, a slight rustling from the hedge separating the parking lot and the garden ten feet away had her frozen. She turned her head to look. Nothing.

The breeze. It's just the breeze.

Gravel crunched. Her heart rate soared and her breathing accelerated.

"Who's there?" she called out in a shaky voice. Silence answered. "Dave, is that you?" More silence tightened her already tense muscles. "All right, if you're trying to scare me, I'll be a big girl and admit you have, okay? Now, come on out. We need to talk."

The silence lengthened. No one answered. That was more unnerving than the furtive sounds. She bit her lip, turned, and strode at a brisk pace toward the hotel, slipping between cars to put as much distance between her and the garden as possible.

Suzanne paused with a hand to her throat, listening. Silence yet again. Then she heard it, what sounded like footsteps from behind her. She whirled. The noise ceased. No one was there. *Maybe I should have kept the gun.* Too late now. No way was she going back to the car.

She resumed her pace, walking faster. Was someone following or was she hearing the wind and what her imagination told her to hear? A pebble tumbled across the asphalt as though kicked by a careless foot.

Suzanne abandoned all pretence of control. She broke into a run and raced for the hotel entrance. Her heart pounding in her ears blotted out all other sounds. Panting, she reached her destination, stumbled up the steps, and jerked open the door. Inside, she whirled and, cupping her hands on either side of her eyes, peered out. Nothing moved.

For the love of God, calm down. No one's there.

She straightened and walked several steps into the lobby.

****

Anger pounded in my ears. There was Suzanne Wayland, alone, in the parking lot. In books, she'd be called too stupid to live. I agreed, but smothered my anger.

I left the hotel to grab another weapon from the car and had just hidden it in the garden when a car door slammed not far away. Peeking through a gap in the hedge, I caught a glimpse of her. She rooted around in the trunk before banging the lid down and leaning against the bumper. A moment later, she headed back toward the front doors.

I mentally cursed. I had missed a golden opportunity. No time to grab the weapon I'd selected. Instead, I picked up one of the rocks lining the garden path. Perhaps, if I hurried I could catch her between cars. But she moved too fast and the distance between us was too far. I made noise and the bitch spooked, forcing me to hunker down behind a car until she disappeared inside. I tossed the rock under a car and vented my frustration by kicking the rear quarter panel leaving several large dents. Damn, damn, damn! I inhaled two or three deep breaths.

Be patient. You'll get her. You can't fail now.

****

The bar beckoned, but another drink was the last thing Suzanne needed. She still clutched the spare key in her hand. Unzipping her purse, she dropped it inside next to Dave's room key, which reminded her of her promise to Zach and Meghan.

She marched up to the desk again and called out, "Any one here?"

The clerk emerged and smiled. "Yes, ma'am?"

"I'd like to change rooms."

"Is there a problem?"

"Yes. Someone has been killed in this hotel, and I want another room. My name is Crocker and I'm in room four-twenty."

The clerk looked confused. "But didn't I just give you a key to room three-twenty-six?"

"Yes. I was looking for my friend. Now, I want another room. It can be next door, across the hall or anywhere. I don't care."

The clerk checked the computer. "I can give you room four-oh-nine."

"Fine." She searched her purse for her key. "Damn, I can't find the key. Let me have the spare, so I can pack."

"Certainly, Ms. Crocker. I'll be right back." He disappeared into the room behind the desk.

Suzanne tapped her foot while she waited.

The clerk finally returned with a frown on his face. "Ma'am, I'm sorry, but I can't seem to find the second key."

"What? You mean you gave my other key to someone else? I'll have you know, I have valuable jewelry in that room." The clerk gazed at the diamonds encircling her throat and dangling from her ears. "What? You think I wear all my jewelry at once? I always travel with a selection. And why the hell am I explaining myself to you? Get the passkey. Now!"

"Ma'am, I'm not sure I can do that."

"The hell you can't. Where's the manager? And don't tell me he's not here. You've had a murder in the garden. Cops are crawling all over the place. He's here and I demand to see him."

Anger and fear roughened her voice. She remembered how easily *she* had obtained Dave's room key. Suppose the killer was holed up in her room waiting for her? An icy finger of fear tickled her spine followed by a gush of adrenaline generated heat. Damn! Why had she come to this stupid reunion?

The desk clerk fumbled for the phone, spoke in a low voice to whoever answered, and then hung up.

"Mr. Nelson will be here in a minute, Mrs. Crocker."

Suzanne waited, glaring at the clerk, until the manager came from the direction of the ballroom.

The clerk explained the situation.

"And I want someone to come with me," she demanded when he finished.

"Of course, Mrs. Crocker, I'll be glad to escort you to your room." He nodded to the young man who handed him two keys—a passkey and one for the newly assigned room. "If you'll please follow me, I'll personally move your bags to the new room."

"Thank you."

She followed the manager to the elevators. He smiled, but said nothing on the ride to the fourth floor. The silence held until they exited the elevator. He handed her the key to room four-oh-nine.

"I'm sure the second key was misplaced rather than given to the wrong person," he assured her. "It's been a very busy night."

"Yeah, I guess a reunion with over two hundred people and a body in your fish pond would qualify as busy."

"And may I have the key you requested earlier? The one that doesn't belong to you."

His voice was polite, but she sensed the disapproval.

"Yeah, yeah, you'll get it when I'm moved. Just open the damned door."

This time he didn't smile, but inserted the key and opened the door. Suzanne pushed past him into the pitch dark room.

"Dammit to hell! Someone *has* been here. I left the light on. And what is that God-awful stench? " She flipped the switch on the wall near the door. Nothing happened. "Shit! If I've been robbed, you'll get your ass sued from here to Sunday."

"Please, Mrs. Crocker, don't jump to conclusions." He moved past her to the wall sconce next to the desk and twisted the knob. Light flooded the room. "I'm sure everything is..." He stopped with a gasp.

Suzanne pushed him out of the way. Dave lay on the floor with something wrapped tightly around his neck. His blackened face and protruding tongue told her he would not be snorting any more cocaine—ever.

Her legs went weak, her throat closed, and the room spun. Clenching her evening bag in clawed fingers, she clasped it to her chest, slowly backing from the room and across the hall until the wall stopped her.

Then Suzanne found her voice and screamed.

Chapter Thirteen

"Do you think we've reached a dead end?" Zach asked Meghan.

She shrugged. They still sat in the bar. "I don't know. We have lots of suspects, a possible motive or motives, tons of opportunity, but not one eye witness."

His forehead furrowed. "Somehow, everything is connected—Tami, Eddie, Suzanne. Meghan, it has to date back to high school."

"If someone is killing off the Fearsome Foursome, then Dave Coryell would be on the list, too."

"And the sheriff can't find him," Zach said slowly.

A little dart of fear zapped Meghan in the pit of her stomach. "Do you think something's happened?"

"Suppose Dave is the killer? Maybe he pitched his line of investment opportunities to Tami and Eddie and they refused, like Suzanne."

"So he kills them?"

"For all we know, he's certifiable." He paused. "Or desperate."

Meghan licked her lips. "It's just a theory. We have no proof. If Dave's left the hotel, he may have done so because his plans for filling the financial coffers went belly up."

Ray Armstrong walked into the bar and pulled up a chair at their table. The sheriff looked tired. The lines on his face had deepened. He removed his hat to run his hands through his, gray-streaked hair.

Meghan did some mental arithmetic. Ray had graduated from high school six or seven years before them, which put him in his mid-forties. The man looked older.

"Anything new?" Zach inquired.

He shook his head. "The last interview is over. The hotel staff can finally get in to clean the ballroom. We do know the stun gun has been wiped clean, and that the electrodes correspond to the burn marks on Annabelle Peterson's neck." He turned toward the bar. "Hey, Jack, can I get another cup of coffee?"

"Yeah, sure, Sheriff. By the way, this is last call. Bar closes in thirty minutes."

Meghan picked up the stun gun again, turning it over in her hands. So small, yet an intricate part of the puzzle.

The bartender brought the sheriff's coffee. Ray added the cream and sugar, took a cautious sip, and made a face.

"Lukewarm," he muttered. He set the cup down. "I still haven't found Dave Coryell.

"Zach and I have a theory. Are you in a mood to hear it?"

"I'm open to all suggestions at this point," Ray replied.

She gave him the details. The sheriff frowned. "That's why I want to talk with Coryell. If he's flown the coop, I need to put out a BOLO on him."

"Has anyone looked in the parking lot for his car?" Zach wondered.

Ray nodded. "We have the make, model, and license plate number. One of my deputies is checking it out now." His phone rang. "Armstrong here." He listened for a few seconds, and then closed his eyes. "Don't touch anything. I'll be right there." He snapped the phone shut and rose.

"What's wrong?" Zach said in a sharp voice.

"Suzanne Crocker found Dave Coryell in *her* room. He's dead…strangled." He rushed from the bar.

Meghan stared at Zach, her stomach turning and her ears buzzing. She gripped the edge of the table as a wave of dizziness swept over her.

"God Almighty," he exclaimed. Leaping to his feet, he ran after the sheriff.

"Wait!" Meghan called. She rose slowly.

Zach hurried back. He braced her with his arm around her shoulders. "Are you all right?"

"Just a little lightheaded. Good Lord above, when is this going to stop?"

He tipped her chin up with his fingers and kissed her. "I don't know. Suzanne could be next."

Taking a deep breath, Meghan regained her equilibrium from both the dizziness and his kiss, and nodded. She pulled away, and then turned back to snatch Zach's stun gun from the table. She dropped it into her evening bag and left the lounge.

"Where's Ray?" she asked.

"Grabbed the first elevator for the fourth floor.

They entered the lift. "What was Dave doing in Suzanne's room?"

"I have no idea," Zach replied.

The doors opened and they rushed to exit. Voices babbled from the hallway on their left. Rounding the corner, a throng of people, some in nightclothes, gathered. She and Zach pushed their way through the frightened guests.

Ray emerged from Suzanne's room.

"Everybody, please go back into your rooms." He turned toward Meghan and jerked his head down the hall. "See if you can help her. Zach, can you handle crowd control until the rest of my deputies get here? I want this hallway clear for official business."

"I'll try." He faced the crowd. "Come on, people, let's do as the sheriff asks."

"What the hell's going on around here?" a man in a bathrobe demanded. "Someone drowns in a goddamned fish pond, and I heard another guest was shot."

"Howard, I want to leave now!" a woman cried in a wavering voice. "I'm scared."

"Then your room is the safest place," Zach insisted.

Meghan didn't wait to hear the rest. She gazed down the corridor. Suzanne knelt and sat on her heels, sobbing and hiccupping, while a man with a helpless expression watched. He looked up at her approach.

Meghan had seen him in the lobby and the ballroom earlier. She crouched next to the hysterical woman and placed a hand on her shoulder. Suzanne flinched and yelped.

"Suzanne, it's Meghan."

Suzanne clutched her arms over her stomach and bent forward until her forehead touched the floor. Her tangled red hair fanned out on either side of her head. She clenched her evening bag in white knuckled fingers.

"Who are you?" Meghan asked the man.

"Mark Nelson, the night manager."

"Why don't you see if you can help Mr. Dunbar

and get these people back into their rooms? I'll take care of Mrs. Crocker. Do you have a handkerchief?"

The man nodded, fumbled in his pocket for the item, and ran down the hall.

Meghan pulled Suzanne upright and wiped her cheeks.

"Come on, Suzanne, get control of yourself. Here," she said handing her the hankie. "Dry your eyes and blow your nose, then we'll leave."

Suzanne hiccupped again, but made an effort to do as Meghan suggested, wiping her cheeks clean of the streaked mascara.

"I w-w-want to go h-h-home," the terrified woman stammered.

"Don't worry, we'll find you a safe place."

"D-D-D-Dave. All b-b-b-black." The crying renewed.

"Can you stand?" She pulled the stunned woman from her knees. Suzanne swayed, clutching at Meghan's upper arms, and buried her face in Meghan's shoulder. Hot tears scorched her skin. She wrapped her arms around the shaky redhead. "It'll be all right."

She glanced toward the scene of the crime. Most of the crowd had heeded Zach and returned to their rooms. The deputies had arrived and relieved Zach of his duties. He stood to one side. The manager was gone.

"Are you ready to go? Most of the people have left."

Suzanne took a step and stumbled. Meghan slipped a steadying arm around her waist.

"You can do it. We'll take it slow."

They walked with hesitant steps down the hallway. The closer they got to the room, the louder the gasps from Suzanne. Zach intercepted them.

"Do you need help?"

"No, I think I can handle her."

Suzanne shuddered and gasped for air, mumbling between breaths.

"I'll take her to the bar before she faints. Maybe a brandy will help calm her. What about you?"

"I'll stay here for a while and see what they find."

Meghan nodded and steered the staggering, breathless Suzanne toward the elevators. The handkerchief remained clutched in her hand along with the purse.

"Let's get you a brandy, okay?" Meghan suggested. Anything to get the poor woman back under control.

"Okay. M-maybe. I-I don't know."

"I imagine just being away from your room helps, doesn't it?"

She kept her voice soft and sympathetic. It worked. Suzanne's gait steadied and she'd ceased the horrible gasping even though she shook uncontrollably on the ride down. Heading for the bar, they passed the ballroom entrance when the door suddenly swung open. Suzanne shrieked and clutched at Meghan's arm. Glory emerged carrying the memorial posters.

"Glory, I thought you'd gone back upstairs," a startled Meghan said, tightening her grip on Suzanne's waist.

"I thought about it, but I'm still too keyed up to sleep, so I decided I'd help with the clean-up." She placed the easel and the boards outside the door and looked at the women for the first time. "Good grief, what's wrong with Suzanne?"

"Help me get her into the bar."

Glory's arm joined Meghan's supporting Suzanne. They entered the lounge, lowering her into a chair. The bar was closed, but Meghan walked behind it, poured a large snifter of Hennessey and returned to the table. She set it in front of Suzanne who tried to raise the glass, but failed. Her hands trembled so hard, the liquor sloshed almost to the rim.

"Here, let me." Meghan took the glass pressing the rim to the redhead's lips.

Suzanne didn't sip. She gulped, and then gagged. A small rivulet of brandy trickled down her chin. Meghan daubed at it with a napkin.

"What's going on?" Glory asked. "Why is Suzanne in such a state?"

"I've got bad news. Dave Coryell's been murdered. Suzanne found his body in her room."

Glory gasped. Her eyes went wide, and she pressed shaking fingers to her lips. "The wicked flee when no man pursueth," she muttered.

Meghan looked at her with a sharp glance. "Proverbs."

Glory nodded. "This is just too horrible. What on earth is going on?"

"I don't know."

"Someone's trying to frame me," Suzanne muttered through chattering teeth. "I didn't kill him. I swear it."

"No one thinks you did," Meghan answered.

The brandy had done its job. Suzanne raised the glass on her own this time and sipped. She still trembled, but appeared more in control.

"I needed to talk to him. So, I went to his room, but

he didn't answer. I got scared because I thought someone was following me."

Meghan drew in a silent breath. "Following you? Where?"

"In the hallway outside his room, and again in the parking lot when I searched his car. I thought I heard footsteps. Then I couldn't find my key, so I went to the front desk to get another. When we opened the door, we found…" She gulped more brandy, pressed the handkerchief to her mouth, and let fresh tears run down her face. All the carefully applied make-up had washed away. Suzanne looked every bit her age.

Meghan looked at Glory whose face was curiously blank. She stared straight ahead as though in a world of her own.

"Glory?" She touched her arm. The blonde jumped. "Are you all right?"

"Oh, yes, I'm fine. Just taking it all in. I thought this reunion would be so special. I worked very hard. I tried to make things run smoothly. I know some people made fun of me, but I truly wanted them to feel welcome. I wanted to do the best job possible. Divine would have. It's the kind of thing she would do."

Meghan stared in consternation, and then realized the woman was on the verge of shock. She snatched the snifter from Suzanne's fingers and held it out to Glory.

"You did a magnificent job. I felt very welcomed. I'm sure most people did. You can't be responsible for the actions of a maniac. Here, have a sip of this."

Glory recoiled. "Oh, no, I couldn't drink spirits."

"Just a sip. You'll feel better," she wheedled.

The lanky blonde placed her lips on the rim and tilted the glass allowing the barest touch of liquor to make contact. She licked, shuddered, and made a face.

"That's awful." She licked again. "How do you stand it?"

"I'm not fond of brandy, but for some reason it calms the nerves."

Zach walked in and pulled out a chair. "Are you all right?" he asked Suzanne.

She blew her nose and shook her head. "No, I'm not all right. I'm scared shitless. He was strangled, wasn't he?"

"Yeah. The killer cut the cord from the lamp on the dresser, fashioned a slip knot, and placed a knee on his back for leverage."

Meghan inhaled sharply. "Just like with Annabelle. Was a stun gun used?"

He nodded. "Got it right in the throat. A heavy dose, too. According to Ray, there are several sets of burn marks. He needed more than one round."

Meghan shivered. "Oh, God.

They found Suzanne's room key on the floor near the desk. Dave must have dropped it. Ray wants to talk to you, Suzanne, as soon as you're able."

She nodded and drained the rest of the brandy.

Zach rose and headed for the bar, then returned with a bottle, and three more glasses. He refilled Suzanne's before pouring one for himself and Meghan. Glory pushed her glass away.

"Nothing for me. I can't listen to any more of this. Please forgive me. I...I need to check on...I mean I need Tom." She rose and left the bar.

"So both of my keys were missing," Suzanne said. "Anyone can get a key. I did for Dave's room."

"You have Dave's room key?" Meghan asked.

Suzanne explained her reasoning to them. "I don't suppose the desk clerk remembers who wanted my key."

"Probably not. The killer must have obtained the second key and stolen yours. Did you leave your purse unattended at any time tonight?" Zach questioned.

"Sure. Any time I went to the bar in the ballroom. So, how did Dave get a hold of my key?"

"Good question," Zach commented. "Maybe he's the one who requested it. He could have been looking for you, too."

"I doubt it. He knew nothing was going to happen between us."

Meghan gnawed on a fingernail. "Any idea when he was killed?"

"Ray says he'd been dead an hour, maybe a little more, but that's a rough guess."

"God, what a mess."

Zach turned to Suzanne. "Tami, Eddie, and now Dave. Have the four of you had any contact since high school?"

"Not much. By our junior year in college, Eddie had flunked out, Tami was stalking her first husband, and I have no idea what Dave was doing. My roommate's family was rich, so I spent a lot of time with her."

"I guess that's one way to get ahead in the world," Meghan said, sipping her brandy.

"God dammit, don't judge me. Money opens doors. I met people through Jennifer, people who counted. And don't go thinking I didn't work for my money. You try hosting a fundraiser for the Chicago Museum of Art and being the chairperson for God knows how many charities. It's damned hard and time consuming."

"All right, all right, I'm sorry."

"Can we get back to the four of you?" Zach demanded. "Someone holds one hell of a grudge. Who would wait twenty years to kill you guys off?"

Suzanne gulped a large portion of her liquor. "I don't know. Maybe because they couldn't find us until this reunion. My name changed, so had Tami's—many times. And as a truck driver, I'm sure Eddie moved around a lot. But why?"

"I haven't got the answer to that. You must have done something to warrant all of this."

"Oh, for God's sake, Dave was always pulling some kind of prank. He Super-glued the locks on the freshman lockers. We all helped. And he and Eddie got a hold of some kind of liniment and dumped it on their teammates' jock straps. Burned like hell. Dave claimed he got that one from some movie." She rubbed her fingers over her forehead. "I don't know. We pulled a lot of pranks."

"What about Tami?" Meghan asked. "She could be damned vindictive. I heard Monica Evans was livid about things she'd said."

"Oh, the cheerleader business. Yeah, Tami was madder than hell. She wanted that head position real bad. She started the rumor Monica was a lesbian."

"Did Monica confront her?"

"Not to my knowledge. Most people didn't want to get on Tami's bad side. Tami was a calculating, manipulative control freak. Dave thought up funny pranks. Tami served up revenge. She didn't even have to have a good excuse. If she thought you'd wronged her in some way, look out."

"That sounds paranoid," Meghan commented. "Was she?"

Suzanne shrugged. "I don't know, but it wouldn't surprise me."

Zach frowned at the redhead. "Who'd she go after other than Monica?"

"Hell, Zach, it's been twenty years. Give me a break. I can't remember everyone she got even with for supposedly slighting her." She paused for a moment. "There was that girl in the drama club. She beat Tami out for the lead in the junior class play. I remember Tami cursing up a storm in the restroom. She threw the trash can clear across the room. Those things were made out of metal and damned heavy, but she tossed it like a wad of paper. Busted the mirror over the basins to smithereens."

"What was her name, the girl who beat her out of the part? Do you remember?" Meghan said.

"Christy? Kristin? Something like that."

"Crystal Bennett?" Zach suggested.

"Yeah, I think so."

"What was the revenge for that?" Meghan asked.

"Vintage Tami Robinson. She spiked the girl's soda at dress rehearsal. When she got sick and couldn't go on, Tami, as the understudy, did."

"Spiked it with what?"

"A laxative. Her parents had to take her to the emergency room."

Meghan looked at Zach who gazed back with a scowl. "That's not only mean, but dangerous. I take it she didn't get caught."

"Tami? Consequences always bypassed her."

"Sounds like they all caught up with her a few

months ago. Was Crystal here tonight?" Meghan didn't remember having seen or talked to her.

"I have no idea," Suzanne replied.

Zach nodded. "I saw her just before dinner. What about Eddie? Where did he fit in with revenge and practical jokes?"

"Eddie was dumber than a box of rocks. His idea of fun was physical. You know, punch a skinny kid on the arm so hard he cried, or trip the class geek in the hallway, and then watch his books and papers fly all over."

"Yeah, I remember," Zach muttered. "I was one of them."

"Could he have hurt someone doing that?" Meghan wondered. "I mean really hurt them, like a broken arm or internal injuries or something?"

"I don't know."

Meghan nibbled on her thumbnail this time. It sounded as though most of the class had motive for hating and killing Tami Robinson, but Eddie, Dave, and Suzanne? Then she remembered a conversation from earlier.

"What about Carol Rutherford's and Alicia Raines's dates?"

"What about them?" Suzanne frowned. Lines etched from her nose to her mouth.

"Alicia said you flirted with them."

"Alicia is full of crap. The guy she was with was bored to tears. I would be if I had a date with Alicia. I spoke with a couple of guys when I ordered from that overpriced bar set up in the ballroom. With one bartender and a lot of thirsty people, it was often a long wait. I talked. I did not flirt."

"Anyone else?" Zach persisted.

Suzanne cast her gaze down, "Lots. I just can't remember offhand." She sipped some brandy, made a face, and pushed the glass away. "I can't handle any more booze tonight."

"How about food?" Zach asked. "You didn't eat much at the banquet. Are you hungry?"

"I suppose. Is the restaurant still open?"

"No, but I know where I can score some roast beef."

"As long as it's food," Suzanne rose swaying briefly.

Meghan stood. "Need help?"

"No, I'm fine. Just tired now. It's been a hell of a night."

****

Suzanne lied. She wasn't fine. She was scared to death. She followed Zach and Meghan into the kitchen and helped pull food out of the fridge, but her mind wasn't on eating.

Dave's face haunted her. She clenched her teeth against the nausea as his blackened face and outthrust tongue refused to leave her mind. And the smell! The stench had been enough to gag a maggot.

It could just as easily have been me. It should have been—twice. Maybe the killer was lying in wait for me to come back, but got Dave as a bonus.

She shivered. Meghan and Zach believed the killer was on some kind of a vendetta. Suzanne agreed. Who could have a held a twenty year grudge allowing the resentment to fester? Dan Masterson had reason. So did Monica and that Crystal person. Other than Dan's veiled threat, none had said anything homicidal. *And I don't even remember seeing Monica or Crystal.*

She racked her brain trying to recall all the people they had wronged back then.

I should have kept a scorecard.

None of them had given a damn about who'd they'd hurt. A twinge of guilt gnawed in her shaky stomach. She pushed the thought away. *For God's sakes, we were kids. Kids make mistakes.*

Carol Rutherford and Alicia Raines hadn't been angels either. Tami had tangled with both of them during their senior year, although what about, Suzanne couldn't remember. Tami hadn't been paranoid, but just plain mean. The former cheerleader enjoyed hurting others.

Suzanne went through the motions of making a sandwich and tuned out most of the conversation Meghan and Zach had going.

She didn't tell them about all the pranks. A couple of them had been directed at the fat girl and the computer geek.

Tami had stolen Meghan's underwear from the shower room and tacked the extra large sized briefs to the bulletin board in the main hallway. Old Ms. Sylvester had removed them before any of the students got an eyeful.

And Eddie must have given Zach hundreds of wedgies—not to mention bruises—in four years. Now, everything seemed childish—not funny.

Meghan poured three glasses of milk, handing her one.

Milk? Suzanne shrugged. Why not? It might help her sleep. She bit into her sandwich and chewed, not tasting a thing. The sick feeling diminished. She finished the food and drank the milk.

"I've had about as much as I can stand tonight," she told the other two. "I'm going to bed."

"But the sheriff wants to talk to you," Meghan said.

"Fuck him. If he wants to question me about Dave, he can wait until later."

"But, Suzanne..." Zach began.

"I'm going to bed!" She turned on her heel and headed for the kitchen doors.

"Wait a minute! Don't go alone. Meghan and I will walk you to your room. Do you have the key?"

"Yes. The manager gave it to me."

Meghan dumped the dishes in the sink. Suzanne exited the kitchen and strode through the lobby, and then paused at the ballroom doors. The easel and memorial board stood where Glory had left them.

She stared at Tami and Eddie's smiling graduation photos. Tremors started in the pit of her stomach and worked their way to her extremities. Shaking, she swiped at the easel's legs with her foot. The boards fell to the floor with a crash.

"Throw those damned things out! I don't ever want to see them again."

Zach picked them up and set them straight. "Relax, Suzanne. You'll be safe in your room. I'm sure the sheriff will post a guard for the night."

Meghan stared at the memorial board. "Zach, look at those dates."

"Which dates?"

"The death dates on Tami and Eddie—May 2nd and June 6th. A little over a month apart. Now look at Clara Sylvester's—July 11th. Another month."

"So, what's your point?" Suzanne mumbled. God,

she was tired. Tired and scared.

"Don't you find that odd?"

"Meghan, what does Clara Sylvester have to do with any of this? Didn't Glory say something about her being in a convalescent home?" Zach commented.

Suzanne sighed impatiently. "She was older than dirt when we were in high school."

"Surely, you don't think her death is connected to the rest, do you?" Zach asked.

"I don't know, but I just find it strange, and if it's one thing I've discovered over the years, it's that nothing is coincidental. Especially murder."

"Meghan, I think we all know what your next novel is going to be about, so can we dispense with the drama? I'm exhausted and want to go to bed." Suzanne turned abruptly and headed for the elevators.

How could that bitch Clara Sylvester have anything to do with this mess? I never realized Meghan was such a drama queen. I'll bet she bumps me off in her next book.

The elevator doors opened on the fourth floor. Suzanne extracted the key from her purse. A quick glance down the hall showed the door to her old room still open. Yellow crime scene tape stretched across the entrance. The rest of the corridor was empty.

She turned to the right and marched to room four-oh-nine, handing Zach the key.

"You go first."

Zach entered and flipped on the lights. A few seconds later he emerged and led Suzanne inside.

"I even checked under the bed," he said with a smile.

"Don't be an asshole. It's not funny."

"I wasn't trying to be an asshole. I was just trying to reassure you."

Guilt washed over her. "I'm sorry, Zach. And thank you, Meghan, for sticking with me tonight. You didn't have to. I haven't been particularly pleasant."

Meghan smiled. "Glad I was there to help." She glanced around the room. "I don't see your things. I guess they must still be in your old room. Would you like me to get them?"

"God, no. That incompetent sheriff will want to interrogate me and all I want right now is to be left alone."

"Well, if you're sure," she said.

Zach opened the door and Meghan followed him into the hall.

Zach turned back to face Suzanne. "Good night. Don't forget to latch the door behind us."

She nodded, closed the door, and slammed the chain into the slot, then leaned her head against the panels. The air conditioner clicking on made her jump.

"Relax. You're safe," she muttered.

But am I? Tami, Eddie, and Dave. They didn't expect to get murdered. Am I next?

"Of course you are." Saying it out loud sent a shiver down her spine. "How safe am I really? Who would I open that door to? Zach? Meghan? A cop?"

She paced the room, her mind still seeing Dave's grotesque body.

Squaring her shoulders, Suzanne walked into the bathroom. Unwrapping the soap, she washed her face. Her reflection in the mirror showed an almost middle-aged woman with terrified blue eyes. She removed her jewelry and set it on the counter.

Suzanne eyed the shower and almost turned it on. The shower scene from the movie *Psycho* flashed in front of her eyes.

"No fucking way," she muttered again.

She returned to the room and pulled down the covers, then unzipped the designer dress, letting it fall to the carpet. Crawling into bed, Suzanne jerked the covers back up. She'd be damned if she'd turn out the lights.

Not tonight.

She swallowed and squeezed her eyes shut. Her heart pounded in her ears. She rolled over pulling the sheet over her head.

A noise from the hallway had her sitting upright. She ran to the door and peered out the peephole. No one.

Back in bed, she heard every noise magnified a hundred times. She crammed the pillow over her head, wondering about sounds she wasn't hearing. Fear bubbled in her chest.

Oh, what's the use? I'm not going to sleep. I may never sleep again. If I am next, I should be thinking of ways to stay alive. I need to get out of here.

Then, Suzanne remembered the spare car key.

Why not? I can take it and head for home. I'll be safe in Chicago.

Before giving herself a chance to think, Suzanne quickly dressed, dumped her jewelry in her bag, and scrounged the key to the Mercedes from its depths. She took a moment to swallow the rising panic. It didn't work. Her hands and legs trembled beyond self-control. She inhaled several deep breaths until the shaking lessened.

She opened the door and peeked around the jamb.

Good, the coast is clear. Suzanne slipped from the room, and pulled the door closed behind her.

The only thing on her mind was escape.

Chapter Fourteen

Suzanne ducked behind a potted palm and waited until the desk clerk left the registration desk, then hurried past when the coast was clear. At the front doors, she paused and peered into the darkness. She'd deal with her bags and the hotel bill later. For once she didn't give a damn about the jewelry remaining in her old room. The parking lot lighting wasn't the best in the world, but she had to remind herself this was not Chicago where everything was lit up like the Fourth of July.

Maybe this isn't such a good idea. I should go back to my room. Meghan's right. The sheriff will post a guard. I'll even answer his goddamned questions.

Then the elevator dinged, the sound echoing through the silent lobby. Panic clawed in her chest and nausea boiled in her stomach. It was the killer!

She jerked open the doors and ran, her hand grasping the railing as she stumbled down the steps. Her heart pounded and her breath rasped from her throat. The car key, clutched in her hand, dug into her flesh.

She stumbled again. The flimsy, high-heeled sandals provided little in the line of practicality beyond a couple of hours on the dance floor. To move faster, she stopped, slipped them off, and proceeded barefoot through the parking lot, then stepped on something.

"Ouch! God dammit!" she blurted, inspecting the bottom of her foot with her fingertip. The touch revealed a slick wetness. She'd deal with that later, too.

That creepy feeling of being followed rolled over her. Suzanne ignored the pain in her foot and raced the last few yards. The space next to the driver's side was empty giving her ample room.

Footsteps rushed from behind her. Suzanne whirled, her heart pounding and her breath stopping somewhere in her chest. She had no time to react. A powerful blow struck her. She cried out and clutched her left shoulder, dropping her shoes, purse, and keys. A tire iron descended again and she raised her right arm in defense. It struck with the force of a Mack truck. Something cracked. Excruciating pain raced through her body. She screamed. The next blow caught her in the side sending her to her knees.

Hugging her arm and trying to breathe despite what felt like broken ribs, Suzanne looked up and saw her attacker for the first time. Man or woman? She couldn't tell. The figure was dressed in dark clothing from head to foot. A ski mask prevented her from seeing a face. She sucked in a deep, painful breath and screamed again. Staggering to her feet, she lunged as best she could. Fear lent her strength. She shoved her assailant hard in the chest and made a grab for the mask. Her fingers curled around the mouth opening and yanked. The woolen hood slid off.

No, it can't be! But it was, and in that moment, Suzanne expected to die.

The next swing of the tire iron caught her on the side of the head. Blood spurted and ran down her neck in a hot stream like lava from a volcano. She fell on her side. Her ears rang and she threw up. She fought to rise. The iron fell again. Ignoring the pain, Suzanne rolled. It struck the asphalt just inches away from her face. In deep survival mode, she had ceased to think or ask herself useless questions.

"Bitch! Do you really think you can get away? I've spent two years planning this. And this time I won't make a mistake."

The weapon swished through the air and found its target. Pain exploded again. Bright stars and flashing lights danced in her head. Her vision blurred. In desperation, she rolled again across the blacktop, the smell of oil and tar making her gag. Her attacker anticipated the move and swung, missing Suzanne's head again. Tiny chunks of asphalt splattered her face, stinging like angry bees.

"Help! Someone help me!" Her voice was little more than a croak.

"No one's going to help, except me. I'm going to help you straight to hell."

Suzanne discovered her body had fetched up next to the car parked one space over. Beyond desperate, she ignored the pain and using her last bit of strength, scooted her head and shoulders under the car praying it would protect her.

A hand grasped her ankle and pulled. "Come out, you whore!"

The pavement scraped her legs and knees. The pain from her broken arm shrieked along every nerve. Suzanne kicked and made contact. The hand released its clasp. Blows rained on her lower legs. Her ankle cracked and shattered, but she no longer had the strength to either scream or move. Pain racked her from head to foot. Blood from her head wounds flowed into her eyes. Tears mingled with the blood. Numbness slowly crept over her body.

Don't let me die. Please God, I want to live.

In the distance, a car door slammed. Suddenly, the assault ceased.

Through the buzzing in her ears, she heard the words, "Five down, one to go."

The ski mask was ripped from Suzanne's clenched fingers.

Blackness descended and in the moments before her mind shut down, Suzanne knew why the murders had occurred.

****

I suspected that psychologically, Suzanne was toast. Finding Dave's body must have been the lowlight of her evening. It was my highlight. Shame I couldn't be there to see it.

The bitch had changed rooms and from my stairwell hideaway I noted the sheriff had not as yet posted a guard. But would Suzanne open the door to me? Given her present state of mind, I doubted it.

Shame I had to ditch the stun gun. It had been useful beyond my wildest dreams. Now, I'd have to improvise.

Then Suzanne's door opened. She stuck her head out, looked down the corridor, and slipped from the room. She clutched her purse in one hand and something else in the other. An alarm fob dangled. A car key. I drew in a ragged breath. The bitch was making a run for it.

I turned and hurried down the steps to the lobby. The front desk was empty. I ran through the ballroom and into the garden, grabbing the tire iron I'd hidden earlier along with the ski mask. Pulling it over my head, I hurried to the parking lot. Hotel security was practically non-existent, but why take a chance? One of those stinking cameras could be operational. I crouched near the front bumper of my car.

Suzanne emerged from the hotel lobby and, casting frequent glances over her shoulder, rushed to Coryell's Mercedes. I followed, keeping to the shadows.

She slowed her pace and fumbled for the unlocking mechanism on the fob.

Now! I rushed forward, tire iron raised.

She whirled, cried out, and lifted an arm to shield her face.

It was too late. I struck, swinging that heavy hunk of pipe again and again. With each thud, with each bone cracking, my heart rate accelerated. Adrenaline gave me added strength. Oh dear Lord, this felt so good. At some point she'd pulled the mask from my head, but who cared? Let *my* face be the last she sees in this lifetime.

"Bitch, bitch, bitch," I crowed with every swing. The tire iron was coated with blood making it hard to grasp. My grip slid in the slippery ooze. I clenched my hands harder.

Blood flowed from her head. I had no idea why she was still conscious. She tried scrunching her head and torso under a car. I grabbed an ankle and pulled. She kicked, so I slammed her legs over and over.

Then in the distance, I heard a car door slamming and voices. My heart pounded in my ears and my breath clogged my throat. I couldn't get caught. Not yet. I wasn't done with my work. I needed to get out of here.

Suzanne lay still, the blood from her broken body pooling around her head. A thin stream crept toward the tire.

The voices grew louder. I wanted to hit her again and again, but there was no time. I could be discovered at any moment. I cast one last look at Suzanne Wayland. She was dead or soon would be.

Only one more to go. I turned and ran.

****

"I want to see if the sheriff needs us any more tonight," Zach said to Meghan after leaving Suzanne.

They approached the crime scene and halted. Zach poked his head around the corner of the door.

"Body's gone." He ducked under the yellow tape.

Meghan stayed put. Novelist or not, she had no desire to see where a man she'd known and spoken with just hours earlier, had been brutally murdered.

A deputy stopped Zach. "Sorry, sir. Can't let you in. Forensics is busy." He glanced toward Meghan. "Are you the people helping Sheriff Armstrong?"

"We've been talking to him. Don't know if it's helped."

"Well, he wants to see you two and Mrs. Crocker. You just missed him. He's headed for the lobby."

Meghan and Zach retraced their steps to the elevator. In the lobby, they spied Ray gazing at the memorial boards by the ballroom. He turned as they approached, a sad expression on his face.

"A damned shame," he muttered.

Meghan alerted him to the timing of the teacher, Clara Sylvester's, death.

"I can't see how she'd be involved, but I'll call the nursing home and the sheriff in the morning. You're right. The timing's too coincidental. Where's Mrs. Crocker?"

"In her room," Zach told him. "She was tired. Said if you wanted to talk with her, it'd have to wait until morning."

"We'll see about that. But first, I want to ask the two of you a few questions."

"About what?" Meghan replied.

"Let's take a load off." Ray walked into the now deserted bar. He took a seat at the nearest table. Meghan and Zach sat on either side of him.

Zach stared at the sheriff. "What do you want to know, Ray?"

"Exactly when were you in Dallas?"

He shrugged. "I'd have to check my schedule, but I think it was in late May or early June. Why?"

"And you said you visited your folks about the same time, right Meghan?"

"Yeah, about. Technically I was in Granbury."

"Where's that?"

"A few miles southwest of Ft. Worth."

"And the two of you never saw each other?"

"No, why should we? I had no idea of Meghan's whereabouts. Ray, what's this all about?"

"And, Meghan, you claimed you were in California prior to that?"

"Yes, I had a book signing tour."

"Did it include Los Angeles?"

"Define Los Angeles. It's a big city. I was in Riverside, Oxnard, and a couple of other places in the area."

"Know the dates?"

"Not off the top of my head, but it was late April or

early May, I guess. Why all the questions?"

Ray held up his hand and turned to Zach. "You admit to being in Los Angeles at that time, too."

"Brentwood. I was helping my folks move. I told you that earlier. Dammit, what's going on?"

"Both of you were in Los Angeles and Dallas at the same time Tami Robinson and Eddie Mancuso were killed."

Meghan gasped. "You can't think either one of us had anything to do with it."

Her mind reeled with the implications. Then she realized how bad it looked. She and Zach had often been on the receiving end of practical jokes and cutting remarks by the Fearsome Foursome. Who's to say either or both of them hadn't decided to get even?

Ray shrugged. "You just said you didn't believe in coincidences. I find it highly coincidental."

Meghan squirmed. Her own words had come back to haunt her. Fear that the sheriff actually believed she might have something to do with the murders made her mouth go dry. She swallowed and cast a glance at Zach, who stared at the officer with an amazed expression.

"Ray, why would either of us kill Tami, Eddie, or anyone else for that matter? I make those trips on a regular basis. Check my schedule," Zach told him.

"I've talked with a lot of people tonight. A few told me that you and Meghan often provided a source of amusement for the so-called in-crowd. Meghan took the insults and embarrassment stoically. Still others found it interesting that you dispatch your fictional characters in extremely gory deaths, kind of like a literary revenge."

"I have an active imagination." Meghan didn't know whether to be angry or scared. Both emotions made her tremble.

"And just how are we supposed to have dispatched Annabelle and Dave?" Zach inquired in an indignant tone.

"You give each other alibis for the former. And one or both of you could have slipped upstairs to kill Dave. For all I know, the two of you have been more than friends for a long time and decided revenge was the best policy. And Zach, you have a stun gun."

Meghan stared at Zach in consternation. His expression was one of disbelief.

"And if I did it, why would I be dumb enough to not only mention that fact, but to actually produce it? If I'm not mistaken, you found a stun gun in a trash can."

The sheriff shrugged again. "You could have had two."

"My God, how could we have known where Tami and Eddie lived?" Her voice shook and her eyes filled with tears.

"Zach knows his way around a computer, and as an author, you know how do research. One of you could have hired a private investigator to track 'em down. As a matter of fact, the two of you make one damned good team."

"But we've been helping with the investigation!"

"What better way to muddy the waters?"

"Ray," Zach said in an incredulous voice. "You can't be serious."

The sheriff removed his hat and ran a hand through his hair, then looked from one to the other. Meghan bit her lip, wanting to box the sheriff on the ear. She clenched her fists to keep the urge under control.

"You've got to admit, it's strange. And I *will* check

your whereabouts on the dates Tami and Eddie died. Wouldn't be doing my job otherwise. You could be helping me just to see what I've uncovered. No reason why both of you couldn't have a stun gun."

"Are you finished?" Meghan asked in a tight voice.

Ray stood and replaced his hat. "Not quite. I have to interrogate Mrs. Crocker."

Meghan wanted to tell Ray to go to hell, but kept her mouth shut. Suzanne would do it for her if the sheriff woke her from a sound sleep.

"She won't talk to you." Zach rose. "She won't even open the door. But she might for Meghan. We'll go with you."

"Unless, of course, you're afraid we'll murder you in the elevator," Meghan snapped.

Ray stared with cold eyes, but capitulated. "All right, but when we're done I want you both to call it a night. You're done with this investigation."

The ride to the fourth floor was silent. Zach slipped his hand in hers and squeezed. She met his concerned gaze and squeezed back. The past twenty minutes hadn't been the best of her life. She still couldn't believe Ray suspected her and Zach of being partners in a murder spree. She forced herself not to kick the sheriff in the ass.

Ray led them to room four-oh-nine and knocked. He tried again when there was no answer.

"Mrs. Crocker, it's Sheriff Armstrong. I'm sorry to disturb you, but we have to talk." Silence met his request and he knocked again, louder this time. "Mrs. Crocker, open up." He waited several seconds. "Would she just ignore me?"

Meghan glared. "Of course, she would. She was

tired, pissed, and scared to death. If you wake her, she'll let you have it with both barrels. Even though she was hysterical, you should have done this earlier."

She was beyond giving a damn what the sheriff thought. *He's an incompetent jerk.*

Ray narrowed his eyes and compressed his lips. "Fine, you try."

She knocked. "Suzanne? It's Meghan. Zach's with us. I know it's late, but please, open the door."

More time and silence passed. Worry and a growing sense of dread rushed through her. "I don't like this. If nothing else, she'd tell us all to go to hell."

Ray whipped out his cell and dialed. "Jamieson, you still in room four-twenty... Call down to the desk and get someone up to room four-oh-nine with a passkey now." He hung up. "Would she leave the safety of her room?"

"I don't know," Zach snapped with a worried expression on his face. "When we left her, she said she wanted to go to bed. I heard the lock click and the chain sliding into place."

"Who would she open up for?" Meghan asked.

"Somebody she trusted," Ray answered with a sharp glance at them.

"It wasn't us," Zach snapped. "We went directly from her room to the crime scene and spoke with your deputy. When we discovered you were looking for us, we came down to the lobby and met you."

Meghan opened her mouth to speak, and then closed it again.

She would have trusted a cop. Oh, my God. Is that the answer? Could the killer be a cop?

It made sense. A police officer would have

unlimited access to the hotel and its grounds. And if a cop showed up at *her* door in the middle of the night requesting she accompany him somewhere, she'd comply. A friend would be the only other person Suzanne would open up for. And Suzanne didn't have a lot of those around here.

Zach? But he was with me.

True there had been a few moments when they'd been separated earlier in the evening, but was that enough time to kill Annabelle and Dave? And there was no way he could have enticed Suzanne to leave the safety of her room.

Or was there? God knows, Suzanne had flirted enough with him tonight. If he'd come to her door with a change of heart, would she open it? Maybe. Oh for crying out loud, what am I thinking? Of course Zach isn't involved. He was with me the entire time.

She swiped a hand across her forehead. Exhaustion muddled her thought processes. It happened all the time when she was in full writing mode necessitating massive edits later. Then another thought occurred.

What if two people are working this? Suppose there's an accomplice—and that accomplice is a cop?

Meghan shivered and moved a step away from both men. She was letting her imagination run wild. The reunion murders weren't part of a novel. They were real. People had died horrible deaths.

The night manager trotted around the corner at a fast pace with a key in his hand.

"This can't be happening," he said. "We can't have another body. The hotel will be ruined."

"Just open the door," the sheriff ordered.

He did, and they all stepped inside. The room was

empty, the bed unmade. Ray checked the bathroom.

"A used washcloth and a towel are by the sink. Looks like she went to bed, then got up and split." He turned to the manager. "Did you see anyone in the lobby in the last half an hour?"

"No, sir."

"Were you on the desk the whole time?" Zach asked.

"No, I was with the night clerk in the back room sorting through some paperwork."

"For how long?" Ray demanded.

"I—I'm not sure. Fifteen, twenty minutes maybe. When I came out, the lobby was empty."

"Damn. Let's search the obvious places."

"Better begin with Dave's room," Meghan suggested. "Suzanne told me she had the key. She got it when she was looking for him."

A search of Dave's room yielded nothing, although Meghan noticed Ray took interest in items on the bathroom counter. He pulled out his cell again.

"Jamieson? Get down to room three-twenty-six. I want it sealed and forensics going over it." He snapped the phone shut. "Looks like the late Mr. Coryell had a private party. Let's head downstairs."

He should have checked Dave's room earlier. He is so in over his head.

Back in the lobby, he turned to Meghan. "Meghan, you try the ladies' room and the ballroom. Zach, you come with me to the bar and the kitchen."

Meghan dashed to the ladies room. The cleaning crew had apparently finished their jobs. The light was off and the place smelled of disinfectant. She flipped the switch and did a quick scan under the stall doors.

No one was there.

In the hallway, she hesitated, looked around, and then slid into the men's room. It only took a few seconds to determine it, too, was empty.

She paused at the ballroom door. Most of the tables had been removed, the stage dismantled, and some of the lights turned off. Without the crowd, the cavernous room looked lonely and cold. She shuddered when her overactive imagination conjured up monsters in the shadowy corners. Suzanne wasn't here. She turned and ran out, meeting Zach and the sheriff exiting the bar.

"Nothing," Ray told her.

"Same here," she replied.

"Well, she has to be somewhere," Zach said. "She can't have just vanished. Would she go into the garden?"

"After what happened there tonight? Not a chance in hell." Meghan rubbed her forehead with her fingers. Where could Suzanne have gone? Something, a tiny bit of information, tugged at her memory. "Damn, what was it she said?"

"Who?" Zach demanded in a rough tone.

"Suzanne. She said something I should remember."

"When?" Ray wanted to know.

"Just a little while ago. After she found Dave. We were in the bar with Glory. I was trying to calm them both down. Glory was in shock, and Suzanne babbled about looking for Dave and how she was being framed. Oh, shit! Why can't I remember?"

"Take it easy, Meghan. Try a few cleansing breaths to clear your mind," Zach suggested.

She complied and tried to recall the conversation in the bar prior to Zach's arrival. Suzanne had talked incoherently about getting the key to Dave's room and feeling spooked because she thought someone was watching her in the hallway and the parking lot. But what else?

"She had Dave's room key and went there to search for a stun gun. She has one and thought maybe Dave had stolen it in Chicago."

"I don't think Dave Coryell zapped and strangled himself," the sheriff retorted in a dry tone.

Meghan waved him silent in irritation. "She had the creepy feeling she was being stalked."

"Stalked? Where?" Ray pressed.

"Outside Dave's room and in the parking…" She stopped. "That's it! She said she searched Dave's car, too."

"Coryell's car keys were in his pants pocket," Ray told her.

Zach heaved a deep breath. "She must have found a spare. Is Dave's car still here?"

"It was an hour or so ago."

"Suppose someone knocked at Suzanne's door, but she didn't answer. Suppose she was scared and decided to bolt," Meghan concluded. "If it was me, and I had a car key, I'd make a run for it."

The night manager approached with the desk clerk.

"Sheriff, Billy has something to tell you."

"Can't it wait?" Ray clasped his cell phone in his hand.

"I guess, but since Mrs. Crocker is missing I thought you'd like to know about the scream."

"What scream?" Meghan, Zach, and the sheriff all spoke at the same time.

Billy cleared his throat. "Well, Mr. Nelson had

been helping me with some paperwork in the back. A few seconds after he left, the phone rang. It was some woman on the sixth floor. She called to say she thought she heard a scream. I know I'm not supposed to leave the desk unattended, but in view of what's happened tonight I went up to check anyway."

"Where were you?" Ray demanded of the night manager.

"Making my rounds. I was checking up on the cleaning crew. I do it every night."

"Go on, Billy." Ray tilted his hat back on his head.

"When I got there, the woman's husband answered the door. He said his wife had fallen asleep with the TV on. He thinks she must have heard the television. He apologized for disturbing me. I came back down, and a few minutes later Mr. Nelson returned."

"Where was this room?" Zach asked.

"Uh, it was room six-seventeen."

Meghan gazed toward the front doors. A chill slid down her arms causing the hairs to rise. "What direction does it face?"

"The front of the hotel."

"Near the parking lot," Ray answered in a low tone.

"Well, the parking lot's off to the side a bit," Billy informed them.

Meghan looked at Zach and Ray. The hair on the back of her neck followed the action of those on her arms.

"Oh, my God," she whispered. "Suzanne."

The three of them raced for the doors, and ran down the steps.

Zach led the charge. "What kind of car does Dave

drive?"

"A Mercedes. Light colored, I think," Ray replied.

In her high heels, Meghan had trouble keeping up with the men. "Any idea where it's parked?"

They stopped momentarily as Ray flipped open his cell and punched a button. "Jamieson, when you searched the lot for Coryell's car earlier, where was it parked?" He listened for a moment. "Thanks." He hung up. "Third row, near the end, over by the garden."

They sprinted in that direction then pulled up short when they spotted the car under a lamppost.

"It's still here. She didn't take off," Zach said.

Meghan walked around toward the driver's side. She gasped when her eyes caught sight of a blue-clad body partially hidden under a car. "Oh, God! It's Suzanne."

Zach and Ray leaped forward and gently eased her from under the car, rolling her onto her back.

Ray placed his fingers on the battered woman's neck feeling for a pulse. His gaze met hers.

"She's alive!"

Chapter Fifteen

Suzanne was alive!

Meghan's heart hammered as she rushed forward to help the wounded woman.

"Don't touch her, Meghan."

Meghan ignored Ray's order, gulped tears, and held Suzanne's hand. Zach crouched next to her. Ray immediately called 9-1-1.

"This is Sheriff Ray Armstrong. I want an ambulance sent to the parking lot of The Grandview Inn stat. I have a critically injured woman. Please alert the ER at the hospital to stand by." He hung up from emergency services and re-dialed. "Jamieson, are you the only deputy still here? Call in Campbell and Thompson. We have an emergency in the parking lot. Someone's assaulted Mrs. Crocker. She's unconscious and bleeding bad. Get forensics out here... Screw Coryell's room. Drug paraphernalia can wait a while. This one is hot—less than an hour old."

Meghan gagged. Suzanne's beautiful designer dress was ripped and blood spattered. Congealing blood caked her red hair. Suzanne's ankle and arm were twisted indicating broken bones. She shuddered at the sight of the stains marring the dress.

Suzanne's face bore no resemblance to the beautiful woman of a few hours ago. Meghan stifled a sob. The metallic stench of blood was overwhelming.

She struggled not to throw up.

"I guess there's no mistake this time." Ray said in a grim tone. "Dammit. Why the hell did she leave her room?"

"I don't know." Guilt gnawed at her insides. "I should have stayed with her."

"Where's that damned ambulance?" Zach snapped at Ray.

"Take it easy. I just called. If you want to help, inform Nelson he's got another victim." Ray glanced at the overhead light several yards away. "Ask him if the hotel has security cameras covering the parking lot."

Zach left while Meghan continued to hold Suzanne's hand, wincing at the sight of the woman's grotesquely twisted limbs. She couldn't just sit here. She had to do something.

"Come on, Suzanne, hang in there. Help is on the way. You're tough. You can do it."

She hoped the redhead heard the words of encouragement. Suzanne could be a real bitch, but she was also a fighter. She wouldn't give up easily. Then a thought occurred.

"Ray, she must have seen her attacker."

"Maybe, maybe not. He might have worn a ski or stocking mask."

"What about the weapon?"

"A baseball bat? A tire iron? Even a hammer. I don't know."

Meghan peered under the cars. "Do you think it's still here?"

"As soon as my men get here, we'll search the parking lot and the garden. The attacker would want to unload it as soon as possible."

"If he attacked Suzanne in the parking lot, he must have returned to the hotel through the front doors."

"Not necessarily. He could have entered the garden, hidden the weapon in the bushes, and slipped in through one of many doors. This is a cool character. He's familiar with the layout of the hotel."

Sirens wailed in the distance. Meghan breathed a sigh of relief. Help was on the way. *It's about time.*

The ambulance cut the noise when it entered the parking lot. Ray ran toward the entrance and flagged them down, pointing to the scene. Two police cruisers turned in a few seconds later. When the ambulance stopped, paramedics piled out.

"I've got to go now, Suzanne. The paramedics are here and will take good care of you. Fight it. Don't let the bastard win."

Meghan rose, picking up Suzanne's discarded purse, car key, and shoes. She stepped back and crossed her arms over her chest as the medical personnel swarmed around the victim. Already Ray had directed his men to the garden. That seemed the most logical place to stash the weapon.

"Meghan, go back into the hotel. This is a crime scene. I'll take those," Ray said, pointing to items in her hands.

Meghan handed them over, and then secured her bag firmly over her shoulder by the slender strap. Blood streaked her arms. She gazed at the men working to save Suzanne.

"BP's eighty over forty, respirations eight and shallow, pulse sixty, thready, and dropping. Come on guys, we're losing her. God only knows what kind of internal injuries she's sustained."

"Fight, you bitch, fight." Meghan hadn't realized she'd spoken out loud.

"Meghan, please," Ray insisted.

"No. I want to stay with her. I'll just stand here."

The paramedics stuck an IV needle in Suzanne's unbroken arm and slapped an oxygen mask over her blood covered face. Meghan held her breath and waited while the men applied air casts on the broken bones. Suzanne never moved.

"Ninety over sixty," the paramedic monitoring vital signs called out. "Pulse and respirations are up, too."

Way to go, Suzanne.

Meghan jumped when an arm draped over her shoulders. "How's she doing?" Zach asked.

"Not so good, but better than a minute ago."

Ray joined them. "What did Nelson say?"

"There are no security cameras anywhere in the hotel."

Meghan jerked her head around to stare. "No cameras? What kind of hotel doesn't have security?"

"According to Nelson, they had cameras, but turned most of them off two years ago in a cost cutting move. What's there now are used as a decoy, a deterrent."

"Didn't work, did it?" she snapped in a tart tone.

"Instead the guards patrol on foot."

"What guards? I haven't seen any all night. What the hell were they doing? Playing Liar's Poker in a back room?" Meghan spat out.

"Relax. There are only two of them. They stroll around the outside, including the parking lot and the garden, once an hour. Most of the locked offices are on the alarm system."

"Are any of the cameras still working?" Ray demanded.

"Nelson admitted he didn't know. He said he hasn't looked at a monitor in six months."

Ray took off his hat, ran his hand though his hair, and grimaced. "Damned jackasses. I hope The Grandview Inn can cover all the lawsuits heading their way."

The paramedics lifted Suzanne onto the gurney brought out of the ambulance. She looked pitiful, barefooted and in the tattered remains of the bloodstained designer dress. Tears gathered in Meghan's eyes. She sniffed. She didn't consider Suzanne Crocker a friend—wasn't even sure she liked her, but no one deserved this.

"BP's one hundred over sixty. Pulse steady and stronger at sixty-five. Respirations improving. Let's transport," the paramedic ordered.

"I want to go with her," Meghan said.

"Let the hospital personnel do their job," Ray told her.

"Please, let me go with her," she begged.

"I'm sorry, ma'am," one of the paramedics finally told her. "We have work to do, but you can follow us to the hospital if you want."

"I want. How long before I can see her?" Meghan persisted as the last paramedic climbed into the ambulance.

"Can't say, ma'am. Could be an hour, could be longer. Take your time. No sense in sitting in a hospital waiting room."

"Is she going to live?"

"She's in bad shape, but her vitals are improving."

He slammed the door, and the ambulance shot out of the parking lot.

"That didn't tell me a damned thing!"

"Come on, Meghan. I need a drink," Zach said.

Their retreat was halted when Ray turned his attention to one of his deputies returning from the garden. "Find anything?"

"Nothing. The lights are too dim and flashlights don't come close to penetrating all the foliage."

"Well, keep looking. The killer wouldn't leave the damned thing lying on the path. Check behind the bushes," Ray snapped.

"Don't forget the koi pond," Zach suggested.

"I hadn't thought of that," Meghan murmured. What better place to hide something than in the depths of dark water?

"Don't worry, we'll check everywhere," Ray replied in an impatient tone. "Why don't the two of you go back inside? Nothing for you out here."

Zach steered her across the parking lot. Nelson met them at the front door. "Is she going to make it?"

"Too soon to tell. We'll be in the bar if the sheriff wants us," Zach informed him.

The night manager nodded, his expression far from happy.

Probably thinks we're going to get blind drunk on his tab. Serves him right if we do.

Meghan ignored the tables and grabbed a stool. Zach slid around the bar and lifted the brandy bottle.

"No, not brandy. Wine."

He opened the fridge under the counter, extracted a half-empty bottle of chardonnay, and poured, then using a glass, scooped ice from the bin. Glenlivet crackled over the cubes.

She sipped, then shoved the glass away and buried her face in her hands. "We should never have left her alone."

Zach pried her hands loose. "And what would she have said if you suggested staying with her?"

"She'd have probably told me to go to hell."

"And you'd have walked away. No one could predict she'd take off. The only person who should feel guilty is the killer." He released her hands and sipped on the scotch. "The bastard obviously thought she was dead or at the least, dying. If she makes it, and got a good look at him, she may be able to provide an ID."

"Assuming he didn't wear a disguise of some sort. I would. To shield my face and clothing from blood spatter if nothing else. Zach, a thought occurred to me earlier." She fiddled with the stem of her wine glass. "What if the killer is a cop, or even one of those security guards? Suzanne would have opened the door to someone like that."

Zach frowned. "I can't think of why anyone in the Grandview Police Department would have a vendetta against these people. Ray and Ron Campbell are the closest in age to us. Ron was a member of the Methodist Church and president of the youth league when I was a teenager. I think he graduated two or three years before us."

"Maybe it doesn't have to be a real cop. Someone could be running around with a fake uniform and badge. Would Suzanne know the difference? Would you? Would I? Would anybody?"

Zach shook his head. "But why would she leave with him? Why even open the door? She was scared and pissed."

"And she wasn't forced to leave. She'd have screamed the house down. Plus, if the killer had a knife to her throat or a gun stuck in her ribs, why attack using a blunt instrument?" She glanced at her watch. "Do you think they have any news yet?"

"Honey, it's only been a few minutes. They're probably just arriving at the hospital. Come on, drink your wine."

"I don't want to drink the goddamned wine. I want to be with Suzanne."

"Why? She's been nasty all night."

"Guilt maybe? I should have stayed with her whether she wanted me to or not." She rubbed her fingers over her forehead, choking back a sob. "Oh, God, I don't know why. I don't even like the bitch. All I know is I want to be with her."

"And do what? Sit in the hospital waiting room? It's going to take a while to set the broken bones, get a CAT scan, and stitch those head wounds. Don't cry, honey, and don't feel guilty."

"At least there would be someone with her, someone who showed some interest in whether she lives or dies." Her voice rose.

"Meghan, calm down," Zach ordered in a quiet voice.

"I don't want to calm down either. I'm mad as hell. I want this maniac caught. I want to know why he's killing off our classmates. These are no spur of the moment events. This took planning."

"There's no need to shout. I want to know, too."

She struggled to lower her voice. "And what if the killer is someone who doesn't have a grudge against the

Fearsome Foursome? What if he just hates everyone in the whole freaking class? Am I next? Are you? And can Ray do a damned thing about it?"

"I'm asking myself the same question," Ray said from the doorway. He entered and took the stool next to her. "Forensics is going over the parking lot, but hasn't found anything. And it's too dark to get much accomplished in the garden. This killer is either very smart, or I'm a lousy cop."

Meghan bit her lip. "Two murders and an attempted murder in less than eight hours are apt to put everyone on edge."

"Maybe I deserve it. I haven't got much in the line of clues, and unless I come up with something, this place is going to empty out tomorrow morning like an erupting volcano, and then the killer could be gone."

"Ray, you look like you could use a drink," Zach said. "Are you still on duty or can I pour you something?"

"I'm still on duty, but go ahead and hit me with whatever you're having." Zach served him. Ray took a long swallow. "Thanks, I'm about at the end of my rope."

"I had another theory," Meghan suggested, and told him about the possibility of a police or security guard impersonator. She stiffened her spine as another thought crossed her mind. "Ray, you said the killer used his knee on the victim's backs to gain leverage. I've watched those reality based cop shows on TV. Isn't that how an officer subdues a fleeing suspect so he can handcuff him?"

"Yes. That's an effective way to maintain control. It isn't easy to throw off a grown man who's kneeling on your back." He ran a hand over his face. "Ah, hell, Meghan, it couldn't be one of my guys. There were too many people here tonight who know us on sight. A stranger in a Grandview police uniform would've been noticed and mentioned during questioning."

"What about the security guards? Would they have had the same type of training?" Zach asked.

"Probably. I've never thought to ask. It's worth checking out. I'll talk to Nelson and the guards."

Meghan tapped her finger against her lips. "Ray, suppose one of our classmates from out of town is a cop or a former cop? Or even a security guard?"

"If that's the case, no one admitted it during questioning, at least not to my knowledge. None of my deputies mentioned it either. I'll ask." He finished his scotch. "By the way, I took your advice and called the police over in Muncie." He shook his head. "Never underestimate the deductive powers of women."

"What do you mean?" she asked.

"I mean, Clara Sylvester's death is listed as suspicious."

"I knew it! Those dates are just too close together. And why a teacher? What was her connection to the Fearsome Foursome?"

Zach shot a quick look at Meghan. "What happened, Ray?"

"According to one of the nurses, she had given Clara her medications and was sitting with her when an emergency in another room called her away. She was gone about an hour. She peeked in on Ms. Sylvester when she returned and found her dead."

"What's suspicious about that?" Zach inquired.

"There was an extra pillow on the old woman's

bed, one the nurse is pretty certain wasn't there when she left. The coroner found cloth fibers in the nasal passages and lungs during autopsy."

"She was smothered?" Meghan said.

"That's the conclusion."

"Could it have been an inside job? Someone who worked there?" Zach wanted to know.

"At the moment, the officials are investigating if a staff member may have had robbery on his or her mind. However, as far as they know nothing was taken. Her watch and rings, along with ten dollars and a bunch of change were in plain sight on the nightstand. Clara also had defensive bruises on her arms. The theory is the person entered the room thinking the old gal was asleep and panicked when he realized she wasn't."

"And he just happened to bring a pillow with him?" Meghan wondered.

"The nurse was *pretty* sure about the pillow not being there, but stops short of swearing to it."

"The police may be right on this," Zach said. "The killer is so scared after she dies, he runs without taking anything. Why would our killer take out Clara Sylvester?"

"No, this was no inside job. There *has* to be a connection," Meghan insisted.

Ray ran his hand over his face. "I have no idea why anyone would want to murder poor old Clara, nor do I understand her connection to students who graduated twenty years ago. We were related, you know."

"You and Clara?" Meghan replied.

"Yeah, her mother and my grandmother were sisters. Made us some kind of cousins, I think. I just thought you'd like to know your hunch was right." He set the glass back on the bar and slid from the stool. "Guess I'll go talk to Nelson. I understand the general manager of the place is on his way in from his weekend cabin on Lake Shafer. You going to the hospital?"

Meghan nodded. "As soon as I change clothes."

"Good idea. I've been in this suit a lot longer than I'd planned," Zach added.

"I'll stop by the ER in a little while," Ray remarked as his phone rang. He answered, listened for a moment, and then heaved a sigh. "All right, I'll send a couple of deputies over. Any fatalities... Well, that's a blessing at any rate." He hung up.

"Something wrong?" Zach asked.

"Three car accident on the highway. Several people hurt, but no fatals. I'll send a couple of guys out to deal with it while I finish up here. It never rains, it pours." He shook his head and left the bar.

Zach finished his drink. Meghan eyed the rejected wine. Might not be such a bad idea after all. She tilted the glass, drinking until it was empty. They walked side by side to the elevators.

"What floor?" Zach asked when they entered the car.

"I'm on the second, room two-fifteen."

"I'm in five-oh-six."

The elevator stopped. "I'll walk you to the door."

Meghan found his actions unnecessary, but endearing. *What I really want is to forget about everything and let nature take its course.* She sighed, opened her purse, and extracted the key. She unlocked the door, and Zach slipped in first to look around.

Meghan held her breath. Was someone hiding in the closet? The bathroom? The inspection took less than a minute. When he returned, he smiled, glanced at the bed, and then shrugged. Forget anxiety. Old-fashioned lust sent heat flooding her body. *Yeah, me too.*

"You're clear. I'll be back in, say ten minutes?"

"Make it fifteen. I want to wash up."

Zach nodded, kissed her, and left. Meghan closed the door behind him, fanning her hot face with the evening bag. Was the hospital really all that important? Another hour wouldn't make much difference, would it? She turned to open the door and call him back. Then Suzanne's bleeding body flashed before her eyes. Her conscience hammered at her.

"Damn," she muttered.

Meghan peeled the dress from her body, tossed it onto the bed, and headed for the bathroom. Washing the make-up from her face and the blood from her arms, Meghan wondered if the doctors and nurses had scrubbed the blood from Suzanne.

She grabbed a pair of jeans from her suitcase and pulled them on, then yanked a canary yellow top over her head. She added socks, slipped her feet into running shoes, and debated the necessity of carrying a purse. Meghan decided against it. Instead, she added twenty bucks to the ID holder that already contained her driver's license and a credit card.

She shoved it along with her cell phone into her back pockets, daubed lipstick on her mouth, and gazed at the stun gun still in her purse. She slipped it out and pressed the red button. Meghan flinched at the zap, but didn't drop it. She jammed the thing into her front pocket. *Won't forget it there. I'll give it to Zach when he gets here.*

A knock startled her.

She glanced at her watch. Zach already? It hadn't even been ten minutes yet.

Honestly, men.

She'd requested the extra time to get her emotions under control. She was angry about the night's events and frustrated at the inability to do anything at the moment about Zach's kisses. She never thought straight when either emotion was present, often saying and doing things she regretted later. And she really wanted to pursue those kisses further.

Certain it was Zach, she gazed through the peephole and, surprised, opened the door.

****

Meghan and Zach are becoming a problem. Both are analytical and intelligent. No wonder that bumbling sheriff allowed them to help with the investigation. He didn't have the brains or the manpower to stop me.

But Meghan and Zach are another story. They could piece it together. The two of them already zeroed in on the past as a motive. It's only a matter of time until the answers click in one of their heads. I'll have to do something about them. I've come too far, have too much to lose, to be defeated now.

I heaved a sigh. I hadn't counted on a seventh or an eighth victim. Maybe number six could wait until later. The road to success is often strewn with rocks. Meghan and Zach represented my boulders. I had to deal with them first. Without them, the sheriff would be clueless.

Together, they're a team. Divide and conquer. That's the strategy. But which one do I chose?

My decision made, I turned to my hotel highway, the stairs.

****

Zach strode out of the elevator on the fifth floor and hurried to his room. Slamming the door behind him, he jerked off his suit coat tossing it on the bed, then kicked off his shoes. His tie, shirt, and pants joined the heap. The bed sagged as he sat to remove his black socks. They hit the floor near the shoes.

He donned jeans, a light blue polo shirt, a belt, athletic socks, and a pair of Nikes. He shoved his wallet, phone, and car keys into his pockets before glancing at his watch.

Why on earth would Meghan need fifteen minutes to change clothes? He could do it in two and be back outside her door in five. Zach decided he had a lot to learn about women.

To kill time, he hung his discarded clothing in the closet, and looked at his watch again.

Swell, that took a whole minute and a half. Now what do I do?

He grabbed the remote and turned on the TV, flipping though channels until finding the news. Two talking heads debated the world situation and the United States' role in it.

He flipped to the Weather Channel. Central Indiana could expect hot and humid conditions for the remainder of the weekend with the possibility of thunderstorms on Sunday afternoon.

The clock on the nightstand said only another three minutes had passed.

This is ridiculous. He shut the tube off. *I'm going anyway. She can either let me in or I'll wait in the hall.*

He jerked the door open and jumped back in surprise.

"Zach, I'm glad you're here. Can I come in? I have

to talk to you."

Puzzled, he stepped aside. "Sure. What's wrong?"

Zach left the door open. Curious and unsuspecting, he faced Tom Ecklund.

Chapter Sixteen

Tom Ecklund rushed past Zach, his hair in disarray and his eyes glazed, as if he'd just gotten out of bed. His expression bordered on panicked.

"Where's Meghan?"

"I just left her in her room. We're going to the hospital. Tom, what's going on?" Zach walked further into his room, leaving the door open.

"The hospital? Why?" The panic on his face changed to sheer horror.

"Suzanne Crocker was attacked a little while ago in the parking lot. She's in bad shape. Tom, what's going on?"

The look on the man's face was scaring him to death. He couldn't decide if Tom was crazy or terrified. Zach cast an uneasy glance back toward the open door.

Tom grasped his head. "Oh God, oh God, no! She's done it again. Oh, Jesus, please help me."

Zach strode forward, and shook his classmate by the shoulders. His voice rose. "Knock it off! What the hell are you talking about?"

Tom gulped, his gaze darting from side to side. Zach shook him again.

"Tom, sober up!"

"I'm not drunk. I was drugged. And now I'm scared. It's Glory. She's the killer. And I think Meghan is next on her list."

Zach's stomach dropped to his toes as a numbing cold swept over him. "What? What makes you think that?"

"I don't know for sure, but I just have a feeling, especially now that Suzanne is dead."

"Suzanne's not dead yet, but she's in critical condition."

Amazement flashed across his face. "She's not? Another mistake. She got away twice." Tom grabbed Zach's arm. "Come on! We have to make sure Meghan's all right."

The man's hysteria fueled Zach's fear for Meghan. *Oh my God! If anything happens to Meghan, I'll die. I can't live without her. Not after finding her again.*

The two men ran from the room.

****

"Glory! What are you doing here?"

Meghan's surprise gave way to concern. Glory was a mess. Her eyes, red and puffy, showed obvious signs of recent tears. Any make-up from the evening had long since vanished. With her washed out blue eyes and pale face, the woman resembled a ghost. Her rumpled gray sweat suit looked as if she'd slept in it. She sniffed and shifted a frightened gaze from side to side up and down the hallway.

"Oh, Meghan, please help me." Glory clutched her stomach and cried, new tears coursing down her cheeks.

"What's wrong?" Meghan reached to pull her into the room, but the distraught woman stepped away.

Glory tugged at Meghan's arm. "It's—it's Tom. I can't find them, and I'm so afraid he's done something bad."

"Bad? Bad how? And what do you mean you can't

find them? Them who?" Meghan pulled back against the determined woman.

"He's with Zach, and I'm afraid," she wailed. "Hurry! There's no time to lose."

"With Zach? How do you know?" Her heart thudded with fear she didn't understand. The woman's babbling made no sense. "Glory, come in and calm down. What's this all about?"

Glory grabbed Meghan's hand again and tugged her into the corridor. "I saw them getting into the elevator, but the doors closed before I could catch them. I think they went down to the lobby. Please, help me."

"Why are you so scared of Tom and Zach being together?" She closed the door to her room and headed for the elevators. Glory, however, veered toward the stairwell.

"The stairs are faster." She rammed the door open and dropping Meghan's hand, grasped the banister.

"Glory! Answer me. What's so urgent?"

Meghan's legs trembled and her heart pounded as the fear increased. Glory's departure from the happy reunion committee member to an incoherent hysteric scared the hell out of her. Glory finally stopped on the landing and turned to face her.

"Meghan, I think Tom's responsible."

"Responsible for what?"

"The killings. I couldn't find him when Annabelle and Dave were murdered. I'm afraid Zach may be in danger, too."

"Why would Zach be in danger?"

"Because you guys are helping the sheriff, and you're getting close to solving the crimes."

Meghan's heart rate soared and her breath caught

in her throat. Tom Ecklund? Quiet, always pleasant Tom, a killer? The image just didn't fit. Her mind had a hard time assimilating the information. On the other hand, how many times in her novels had the quiet ones been the killers? A lot. The quiet ones who allowed things to fester were always prime candidates for being serial killers. *But this isn't a story. This is real life.*

"Why would Tom kill anyone?"

"He hates them all. They made fun of Divine and after she killed herself, he blamed everyone for sending her over the edge. And he wasn't in town when Tami, Eddie, and Ms. Sylvester died."

"What's Divine got to do with this?" The ramblings, making less and less sense, confused her. They also scared her. Glory's panic-stricken face and words fueled Meghan's fears. *Oh God, what if she's right? What if Tom does want to kill Zach, and then me? I couldn't stand to find Zach's body. Not when I think I'm in love for the first time in my life.*

Glory continued down the stairs. If she wanted an explanation, Meghan had no option but to follow. Fear and a growing sense of dread overwhelmed her. She wanted that explanation.

"Glory, tell me, what does Divine have to do with this?" She put on a burst of speed to catch up to the woman galloping down the stairwell.

Glory paused on the landing below, her breath rasping in and out. "He was in love with her. Still is. He only married me because I look like her. I tried to be just like Divine for him, but it was never enough. He gets drunk and forgets who I am. Calls me Divine. He's not normal, Meghan."

She whirled and continued on. Meghan followed.

They reached the lobby and jerked open the door. The area was empty.

Tom in love with Glory's sister? She could see that, but to marry the younger sister as some kind of substitute sounded crazy. Then she remembered Tom's stumbling actions in the bar earlier in the evening before Dave's murder. Meghan sucked in a ragged breath. Crazy? *Oh, my God, no.*

"We need to find the sheriff."

"No time to look. We need to confront Tom now. He'll hurt Zach, and Zach won't see it coming. He won't suspect. If we find them, we'll be witnesses. Tom won't do anything with witnesses, and he won't hurt me. Then Zach can subdue him while one of us gets the sheriff," Glory said, still breathless and sobbing. She grabbed Meghan's hand again and tugged. "Quick, the ballroom!"

Meghan tried to control the ever-increasing terror. Her legs trembled, and her breath rasped in her throat. Frightened for Zach, she tried to pull free, but the woman's grasp on her hand tightened painfully.

"Why the ballroom? Maybe they went out front."

"Too busy and well-lit. Tom would get Zach into a more secluded place."

"Glory, stop! We don't even know where to look. We need Sheriff Armstrong. Given what's happened tonight, Zach will be careful."

Glory burst through the ballroom doors. The younger woman's panic and hysteria were infectious. Meghan followed, a ball of anxiety and fear knotting in her stomach. The room had minimum lighting. The table rounds, not yet put away, leaned against the walls.

Glory pointed to the open terrace door. "The

garden. He'd have gone out through the terrace to the garden. Hurry, Meghan!"

The urgency in Glory's voice sent a cold chill down her spine.

Then Glory cried out and clutched her calf. "Cramp," she cried out with a gasp. "Hurry, Meghan! You can catch up to them."

Against her better judgment, she ran past the woman for the terrace doors. If Tom Ecklund was the killer, then she had to find Zach. He was fit and would put up a hell of a fight, but Tom would have the element of surprise.

She plunged onto the dimly lit terrace and paused at the top of the steps.

"Tom, Zach, are you out here?" Only the chirping insects answered. "Zach! Where are you?" She dashed down to the path, and then slowed her pace when she almost fell.

"Which way would they go, Glory, and how long ago did you see them?"

She didn't wait for a reply and turned left toward the koi pond. A few seconds later, it dawned on her Glory had not followed. She whirled. Her breath and her mind froze.

****

Zach and Tom raced down the stairwell.

"Why would Glory want to hurt Meghan?" Zach said, gasping as he ran.

"You guys got in the way of her plans." He yanked the door to the second floor open.

They ran to Meghan's room. Zach pounded on the door.

"Meghan!" He waited less than three seconds

before repeating his action. "Meghan! Open up!"

"Oh, God, please let her be in there," Tom muttered.

"Damn! She's not here." They raced back to the stairs, stumbling out in an empty lobby.

Zach looked around, his heart slamming against his ribs and his breath ragged. The front desk was once again unattended, but the light in the small back room was on.

"Hey! We need help!"

Billy emerged, his eyes wide at the sight of the two men.

"I need the passkey to room two-fifteen. Now!"

"I can't do that," Billy protested. "I may never hand out another key again."

Zach leaned over the counter and grabbed the young man by his tie, yanking him forward.

"I said give me the goddamned key now! A woman's life is in danger!"

Tom pulled at Zach's arm. "She's not in the room. Glory wouldn't do anything there. She'd get her to leave."

"Where's the sheriff?" Zach yelled, keeping his hold on Billy.

"He—he's in the security room questioning the guards."

"Get him!"

He released the man's tie. Billy picked up the phone and dialed. "Uh, Sheriff, you'd better get out here. I got trouble." He hung up, backing away from the two men.

The sheriff emerged from a back hallway with Mark Nelson. At the same time, the remaining two deputies stepped in the front doors.

"What's wrong, Zach?"

"Meghan and Glory are missing."

Ray's eyes sharpened. "You think the killer's got both of them?"

"I think Glory's the killer," Tom informed him.

"Meghan's not answering the door to her room. She should be there."

"Get the passkey and go check," Ray snapped at the hapless desk clerk. "Campbell, go with him. Let me know what you find. Jamieson, you checkout the parking lot."

"We just got back from there. It's quiet."

"Goddamn it! Check it again!"

The deputies turned and ran, one through the front entrance and the other toward the elevators.

"Any idea where Glory and Meghan might have gone?"

"Why would Meghan go with Glory? She's not stupid," Zach claimed.

"My wife can be very persuasive. She knows exactly which buttons to push. She'd use you, Zach. You've been with Meghan all evening. It's obvious the two of you are close." Tom gazed around the lobby with a haunted look in his eyes. "The garden. If she wants to kill Meghan, she'll try for the garden. It's dark."

They ran to the large double doors of the ballroom that earlier in the evening had opened to a crowd of happy people. Zach wrenched open the door and rushed in, then paused in the semi-darkness to scan the room.

"One of the terrace doors is open," he exclaimed, pointing.

A scream echoed from outside. Ray drew his gun and raced for the terrace, pushing Zach and Tom out of the way.

"Stay back," he ordered.

Both men ignored him and pounded after the policeman.

A second scream shattered the night.

****

Glory stood at the bottom of the steps six feet away, a tire iron in her hands. The look on the woman's face in the feeble light was just short of grotesque. Her lips were drawn back in a snarl and her pale eyes glowed. Meghan didn't need to be told, she'd been a fool. Her heart hammered and her knees went weak.

"Glory?"

"I'm sorry, Meghan, but you had no business sticking your nose into this." She stepped forward and swung the tire iron like a baseball bat.

Meghan leaped back. The end of the iron caught her in the side and spun her around with a gasp. Pain radiated through her torso.

"Glory, for the love of God, don't do this. Think! You'll never get away with another death. I'm not Suzanne."

"That bitch! 'And I will execute great vengeance upon them,'" she muttered.

Meghan's mind snapped back to all those years in Catholic youth and parochial grade school. Long forgotten Scriptures funneled into her brain.

"Ezekiel. Chapter twenty-five, verse seventeen," she said, gasping.

The weapon descended again. She jumped sideways, and Glory missed by inches, the breeze from the swing kissing Meghan's cheek.

"'The wicked shall not be unpunished.' Proverbs, eleven, twenty-one." The crazed woman swung, this time making contact with Meghan's arm.

She cried out in pain, and her arm went numb. "'Thou shalt not kill!'"

"'An eye for an eye and a tooth for a tooth,'" Glory quoted back along with another swat with the tire iron.

She missed, and Meghan circled to the left. Fleeing into the garden was not an option. She didn't know the layout. Glory did. The terrace loomed above her. If she could make it to the steps, she had a chance.

"'Vengeance is mine.'" Maybe trading Bible verses would distract Glory from her mission. Meghan hoped she remembered enough of them. "Why, Glory? Why kill them?"

"It's in the diary."

"What diary?"

"Divine's. I found it and read it. It's all their fault."

"Glory, put the tire iron down."

"'The eyes of the wicked shall fail, and they shall not escape.' Job, eleven, twenty."

A vicious chop to the head had Meghan jumping back just in time. Glory circled, in the opposite direction cutting off the steps to the terrace.

"'Judge not lest ye be judged.' Matthew, seven, one."

Meghan kept her eyes on Glory's face trying to anticipate the next blow. The woman telegraphed it. Meghan stumbled backwards and fell to avoid being hit in the side.

Glory closed in. Her eyes glowed with what Meghan assumed was righteousness—or insanity.

Reasoning with her was out of the question.

"Zach! Help!" she cried out. Her ears roared from the blood pounding in them, and she wasn't sure if she had screamed or whispered.

"You fool, he's not coming to help. I watched him get in the elevator and go to his room on the fifth floor. He's sound asleep."

"No, he was changing clothes. We were going to the hospital to see Suzanne."

"She's dead."

"No, Glory. She's alive and can identify you." She had no idea if any of it was true.

"Liar!" She swung the tire iron wildly at Meghan's head, but in her rage, missed. "It's a sin to lie!"

"'Fear God and keep His commandments.'"

"'The name of the wicked shall rot,'" the insane woman screamed.

The iron swished through the air again. Meghan rolled to her right and attempted to rise. Glory's foot lashed out and caught her in the chest. She fell back. Glory wielded the weapon again and made contact with Meghan's leg. She cried out and rolled. Didn't anyone in the hotel hear the commotion? Something dug into her hip.

The stun gun! I have a chance. She fumbled to remove it. Out of the corner of her eye, she saw the tire iron aimed at her head.

"'The righteous shall rejoice when He seeth the vengeance.' Psalms!" Glory shrieked. The weapon descended.

Meghan rolled at the last moment. The tire iron struck the ground. She rolled again and regained her footing.

"You see, Glory. I'm faster than Suzanne." While she spoke she tried to wedge her hand into her front pocket and cursed the tight jeans.

Glory didn't answer, but swung again. The blow hit Meghan just above the left knee. She cried out and crumpled backward onto the steps. She twisted to the left in desperate attempt to avoid a whistling chop, the sharp stone of the step digging into her side. The iron struck where she'd lain.

Her attacker's movements slowed. Glory panted with exertion. Her aim was not as accurate as a minute ago and the blows, while painful, had diminished in intensity. Still, she raised the bar again. Meghan rolled to the right and Glory missed, the step taking the brunt of the blow again. The edge of the flagstone bit into her wrist. Blood flowed hot and warm into her hand, but her fingers finally touched the stun gun.

The whoosh of air told her the tire iron was on the move. This time she didn't move fast enough. It caught her on the shoulder. She screamed and grasped for the slender rod. It was slick with a slimy, jelly-like substance. Blood? Hers or Suzanne's? Glory wrenched it away, hoisting it over her head. Meghan waited until the weapon began its downward arc, and then rolled to the left. At the same time, her fingers wiggled the stun gun from her pocket.

Glory's momentum carried her forward. Unable to stop, she screamed and stumbled against the step, then fell forward, the tire iron falling from her hands.

Meghan staggered to her feet, switched the stun gun on, and charged.

Glory crouched, reaching for the bar just as Meghan made contact with the side of the woman's neck. She pressed the red button. The current flowed, sizzling and crackling. Glory jerked, and then fell onto her back.

She finally released the button and gazed at Glory's unmoving body, her eyes wide and staring.

Oh, my God, I've killed her.

Then the woman's eyes shifted from side to side, and an odd gurgling sound emanated from her throat.

Meghan sobbed and fell to her knees at the foot of the stairs. "'With malice toward none; with charity for all.'"

She was so exhausted and frightened, she didn't hear anything until a voice boomed, "Don't move. Stay where you are!"

She looked up. Ray stood on the terrace with gun drawn. Zach and Tom burst through the doors behind them a second later.

"Help me," she said in a weak voice.

Ray stared at Glory on the steps. "What happened?"

Holding up the stun gun, Meghan declared in a shaky voice, "I zapped her," then pitched forward in a dead faint.

****

"I'm okay, really, I am," Meghan insisted, looking into Zach's worried eyes. "Just some cuts and bruises."

"Are you sure?"

His hand gently stroked her arms and ribcage. She sucked in a deep breath as pain jabbed her side. Tears filled her eyes.

He muttered something obscene under his breath. "You could have some broken ribs. Damn, I should never have left you alone, even to change clothes."

She stroked his cheek and blinked the dampness from her eyes. This man was a keeper.

Her fainting spell hadn't lasted long. She'd regained consciousness being carried through the ballroom in Zach's arms. It was a nice way to awaken.

"You should go to the hospital for x-rays and stitches," the paramedic said, bandaging her right wrist.

"I will in a while."

"I've never been so scared in my entire life," Zach said. "When Tom told me he thought Glory was the killer and that you may be in danger, I didn't know what to do. It sounded like the ranting of a madman."

"She came to the door and told me Tom was the maniac and that *you* were in danger."

She and Zach sat on the sofa in the lobby. Her gaze slid over to Glory who was seated a few feet away in a chair, her hands handcuffed behind her back. She swayed back and forth. The tangled hair escaping from the bun hung beside her face. Tom crouched in front of her, his hands cradling her face.

"'The memory of the just is blessed.' That's Proverbs. Chapter ten, verse eleven, I think, or is it seven. I can't remember. Mama will beat me for forgetting," Glory mumbled.

"No, she won't, honey. I won't let her," Tom replied with a sob.

"You're so good to me, darling. 'A man's foes shall be they of his own household.' That one is Matthew ten, thirty-six. I know that's right. I remember it. I used to tell it to Glory after Mother beat us. Where is Glory? Wasn't she here a little while ago? I have to protect my little sister."

Meghan glanced at Zach.

He shook his head and murmured, "Psychotic. Completely around the bend."

Ray walked up to them. "Sometimes she's Glory and sometimes she's Divine. Tom says she started slipping about a year ago. Had nightmares and kept referring to Divine like she was still alive. Had entire conversations with her dead sister. Scared the hell out of him."

"Why didn't he get her to a doctor?" Zach demanded.

"He did. The doctor prescribed medications and therapy. Tom thought both had worked. Said she seemed better." Ray shook his head. "Also told me the Prescott household was like living in hell. The old man screamed about hell and damnation, and the mother beat the crap out of them."

"We all knew the Prescotts were odd, but never abusive," Meghan replied. "At least, I didn't."

Ray shook his head. "I feel damned sorry for Tom."

"I just wish he'd paid more attention. He might have seen this breakdown coming." Zach's voice was low-pitched, but hard.

"He loves her. I guess he couldn't believe she was so far gone. What's going to happen to her?" Meghan asked.

"She'll go to jail tonight. We'll put her in an isolation cell until a judge can order a psychiatric evaluation, hopefully tomorrow. I'd have to say a mental institution is her next home."

"She must have suppressed things for years," Zach said, shaking his head and brushing his hand down Meghan's cheek again. "I wonder if Clara Sylvester knew. She often seemed to hover over the girls during youth night meetings at the church."

"I think we'll find a motive for Clara's death through that," Ray confirmed. "Maybe she knew about the abuse, but said nothing."

"Could be." Meghan shook her head. "I still can't believe I bought her story. She was so convincing with the fright in her eyes and the tears streaming down her face," she lamented. "She just seemed so…so harmless. Thank goodness, I was at the bottom of her hit list. God, she looked so frail, who would ever suspect she had that kind of strength to strangle and swing a tire iron?"

Zach sighed and ran a hand through his hair. "None of us thought Glory could kill five people, attempt to kill a sixth, and critically injure a seventh."

"Yeah, but I'm an author. I should know better. No fictional heroine would be so stupid as to do what I did."

"You weren't stupid, just unsuspecting."

"Same thing. I also can't believe nobody heard me screaming."

"It's four in the morning. People are asleep with the windows closed and the air conditioning on. Hell, we didn't hear anything until we were in the ballroom." Zach turned his gaze to Ray. "Any word on Suzanne?"

"The last I talked with the hospital, she was doing well. Her vitals had returned to normal, and while she's still unconscious, the doctors expect her to come out of it."

"Thank God," Meghan said with a sigh. "Where did Glory get the tire iron? She didn't have it when she came to the room. *That* I'd have noticed."

"After whacking Suzanne, she must have re-entered the hotel through the ballroom from the terrace. She hid it behind the draperies by the terrace doors. We found blood on the fabric. I'm sure we'll find the weapon came from her own car."

"And I was so distracted by her hysteria, I never noticed that she'd changed clothes from earlier. When we were in the lobby, she had on navy blue slacks and a long sleeved T-shirt. When she came to the room, she wore a gray sweat suit. Must have had Suzanne's blood all over her."

Zach glanced at Glory. "She missed her calling. She'd have been a great actress."

The paramedic finished with the bandages and rose. "I still recommend the hospital."

"I'll see she gets there," Zach promised.

Meghan's attention turned back to Glory and Tom.

"Divine was the best sister in the whole world."

"I know, honey. She loved you very much," Tom soothed in a soft voice.

"Did you hear? Meghan and I exchanged Bible verses on the terrace. She knows a lot of them." Glory's gaze turned toward Meghan. "You did good, Meghan. But that last quote wasn't biblical."

"I know, it was Abraham Lincoln. I ran out of Bible verses. You remembered more than I did."

"Oh, Daddy made us recite them every night. He'd give us a quote and we'd have to name book, chapter, and verse." She gazed off into the distance, with blank eyes, her head cocked to one side and her face still as though listening. Glory's lips curled into a strange smile. "Good one, Divine. Revelation, chapter six, verse eight."

Two policemen stood next to Glory. "Time to go, ma'am."

"Are we going home now, Tom?"

"Soon. You go with these men and have a good night's sleep. We'll talk in the morning."

The men helped Glory to her feet and led her away. She turned at the doors.

"Aren't you coming, honey?"

Tom smiled through his tears. "I'll be along in a little while. I have to pack."

"Oh, yes, of course. How silly of me." The entrance doors closed behind her.

Tears welled in Meghan's eyes.

Tom looked at her and said, "I'm so sorry. She really isn't...she doesn't..." He didn't finish. Just shook his head and turned toward the elevators.

Meghan wanted to say something comforting to the poor man, but for once in her life words failed.

"Come on," Zach said, placing a hand under her elbow and pulling her upright. "To the hospital. I insist."

Ray removed his hat and scratched his head. "This has been a hell of a night. What was that last thing she said about a revelation?"

Meghan let the tears overflow. "Revelation, chapter six, verse eight. 'I looked and behold a pale horse; and his name that sat on him was death.'"

Chapter Seventeen

Meghan opened one eyelid, and then shut it again against the sunlight flooding the room through the window. She rolled over, her arm making contact with someone lying next to her in the king-sized bed. In spite of the bright light, she opened her eyes.

Oh, yeah, Zach. She remembered him saying he wouldn't leave her alone during what had been left of last night. The pain pill the doctor gave her at the hospital had kicked in sometime on the ride back to the hotel. Everything after that was hazy.

Meghan peeked under the sheet. Her jeans and the canary yellow top were gone, but the underwear remained in place. *Nothing happened. Dammit.*

Still groggy, she leaned on an elbow and gazed over Zach's body to the clock on the nightstand. Nine-thirty. Oh, well, four hours of sleep was better than nothing.

Flopping onto her back, she used her right arm to shield her eyes from the invasive sun. Exhausted from last evening's events, they'd forgotten to close the drapes.

At the hospital, Meghan had refused all treatment until seeing Suzanne. The redhead was tucked away in ICU with tubes and wires running from her body to beeping machines. Although unconscious, Suzanne muttered and moved restlessly. The doctors gave a cautious prognosis she would soon wake. Meghan stood by her earlier assessment. Suzanne was a fighter and would live.

A bandage scraped at her forehead as she raised her arm, peeling back part of the gauze to examine her wrist. Ten stitches had taken care of the cut. Luckily, it hadn't been deep, just ugly. Her fingers probed another bandage on her head near the hairline. It hurt like hell, and couldn't remember how it had happened. Perhaps when she'd fainted. She moved her leg and winced. Damn, she hurt, but not as badly as expected.

The phone rang scaring her half to death. Zach fumbled for the receiver and answered with a sleepy hello.

"Yeah, this is Ms. Donahue's room. Who's this… Really? That's great. Any specific time… Let us get cleaned up and something in our stomachs. We'll meet you there."

"Who was that?" she asked when he'd hung up.

"The sheriff. Suzanne's awake and wants to see us. She's already demanded a private room. The doctors have okayed an hour for visitors at one o'clock." He turned his head to gaze at her. "How are you feeling?"

"I'll let you know as soon as I get out of bed and try to walk."

Zach chuckled, threw back the covers, and sat up. "Hungry?"

"Starved."

He rose, and she admired the tanned, well-buffed body of the former computer geek. He looked damned sexy in his boxers. A shot of shame stabbed her in the gut. Never would she admit to Zach that she'd doubted him last night. Her gaze slid up and down his body again. Yeah, she was starved, but not necessarily for food. She considered doing something about it.

"In that case, why don't I call down for room service while you grab the shower first? What do you want to eat?"

Meghan had an answer, but knew Zach referred to food. A warm gush of heat pooled in the pit of her stomach. Desire plucked at every nerve. *Oh, the hell with it. I don't care how many bruises I have, he's worth it.*

Zach was reaching for his jeans when she murmured, "I'd like to start with your ear lobe, then work my way down to your neck before moving on to that chest. Want me to go on? I'm a writer. I can get very descriptive."

Zach grinned, dropped the jeans, and crawled back into bed, straddling her hips and bracing his arms on either side of her shoulders. "Yeah? I'm more of a hands on kind of guy."

His hands slid under the pillow, raising her head. His lips took hers in a hard demanding kiss. The heat turned into flames. The suppressed passion of the night before consumed Meghan. His tongue stroked while his hands caressed her skin, sending shivers of pure delight throughout her body.

She groaned deep in her throat, kissing him back.

Zach pulled away. "Are you sure you're up for this?"

Her hands ran up and down his back before slipping under the waistband of his boxers where she kneaded his tight derriere.

"Oh, yeah, and then some. I can feel you are, too."

Zach smiled, his nimble fingers unclasping her bra.

She struggled out of it, while he peeled her panties down her legs and off. Both items hit the floor. His boxers followed. Naked, they paused for a moment, staring.

"God, Meghan, you're gorgeous. I want you so bad, I hurt."

Her hand slipped over the sculpted muscles on his smooth chest. "I know. I feel the same."

His mouth descended again to claim hers. Ignoring a sharp pain in her hip, they rolled and thrashed across the bed like two animals with teeth nipping and hands stroking. The blood roared in Meghan's ears. She cried out when his teeth found the erect centers of her breasts. Hot darts of raw desire stabbed deep inside her core. Her hand caressed and squeezed his erection, the heat burning her palm.

Then Zach's fingers touched the slick warmth pouring from her. His thumb massaged the sensitive pinpoint at the junction of her thighs. She cried out— just sound, no words were possible from a body consumed with the fire of passion. Her hips pumped as his fingers played her body like a musician would his instrument. Meghan throbbed from head to foot. Soft sobs burst from her throat. An internal spring wound tighter and tighter. She needed satisfaction now.

Zach rose and nestled between her knees, and with a groan, thrust inside her pulsating body. Once again, she ignored the painful reminders of last night's confrontation and clasped her legs around his hips.

He moved slowly, and then faster. She burned like a torch, matching his fierce strokes. Meghan opened her eyes. Zach's eyes were closed. The tendons in his neck corded with the strain. His mouth stretched onto a grin of what she assumed was pure desire.

She understood. The spring coiled, ready to release. She closed her eyes again and rode the fiery sensations wanting to achieve that final destination, yet unwilling to have it end.

With suddenness she hadn't expected, the spring snapped. Hard, deep contractions of pleasure ripped through her. She screamed Zach's name.

Then Zach, thrusting one last time, buried his face in her neck. He cried out hoarsely. She felt his climax pulsating inside her. Meghan rode the wave until it crashed onshore again and again until finally dissipating.

Her legs loosened their grip and fell limply on the bed. Zach, arms quivering, rolled and collapsed beside her. Neither spoke. The only sound in the room was their breaths rasping in and out of their lungs.

"Oh, wow," Meghan murmured when she could speak.

"Yeah, wow," Zach echoed. He rolled over and nuzzled her neck, while his hand smoothed over her breast.

"Hmm, continue doing that and I might consider round two."

"I'm game if you are."

"Satyr."

He laughed. "First time a woman's ever called me that."

"What do they usually call you?"

He didn't answer. His fingers pinched her nipples into hard centers again, while he sucked at the pulse point on the side of her neck.

Her body responded with a throb. Meghan inhaled

a sharp breath. The spring tightened again. She rolled Zach onto his back and, throwing a leg over his body, straddled his hips. His hands kneaded her breasts. Groaning, she leaned forward until his teeth captured an erect point.

With Zach fully aroused, she guided him to the entrance of the rekindled flames. His hands abandoned her breasts and clasping her hips, jammed her down hard.

Meghan cried out, and then rode his thrusts, her body twisting and turning as the fire raged. Within seconds, she climaxed again. Zach followed, his cry of satisfaction mingling with hers. It was short, fast, and fabulous. She bowed her head and sobbed into his chest, then rolled off to the side.

"I never expected..." She couldn't finish. Tears still formed in her eyes.

His fingers intertwined with hers. "I know. Me neither. I thought I'd need more time before... Well, you know. Oh God, Meghan, you have no idea how many nights I laid awake thinking about you twenty years ago. Your eyes, your smile were always on my mind."

"What did you see in me? I was overweight and not too graceful."

"I saw a girl who always had a kind word for others and knew instinctively you felt things deeply. I wanted so badly to ask you out on a date, and never could screw up the nerve to do it."

"Funny. I sometimes thought about you, too. It was so chaste—a movie, a pizza afterward, even a goodnight kiss on my front steps." She sighed. "I'm glad I got so much more than the kiss."

Zach raised her hand to his lips. "Me too, sweetheart. We both got it all."

I love him. I think I always have. Exhausted, she closed her eyes.

****

The movement of the bed woke her. Zach had risen and once again reached for his jeans.

"H-m, what time is it?" she murmured sleepily.

"Almost eleven. Do you want breakfast or lunch?"

"Breakfast if they're still serving it." She wouldn't have minded a third helping of Zach.

Instead, she tossed the covers back and swung her legs over the side of the bed, groaning when darts of pain jabbed at her body.

"Hurt?" Zach asked, pulling on his jeans. "Maybe we shouldn't have…"

"I've heard it said that great sex masks pain. Apparently, it's true."

"At least you're calling it great. I considered it fantastic."

Meghan chuckled. "Don't get into a war of words with me. I'm a writer, remember?" She looked at the bandage on her wrist. "I take it I'm not supposed to get this wet. How do I bathe and accomplish that trick?" She had a suggestion—like the two of them in the shower.

"The doctor said to keep it as dry as possible, but gave me fresh bandages just in case. What do you want to eat?" He pulled the light blue polo from last night over his head, and lifted the receiver.

I'd love a lifetime of you for starters. Honestly, men can be so dense sometimes.

Breakfast, however, sounded good. "A bunch of

those little link sausages, two scrambled eggs, biscuits with lots of butter, fruit of some kind, tomato juice, and coffee—lots of coffee." She limped toward the bathroom.

"No low-cal cereal this morning, huh?" he questioned with a grin.

"If I'd had more fat on me last night, that tire iron might have bounced better. Besides, I just had a lot of exercise," she said, gathering fresh clothing and closing the door on Zach's laughter.

****

With a long stint in a hot shower and a full stomach, Meghan checked out of the Grandview Inn. The manager had personally apologized to her. She and Zach were among the last of the classmates to leave. He told them most of the people had no idea of the events in the wee hours of the morning. She suspected the hotel had threatened any employee with dismissal if they talked.

Meghan and Zach drove to the hospital. She shifted in her seat, trying to find a comfortable position. Time was bringing out the pain. Her torso and upper thighs were a mass of bruises, all turning interesting shades blue, violet, and black. Not even the make-up she'd slathered on could hide the purple coloring along her jaw. Zach had replaced the bandages on her wrist and head with a dedication she found endearing. Naturally, she thanked him with a long kiss. If time hadn't been so tight, they'd have graduated from kissing to more athletic endeavors.

"I'm anxious to hear what Suzanne has to say," she commented.

"I talked to Ray again while you were in the

276

shower. He said she was having problems with some details, but the gist of it was she left the room of her own accord. She was scared, had the spare key to Dave's car, and only one thought—to get the hell out of Grandview."

"And leaped from the frying pan into the fire." *Did I really just use that old cliché?*

"More or less. Glory must have been stalking her."

"Maybe she even planned on using the same routine with Suzanne as she did with me," Meghan said. "Although, I doubt Suzanne would have been as gullible. She'd have told Glory to go to hell."

"You're not gullible, just caring." He clasped her hand and lifted it to his lips.

Zach pulled into the parking lot and steadied Meghan with his arm around her waist as they walked into the hospital. He didn't have to, she could walk just fine, but liked the comfort of his arm. It spelled permanence, something she wanted more than anything.

A few minutes later, they stopped in front of room three-oh-four, and walked in the open door, greeting the sheriff and a battered Suzanne.

****

Suzanne didn't want to talk to anybody. Inside the bandages encasing her head, a jackhammer pounded away. She visualized chunks of her brain chipping off. The bulky casts on her ankle and arm made movement difficult. She sported a black eye, and more bruises than she could count. But thank God, no vital organs had been damaged. Why was a mystery. She was, however, alert.

"Holy crap, what happened to you?" she asked when she saw Meghan's bandages. "Don't tell me you tangled with that psychotic bitch, too."

"I'm afraid so. How are you feeling?"

"How the hell do you think? I'm hurting like a son of a bitch, my head feels like it's going to fall off, and I'll have to walk with crutches if and when I ever get out of the Hotel Walking Wounded here. I can claim two chipped teeth, plus I have twenty six stitches in my head." She paused for breath. "But I'm grateful to be alive." She shot a glance at Ray. "I assume you're in custody of my jewelry."

Ray nodded. "Your purse is in the safe down at the station. The hotel is holding everything else that was in your original room. Suzanne, I need to know exactly what happened."

He pulled up a chair and sat. Zach eased Meghan into the other one, and leaned against the window sill.

Suzanne stared at the ceiling wondering where to begin. She started with why she left the safety of her room.

"I was going to drive north until I got to another town and motel. I thought I'd be safe. Wrong conclusion."

She related the attack in as much detail as she remembered. "I knew that if I didn't protect my head, I was a goner. For a while there, I thought she'd succeeded anyway. I assume you found the ski mask?"

Ray nodded. "It along with the bloodstained dark clothing she wore last night. All were carefully folded in her suitcase."

"Psychotic bitch," she muttered again.

"Suzanne, why would Glory want to kill Tami, Eddie, Dave, Clara Sylvester, and you?" Ray asked.

"Clara Sylvester? I have no idea why she'd want

that old crow dead, but I've got an idea about the rest of us."

"Glory said something about a diary. Did you know Divine kept a diary?" Meghan questioned.

"No, why should I? A diary? What was in it?"

"I haven't read it, but Tom confirmed its existence this morning," Ray told her. "He's looking for it."

"Knowing Divine, she probably gave a detailed account of vivid predictions regarding the futures of damn near everybody she knew," Suzanne replied.

"Vivid as in hell and damnation?" Meghan suggested.

The redhead shrugged, and then winced at the sharp stab of pain the action produced. "What else?"

"Suzanne, what *can* you tell us? Most of what Glory says isn't coherent, but I gather it dates back to high school. What happened?" the sheriff demanded to know.

Suzanne closed her eyes and shuddered. All these years, buried in her subconscious, she'd known what they'd done would come back to haunt them.

"I can't believe some insignificant, juvenile prank has caused all of this."

"We gathered this had something to do with Divine's suicide," Zach added.

"Divine was the perfect target for practical jokes and Tami's sharp tongue."

Meghan nodded. "I remember. Divine didn't take biology because she said cutting up a body was a sacrilege—even animal and reptile bodies—and against her religion."

"When we were in junior high, she called out the janitor when he caught a mouse in a trap. She was sanctimonious as hell, and quoted Bible passages whenever she wanted to get her message across," Suzanne told them.

"Yeah, I can relate to that," Meghan murmured.

"Pissed off a lot of kids. Everyone made fun of her behind her back and some, like Tami, directly to her face," Suzanne replied stating the obvious.

"We used to talk at church. She knew what was being said. It hurt. She didn't have many friends," Zach informed them.

"Maybe she was scared to have friends," Meghan answered.

"Her home life must have been something else," Zach commented. "The Prescotts went to church, but didn't mingle with the rest of the congregation. Thought we were all sinners and hypocrites for showing up at Sunday worship to pray, and then going home to sin for another week. Her father once told me to stay away from Divine. I'd said hello. Luckily the old man didn't attend the youth night meetings. We'd talk a lot then. Divine was a nice kid. She deserved a friend."

"I don't ever remember Divine attending a school function," Meghan added. "I guess anything that was fun or pleasurable was considered a sin in the Prescott household."

"Yeah, yeah, whatever. Like I just told you, she was an easy target," Suzanne continued. "The way she dressed—mid-calf length skirts, long-sleeved blouses buttoned up to her chin, dark-colored stockings, and really ugly shoes—didn't help."

"So, how did this juvenile prank bring on multiple murders twenty years later?" the sheriff asked.

Suzanne sighed. She recalled every detail of that

summer and its aftermath, wishing like hell she could erase them from her mind.

"It all started with Tami on graduation day. Tami loved to push the envelope of decency and propriety. Why should the day we got our diplomas be any different?"

She pressed the button on her hospital bed and waited for the top to raise her into a sitting position, stifling a groan as her body adjusted.

"It was early June and hotter than hell. Those polyester gowns were like fabric saunas. Our assembly area was the parking lot next to the gym—not a speck of shade in sight. We were all sweating like horses when Tami said something like 'I can't stand this anymore,' and split for the restroom. She came back a few minutes later with a grin on her face.

"Eddie, Dave, and I stood together, fanning ourselves with our caps. Tami approached, unzipped her gown and flashed us. She was buck naked."

She fumbled for the pitcher of water beside the bed. Ray rose, poured a cup, and handed it to her. She drank and leaned back against the pillows. Her head and shoulder hurt like hell. As soon as she was done with this, she'd pop a pill and let sleep take over. Anything to blot out the memories.

"A bunch of kids saw it, including Divine. Most laughed, but Divine stalked over. She told Tami something along the lines of, 'You'll burn in hell for that. Repent your ways or face the eternal flames.' She had the bad taste to stick her finger in Tami's face.

"Tami, being Tami, told her to cram her Bible up her ass. More words were exchanged and the decibel level rose until Mrs. Hardy, the home ec teacher, came over and asked what was going on. Divine, in that sanctimonious voice, told her. Mrs. Hardy escorted Tami to the restroom and made her put her clothes back on."

"Tami Robinson was always a handful," Ray muttered. "Pretty as a picture, but a handful. Told her daddy that, too. Guess he didn't know how to deal with a teenage girl by himself after his wife's death."

"Tami didn't give a rat's ass about anyone other than herself," Zach told him. "As long as she was the center of attention, she was happy."

"Go on, Suzanne," Meghan prompted. "What happened? As I recall, graduation went smoothly."

"We were lining up for the processional when Tami returned. She was furious at having been marched away in front of the entire senior class. I remember her grabbing Divine's arm and saying, 'I'll get you for this. You want to know about eternal fire? Well, get ready, because I'm about to make your life a living hell.' Tami was still seething that night.

"The four of us copped a bottle of Jack from somewhere along with some weed, and drove out to Samson's Lake. We'd gone through about two-thirds of it when Tami suddenly laughed. 'I've got it. I know how to get even with that Bible-toting bitch.' Her idea was to have Eddie and Dave write Divine's name on every men's room wall in the city. You know, for a good time call Divine at, and then give her phone number.

"We were pretty wasted and thought it was funny. So, we piled into the car and stopped at every convenience store, truck stop, and gas station we saw. If it was public, we hit it. We finally ran out of booze and pot and went home. The next day Tami called. She wanted to expand on the idea."

"Expand? How?" Zach asked.

"Tami's father not only owned the local newspaper, but a printing company as well. She stole the key, and the four of us sneaked in on Sunday. All we needed was a copier and twenty minutes. We popped off a hundred copies of a poster that said much the same thing as the graffiti. We couldn't work during the day, of course, but at night, we stapled those posters to trees and telephone poles, and slapped them on car windshields. Tami finally lost interest when it came time to leave for college. Shopping replaced revenge."

"I remember Mr. Prescott came in one day with one of the flyers in his hand, screaming it was the work of the Devil and how I should arrest him," Ray said.

"Arrest who? The Devil?" Meghan wasn't sure.

"I guess so. Old man Prescott didn't often make sense. At any rate, he claimed calls were coming in to his house day and night. About a week later, he stormed in again. Divine was walking home from prayer meeting the night before, and saw Tami on Columbus Avenue with a bunch of papers in one hand and a stapler in the other. I talked to Tami. Naturally, she denied everything."

"Naturally," Zach said.

"And I couldn't prove it was her. The whole business stopped a couple of days later. I thought that was the end of it."

"I didn't know you'd talked to Tami," Suzanne replied. "That might explain why Tami lost interest, although Tami Robinson wasn't afraid of, or intimidated by anyone, not even the police."

She sipped more water. The sudden switch from revenge to college had been a relief. Suzanne had tired of harassing Divine. Soon they'd all gone their separate ways. Tami had chosen Indiana University where both fun and men were in large supply. She hadn't been sorry to see the so-called friendship cool.

"I don't understand how Glory fits into the picture," Zach said. "She was much younger than Divine, wasn't she?"

"By five or six years, I think," Meghan told him. "I remember her as kind of a gawky kid with a perpetually earnest expression on her face. Ray, what did Glory tell you?"

"Not much. When I questioned her last night, she rambled, sang hymns, quoted the Bible, and declared everyone she killed deserved to die because they were responsible for Divine's suicide."

"How?" Zach asked.

"I don't know. Maybe the graffiti and posters depressed her. Maybe old man Prescott convinced her everything was her fault, and she was going to hell. I'll need to read the diary when Tom finds it," Ray answered. "If he doesn't find it this morning, I'll have to issue a search warrant for the house."

"You should have ordered it anyway. Doesn't sound like stability was a family trait," Suzanne said in a crisp voice.

Zach stared with a disapproving expression. "No, but it was still a mean thing to do. Didn't your conscience nudge you just a little when you heard about Divine's death?"

Hell yes, her conscience had done more than just nudge. It *had* been mean and she was sorry she'd been involved, but over the years the incident had faded. Suzanne defended herself when three pairs of eyes turned her way.

"Hey! Gimme a break. We were eighteen. None of us ever thought beyond the moment. Did I wonder if Divine *killed* herself because of that silly prank?" She paused and shrugged wincing again. "The thought crossed my mind, but life goes on, and I forgot about it. Last night, Glory relished telling everyone who'd listen all about Tami and Eddie's deaths. I think she wanted to scare Dave and me—maybe even put us on notice. Should have realized then the crazy bitch knew more than she let on."

"So, five people died, and two others came under attack, because you were eighteen and stupid," Meghan spoke in a clipped tone.

"Don't get prissy on me. I didn't have to tell you a damned thing, so get off my back. That's all I'm saying. Go lock that nutcase up in a padded cell where she belongs, and tell Tom Ecklund and the Grandview Inn to get good lawyers. They're both going to need one." She rubbed her aching forehead. Maybe a pain pill would relieve the pounding. Besides, she was tired of defending herself over something that happened so long ago. She wasn't ready yet to acknowledge guilt. "Interview's over. I'm tired, and my head is splitting. I'd appreciate it if you'd all leave."

Her three visitors rose and filed out of the room without another word—no goodbyes or hope you feel better on their lips. The door closed with a swish. *The hell with them.* She stared out the window through a veil of tears.

Meghan was right. She'd been so stupid. They all

had. *Stupid and thoughtless.* No amount of justification could erase the consequences of their actions that summer. Now, alone, she allowed the guilt to surface. Five people had died not knowing why, and she bore part of the responsibility for the tragedy. The tears overflowed and coursed down her cheeks.

"Oh, God, Divine, I'm so sorry. Please forgive me."

Suzanne buried her face in her hands and sobbed.

Chapter Eighteen

Zach and Meghan followed the sheriff to the hospital waiting room and claimed space on the vinyl sofa.

"Can I get you something to drink?" the sheriff asked, pausing in front of the vending machine.

Meghan shook her head. "No thanks."

"Me neither."

He pumped change into the coin slot, made his selection, and then sat in a chair. The lines etched on his face had deepened over the past few hours, and Meghan could almost feel his weariness.

"I still can't believe Glory Ecklund killed everyone. I can't wait to get a gander at that diary," Ray muttered. He rose, wandered over to the window, and squinting in the bright sunlight, tilted a soda can to his mouth.

Suzanne was right about one thing—Ray should have a team searching Tom and Glory's house right now. The diary was evidence regardless of what it contained. *A lifetime of friendship can't be in the equation.*

"But how did she pull it off? Has she said anything coherent?" Meghan wondered. "I mean, trips to California and Texas take time. Didn't Tom question his wife's whereabouts?"

"She was more lucid this morning and talked

willingly with a lawyer present. Tom is the regional manager of an insurance company. Once a month he travels to the home office in Chicago for meetings. He leaves Tuesday afternoon and returns Thursday night. Tami, Eddie, and Clara were killed on Wednesdays," the sheriff informed them. "She told us everything with the certainty we'd understand why she had to do it."

"And therefore, it was perfectly all right," Meghan concluded.

"So, Glory flies to Los Angeles and Dallas, rents a car, puts the phone at home on call forwarding to her cell in case Tom checks in, and then hops a flight back before he knows she's been gone," Zach speculated.

"And because she's a bit of a recluse and the time frame is so short, neighbors don't notice she's out of town," Meghan added.

"We'll verify the flights." The sheriff turned to face them. "Glory's one of those people who blends into the woodwork. You notice her, and then forget her. I talked to the hotel manager this morning and found out she had often visited the premises with the excuse of checking on things concerning the reunion. She had ample time to scope out all the entrances, exits, garden pathways, and the corridors on every floor.

"By the time the reunion rolled around, she knew which rooms had been assigned to Dave and Suzanne. According to the reservations clerk, Glory requested a room across the hall from her best friend, Suzanne Crocker."

"It made keeping tabs on Suzanne that much easier," Zach said. "All she had to do was look out the peephole or crack the door."

"She knew exactly where to hide and when to

strike," Ray agreed.

"And the hotel security guards?" Zach asked.

"When Tom was out of town and she wasn't busy killing classmates, Glory cased the parking lot and timed the guards' rounds. They're creatures of habit, never varied their routine."

"And all because the hotel, in order to save money, didn't have jack for security cameras," Meghan asserted in a bitter voice. She was still angry about that. If cameras had been present, in the hallways and the outside areas, the victims might still be alive to tell the tale.

"I doubt if Glory even thought about cameras," Zach said. "She isn't exactly up on the latest technology. A cell phone is about as hi-tech as she goes."

"And a stun gun," Meghan reminded him.

Ray drank from the can again. "Lawyers are scrambling as we speak. I'm sure Suzanne, Eric Peterson, Dave Coryell's relatives, and God knows how many others will file lawsuits against the hotel."

"You know, I never thought of this as a psychological murder. It wasn't until I suggested the link with Tami and Eddie before that particular light bulb went off," Meghan mused.

"If Glory had thought it out, she'd have never used the reunion to kill Dave and Suzanne," Zach commented.

"But she had to kill when Tom was out of town, and his meetings were in Chicago where Dave and Suzanne lived," Meghan responded.

"That's true, although the chances of them crossing paths were slim," he agreed.

Ray shook his head. "Glory was crazy, clever, and sloppy all at the same time. We've spent most of the morning checking credit cards and ATM withdrawals. She left a mammoth paper trail, but like most killers, probably figured no one would suspect her."

"If she thought about it at all," Meghan said. "She was on a mission."

"You're probably right," Ray replied. "I got the California and Texas files this morning. The police in Malibu found a set of kitchen knives in a trash can down the street from Tami's home. The chef's knife was missing. A clerk at a local grocery store remembers a woman buying several bouquets."

"All caught on security cameras, too, I'll bet," Meghan said.

Ray nodded. "The police checked those out first thing when they saw all the flowers. In Texas, a red pick-up was stolen from outside a bar in Mesquite, twenty miles from Harrison. It was later found a block from where it was stolen with massive front end damage. Also had blood and fabric caught in the grill. They matched Eddie's.

"Both the knife and truck contained a set of unidentified fingerprints. I'm sure they'll match Glory's, and I'm certain the Muncie police found the same in Clara Sylvester's room."

Zach's eyebrows rose. "She didn't wear gloves for any of this?"

"Apparently not."

"God, she wasn't even trying cover her tracks or be clever," Meghan murmured.

Zach shrugged. "She wasn't into clever, just revenge."

The sheriff finished his soda and tossed the can into the trash. "When I talked to her at the station, Glory kept saying it was God's will they should die, an eye for an eye."

"I guess the gospel according to Daddy Prescott bore fruit," Meghan replied, a trace of bitterness remaining.

"I still say she could've nailed Dave and Suzanne in Chicago. Accompany your husband to Chicago on the excuse of visiting the museums or something. Neither one of them would be hard to find. They both led high profile lives," Zach insisted.

"Too high a profile. Getting close would have been tough. Someone might remember her. Besides, Eileen told me Dave and Suzanne were among the first to confirm they'd be attending the reunion," the sheriff said heading for the door.

"She didn't need to go after them. They were coming to her, and on her turf," Meghan murmured. "What happens now?"

"She won't do jail time. A mental institution for the rest of her life is more likely."

Tom walked into the waiting room, his expression shifting from anger to sorrow and back again. A Grandview deputy stood in the doorway, a frown on his face.

"Meghan, I'm so sorry. Are you all right?"

"I'm fine. She was too desperate and exhausted to put much force behind the blows, although at the time it hurt like hell. I still feel like I've had a close encounter with a battering ram."

His chin quivered, and his eyes glazed with a haunted look. "She drugged my drink in the bar. I always have a small whiskey in the evenings. Glory's been taking Valium for months. Whiskey for me, Valium for her. It helped ward off her nightmares. I suspect she concealed one or two in her purse, and spiked my drink. I never expected it."

"Tom, I'm…" she began, but Tom ignored her and continued talking.

"I knew something was wrong. I was too sleepy for only having had a couple of drinks. I woke up and found Glory gone. Scared me. I wondered at dinner how she knew so much about the murders. I had to find her before she did something bad. Guess I was too late."

"You suspected she was behind the murders? Was she always…" Zach paused as if to find the words.

"Unstable?" Tom finished. "Yes. I married her two weeks after she graduated high school. I'd known her for years through the church. She used to talk and confide in me. Her father was a verbally abusive SOB. He thundered and thumped the Bible, but her mother doled out the physical punishment—cane beatings and belts. Glory showed me the welts on her back. I thought if we got married, I could protect her. It worked for years. I didn't suspect anything until last night. Guess I didn't do such a great job."

Meghan blinked tears from her eyes. Never had she heard anything so noble or so tragic. She sniffed. Zach's arm encircled her waist. He fumbled in his jeans pocket and shoved a handkerchief into her hand. She daubed her eyes.

"You did your best," Zach said. "When did it fall apart?"

"When she found Divine's diary. We moved into

the family home after her mother died. The woman never threw anything away. Boxes and boxes of crap were stored in the attic and the basement. Glory was clearing stuff out and found the diary. She told me it contained ordinary, everyday girl-talk and chit-chat. I should have known better. Divine didn't indulge in chit-chat. If she kept a diary hidden from her family, then she had something important to say."

"Have you found it yet?" Ray demanded. "I'd like to read it when you do."

Tom nodded. "You will. Glory became withdrawn, but when Eileen called to ask if I'd sit on one of the reunion committees, Glory leaped at the chance, volunteering to help locate lost classmates. I thought it was a blessing in disguise. It got Glory interested in something again."

"She found Tami and Eddie," Meghan said. "We know why she sought revenge. Suzanne told us about the practical joke that got out of hand."

"I know about the prank. It's in the diary. But Suzanne couldn't tell you why Divine committed suicide because she didn't know."

"Know what? You've read the diary?" Ray asked, his eyes boring into Tom's, and then shifting to Zach.

Tom returned Ray's stare. "I found it on the desk when I woke up from the drug. It was open to the last page. I read enough to know Meghan was in danger. That's when I went to Zach's room to inform him and help with the search."

"Why did she kill herself?" Zach wanted to know.

Meghan wasn't sure she wanted to hear the answer. Ray and Tom stood twenty feet apart staring at each other like two gunfighters about to draw. Zach's arms contracted, biting into her waist as he tensed.

Tom broke eye contact with Ray and turned his attention back to Meghan and Zach. "She wrote everything that happened in the diary. All those flyers and graffiti paid off. While walking home from church one night, Divine accepted a ride from the wrong person. She was raped."

Meghan gasped. "Raped? And no one suspected?"

"Who did it?" Zach said in a hoarse voice.

Meghan sucked in a startled breath, looked at Zach, and then Ray. "Did you catch the bastard?"

"This is the first I've heard of it. Neither Divine or her parents ever reported anything like that," he denied emphatically.

"Given her background, I can see how she'd keep it to herself," Zach commented.

"She told someone," Tom confirmed in a quiet voice. "She told a member of the Methodist Church—a teacher at the high school."

"Clara Sylvester." Meghan guessed in a hushed tone.

Tom nodded. "According to the diary, when Divine feared she was pregnant, she broke down and confided to Ms. Sylvester. But Clara Sylvester didn't believe her, called Divine a liar and unbalanced."

"Now, we know why an old woman died," Zach said.

Ray waved a dismissive hand. "I doubt any of this is true. Surely her parents read the diary. If the Prescotts didn't contact Sheriff Hilliard, then I'd have to believe they thought it was bunk."

"Neither Jonah or Sarah Prescott read it. Their daughter committed the ultimate sin—taking her own life. I'll bet Divine's things were packed and stored the next day. The diary is a large spiral notebook. It looks like any other high school composition book," Tom told them.

"Did she name her attacker?" Zach insisted in a low voice.

Tom turned to nod at the deputy who stepped into the room, and then returned his gaze to the two men. Zach shifted his weight on the sofa. The sheriff licked his lips.

"Yes. On the last page, written just before she hanged herself. But it wasn't the last entry. Glory had several additions, including the details of how she killed Tami, Eddie, and Clara. I found three obits stuck in between the pages. She also listed six names—five of them crossed out with heavy pencil strokes. Tami Robinson, Eddie Mancuso, Clara Sylvester, Dave Coryell, and Suzanne Wayland. Meghan's name was penciled in with a question mark beside it, like an afterthought." Tom paused and closed his eyes. "The last name is Ray Armstrong. You're responsible for Divine's death, Sheriff. You raped her. It's there in Divine's handwriting."

Ray's expression was a cross between incredulous and outraged. "What? You're nuts!"

A sharp pain slashed through Meghan's head and the room spun at Tom's accusation.

Ray? Divine named Ray as her assailant?

She shuddered. Had the poor girl been as crazy as her younger sister?

"You were the one person in Grandview, Divine Prescott would have trusted. She'd have accepted a ride with a deputy sheriff, especially in view of the obscene phone calls those flyers and the graffiti produced," Zach said.

"That's insane! I never touched Divine Prescott, and if she says I did, she's lying. No wonder Clara didn't believe her," Ray stated. A line of sweat coated his upper lip.

"Clara Sylvester was your mother's cousin. You could do no wrong in her eyes," Tom insisted. "She was involved in each of your election campaigns. I can't imagine why Divine would tell her anything."

"Because Clara had the knack of inviting confidences, of listening and saying the right things. That's what made her such a good Methodist youth advisor," Zach told him. "Divine either didn't know, or forgot about, her devotion to the Armstrong family."

"This is nuts. Are you going to believe me or the ramblings of a clearly deranged young girl? After twenty years? There's no proof." His voice changed from angry to scoffing.

"Divine was eighteen, so that eliminates statutory rape. There's no statute of limitations on rape if force, a weapon, or drugs are involved. It had to be force. Divine wouldn't have consented. Did you handcuff her to the door? Did she scream and kick? Maybe beg?" Tom asked softly.

"You're crazy and still don't have any proof!" The sheriff wiped the sweat from his lip with his shirt sleeve.

"The Wednesday evening youth meetings were over by eight-thirty. If Divine stayed to help close up like she often did, then she would have been on her way home by nine or nine-thirty. It was summer. In those years, Grandview was on that double daylight savings time. Nine o'clock would be dusk. I'm sure someone must have seen the patrol car—maybe even noticed Divine getting in," Tom continued.

Ray slapped his hat on his head and glared at all of them, then strode to the door.

"A lot of years have passed. I doubt if anyone would accurately remember one specific summer night twenty years ago. You have no proof," he repeated, and then left.

"He's right," Meghan said breaking the silence the accusation and Ray's departure caused. "An old diary of a parentally abused girl who killed herself is not proof. And there's no DNA evidence."

"I know," Tom replied. "But I called in the State Police to investigate. I'll let them take over." He shook his head, and then nodded toward the deputy. "I hoped he'd confess and could be locked up today. Guess that was wishful thinking. Ray's probably right. No one will remember."

The deputy, silent until now, finally spoke. "I wouldn't be too sure of that. I joined the force a couple of years after Ray. Whenever he was on patrol, he always stopped between eight-thirty and nine o'clock at The Cozy Corner Café for coffee."

"That's only two blocks from the Methodist Church," Zach added.

"And the route Divine would have taken home," Meghan reminded him. "Oh, my God, I feel sick."

"Don't we all," Tom said.

"Are you saying Ray was the main target and that the others were…what, practice?" Zach wondered.

Tom heaved a tired sigh and shrugged. "I don't know. She hated them all. If they hadn't harassed

Divine, she'd have never been raped."

"When did you start to suspect Glory?" Zach asked.

"When Eileen found Annabelle's body. Glory had disappeared from the ballroom. In spite of her reunion duties, she'd been brooding and morose the last three months. I worried the medications weren't helping. Obviously, she'd stopped taking them. She told me she was fine, just nervous about the reunion. I wanted to believe her. But she knew so many details about Tami and Eddie's deaths, it made me uneasy. At first, I thought Eileen had told her, but when I cornered her in the bar later, she claimed the police from California and Texas only asked if the invitation was legit."

"No wonder Glory fainted when Suzanne strolled out from behind the plants. Her first failure. She must have gotten one hell of a shock," Meghan concluded. "I wonder how she enticed Dave to Suzanne's room."

Tom walked over to a chair and sat. His face twisted, and he blinked his eyes rapidly but failed to suppress the tears.

"I spent several hours with her, our lawyer, and the doctors this morning. She's holding nothing back. She slipped the room key into his coat pocket in the bar. Dave was drunk. When he found it, he expected Suzanne."

"So, she zapped him with the stun gun and had an easy victim," Zach said. "Did you know about the stun gun?"

Tom shook his head. "Never had a clue."

"And she was sitting next to me in the lobby when the subject came up. Remember? She high-tailed it out of the room shortly afterward," Meghan replied, turning to Zach.

"She ditched it, and then stalked Suzanne," he finished.

A strangled sob escaped from Tom's throat.

Meghan shifted in her seat to ease aching muscles. "And Suzanne played right into her hands by trying to run. Poor Glory, both verbal and physical abuse."

Tom wiped his eyes. "Divine was her protector."

"Protector? In what way?" Zach inquired.

"Old man Prescott preached fire and brimstone every night believing the Devil was in both of his daughters. But her mother was crazy, and I mean the certifiable kind of crazy. It was her duty to beat the evil out of her daughters. The girls feared her."

Meghan groaned. "Oh, God. None of us ever suspected."

"The clothes they wore would hide the bruises and welts. It still doesn't explain the protector part," Zach said.

"The abuse brought on nightmares. Glory would wake up screaming in the middle of the night. When her mother came in, Divine would take the blame. In Sarah's twisted mind, the Devil was still in residence, so Divine took the beating for her sister. Glory was twelve when Divine killed herself. There was only one target for the next six years."

"God, how warped can a person get?" Meghan demanded angrily. "How could she do that to her own children?"

"She believed that because they were women they were therefore a constant temptation to men and the Devil. Told her daughters that Satan was a coward and would leave to avoid the pain." Tom buried his face in his hands. "I honestly thought I could help by marrying her. It worked for a while, too. Glory knew she was safe with me. I replaced Divine. I should have taken the diary away from her and burned it."

"Glory would still be disturbed," Meghan told him in a gentle tone.

"Yeah, but five people would still be alive." Tears filled his eyes again. "If I had been more observant, I might have seen it coming."

Zach shook his head. "How? You had no idea what she was planning or that she'd gone to Malibu and Texas while you were in Chicago. It's not your fault. You did everything you could."

"I suppose, but I'll never get rid of the guilt." He raised his eyes to Meghan. "She hadn't planned on ditching the stun gun, and wanted me to thank you for warning her. She's read your books and knows you have an eye for detail. She was afraid you'd remember her big purse. Then she realized you had linked Tami and Eddie's deaths to the reunion and had questioned other people. She decided to eliminate you, Meghan."

"I'd still be around," Zach reminded him.

"She saw how it was between the two of you. In her mind, you'd be too upset about Meghan to cause any harm."

Tom rose, walked stiffly toward the door, and turned hesitating as if about to speak. Instead, he shook his head and left with tears running down his face.

Meghan's eyes welled. "God, I feel so sorry for him."

"I guess if my wife turned out to be a mass murderer, I'd come apart at the seams, too."

"Do you believe Divine's diary?"

Zach nodded, tightened his arm around her waist, and kissed her temple.

"It was her suicide note. People generally don't lie when they're about to pull the plug. I just hope the state police can bring Ray to justice. Ray acted guilty as hell. I think he knew twenty years ago why Divine killed herself."

She rested her head on Zach's shoulder. "You think she told Ray about being pregnant?"

"What would you do?"

She drew in an angry breath. "I'd confront the son of a bitch. He was already married at that time, wasn't he?"

"Had a kid, too. I'll bet she told him, and he refused to believe it or convinced her to get rid of it."

"No, not Divine," Meghan said emphatically. "Abortion was a heinous sin. If she was pregnant, everyone would soon know, including her parents. Can you imagine her mother's reaction to *that*?"

"*If* she was pregnant, the coroner either didn't say anything or her parents hushed it up."

"My guess is it was always in the autopsy report. The Prescotts just never asked to see it. And since it was obviously a suicide, the case was probably closed without the details ever being revealed," Meghan remarked, raising her head and wiping her eyes. "You're right. Either way, Ray Armstrong knew why she did it. I guess we'll never know exactly how Glory's mind worked, but what better way to kill the man who raped your sister than to lure him to the reunion with a murder?"

If I were writing this, I'd use it as a plot strategy. It's brilliant.

Suddenly, her creative urges kicked in. She couldn't wait to start a new book.

"I wonder how on earth she would have killed Ray?" Zach mused.

"She managed Dave just fine."

"But she ditched the stun gun."

"Maybe she planned on retrieving it later, or maybe she made another plan when word got out about the stun gun. *Maybe*, she just didn't know and decided to wing it." She paused, and then sighed. "God, let's get out of here."

Zach helped her to her feet. "I'm with you. I don't think I'll attend the twenty-fifth reunion."

They exited the hospital and walked to the car. Before opening the passenger door, he stopped and gazed into her eyes.

Meghan's heart knocked against her ribs, and her nerves danced when he placed his hands on her shoulders.

Zach lips curved into a sexy smile. "Do you have to return to Raleigh right away?"

"Not for a couple of weeks. I tied the reunion into a two week vacation."

"Any place special?"

"No. I was going to let the wind blow me somewhere."

He arched his eyebrows. "Ever been to Phoenix?"

"Can't say that I have," she replied, not at all surprised when her heart rate accelerated.

"I have a three-bedroom house in town, and own a dude ranch near the Grand Canyon."

"A dude ranch? You're kidding."

"Not at all. It's a great investment and very

relaxing. I don't know about you, but I can use a rest."

"Is that an invitation?"

His smile deepened into a grin. "Definitely."

She teased him for a moment, pretending to think, and then laughed at his anxious expression.

"Make the plane reservations. I'll go shopping for jeans and cowboy boots. Yee-haw!"

"Don't forget a hat. You'll need one of those. It's August and the sun is brutal." Zach stared into her eyes. "I love you, Meghan. Let's make this the start of the rest of our lives."

"Are you proposing?"

He smiled. "Yeah, I guess I am. Could have done it better, but I'm new at this love thing."

"I think you did it beautifully."

"You haven't said yes yet," he reminded her.

Tears welled in her eyes. "Of course, I'll say yes. I love you, too."

He pulled Meghan into his arms, kissing her soundly. She ignored those stabbing jabs of pain as her bruises protested until she came up for air.

"You'll make one hell of a cowgirl."

"I suppose you own all the correct cowboy gear? Does that make you a real cowboy?"

"Of course," he answered, his lips nuzzling her ear.

She shivered and welcomed the throb from deep inside her. "And you know how to ride horses?"

"Hmm," he murmured from the vicinity of her neck.

"I don't," she whispered, snatching his ear lobe between her teeth.

The throb intensified, sending little flames licking along her nerves.

"I'll teach you." His lips nibbled lightly on her chin.

"I have a better idea. As the song goes, 'Save a horse, ride a cowboy.'"

He laughed, and then covered her mouth with his.

Epilogue

Excerpts from the Grandview, Indiana News-Journal:

August 31st

"Grandview Sheriff Raymond Armstrong was officially placed on administrative leave by Mayor Travis Connor pending the investigation of a twenty-year-old rape accusation made by Thomas Ecklund on behalf of his late sister-in-law, Divine Prescott. Mr. Ecklund is married to Glory Prescott, sister of the deceased, who is currently being held in…"

September 20th

"After evaluations by three state approved psychiatrists, Judge Randolph J. Hennison today sentenced Glory Prescott Ecklund to The Indiana State Sanatorium for the Criminally Insane where she will remain until doctors deem her fit to carry out her sentence of life in prison for the murders of…"

November 6th

"Today mayor-elect, John Hamilton congratulated his opponent, Dan Masterson on a well-run race and looks forward to working with the City Councilman in the future.

Businessman Hamilton won in a landslide of close to 3-1…"

November 15th

"Two fishermen reported finding the body of suspended sheriff Ray Armstrong in his car parked on the north end of Samson's Lake. Cause of death is pending an autopsy, but witnesses revealed a gunshot wound to the head. Sheriff Armstrong's police issued Glock was found next to the body.

The Grand Jury recently indicted the former sheriff on rape charges when, after twenty years, an old coroner's report was discovered stating that Divine Prescott, aged eighteen, had been three months pregnant at the time of death.

Acting Sheriff Ron Campbell released the following statement: "We are indeed saddened by this tragedy. Ray Armstrong was a dedicated law enforcement officer and a valued member of the community. The sheriff's office has no comment on the accusations against Sheriff Armstrong."

E-Mail from Thomas Ecklund to Zachary Dunbar:

Ray Armstrong committed suicide early this morning in his car with a single shot to the head. One of the men who found him told me he read a note left on the front seat. In it, Ray confessed to having raped Divine.

When I told Glory, she quoted, "The Lord shall return thy wickedness upon thine own head." The book of I Kings, chapter two, verse forty-four.

I know other appropriate quotes: "Nature has but one judgment on wrong conduct—the judgment of death." Oliver Wendell Holmes.

"Preserve me, O God, for in thee I put my trust." Psalms 16:1

Divine can rest in peace. It's over.

~Tom

A word about the author...

Suzanne was born and raised in Indianapolis, Indiana, but has had the privilege of living in many areas of the country. Currently, she and her husband call Ft. Lauderdale, Florida home.

When not creating murder and mayhem along with romance, she loves traveling to see her 6 grandchildren in Memphis, Tennessee, and in Rockford, Illinois.

Thank you for purchasing
this publication of The Wild Rose Press, Inc.
For other wonderful stories of romance,
please visit our on-line bookstore at
www.thewildrosepress.com.

For questions or more information
contact us at
info@thewildrosepress.com.

The Wild Rose Press, Inc.
www.thewildrosepress.com

To visit with authors of
The Wild Rose Press, Inc.
join our yahoo loop at
http://groups.yahoo.com/group/thewildrosepress/